Rook-Shoot

Rook-Shoot

Margaret Duffy

St. Martin's Press
New York

Library of Congress Cataloging-in-Publication Data

Duffy, Margaret.
  Rook-shoot / Margaret Duffy.
      p.   cm.
    ISBN 0-312-06456-X
    I. Title.
  PR6054.U397R66   1991
  823'.914—dc20   91-19985
                                                                         CIP

First published in Great Britain by Judy Piatkus (Publishers) Limited.

First U.S. Edition: December 1991

10 9 8 7 6 5 4 3 2 1

Strategy

'A certain amount of stupidity is necessary to make a good soldier.' Florence Nightingale, letter to Sydney Herbert from Scutari, January 1855.

When an army officer is asked to resign from MI5 because he fails to prevent a subordinate shooting and killing a prominent member of London's underworld this does not mean that disgrace automatically follows, even when the officer in question has previously conducted himself in the manner of an avenging angel. The mitigating circumstances of the incident – Terry Meadows had been kidnapped and abominably ill-treated – went in favour of Meadows himself, and, as the officer in question, Patrick Gillard, would have been the first to agree, this was entirely right. For Gillard had known precisely what he was doing in that couple of seconds when he had not forbidden Meadows to use the gun he had just snatched from the floor. There is no doubt that Meadows would have obeyed such an order for there was a perfect working relationship between the two men.

A completely unforeseen circumstance following this episode was that a newspaper somehow got hold of the story. The pity of it was that it was not the kind of newspaper to associate itself with tales of lurid nature and dubious authenticity which could be discounted. The facts were reported in cold, stark prose and started yet another clamour concerning the accountability of the security services. This army officer, snarled other, less responsible publications, was also head of the security team that managed the Prime Minister's travel

1

within the United Kingdom but outside London. Very soon, Gillard found himself out of that job as well.

It was not the right time for a priest's son to reflect on whether this was the moment to follow in his father's footsteps, something that I think he has always promised himself. No, one does not go cap in hand, when everything else has failed, into this kind of vocation. And Gillard was, after all, still in the army. He took counsel from me — for I am his wife — and his family and waited to see what the army would do with him.

The army, obviously with a few reservations of its own, sent him on indefinite leave.

Further news arrived at our Devon cottage in early October when Patrick had been at home for almost three months. The buff-coloured envelope that looked as though it had been made from thrice recycled paper was of unmistakable origin. I followed the sound of wood being chopped and found Patrick in the garage.

'Your fate,' I said, holding it out to him. 'And the electricity bill.'

Patrick wiped his hands down the sides of his jeans and took the envelope from me, hesitating for a moment before slitting it open.

'A tour of duty licking stamps on the Rhine?' I hazarded, determined, if at all possible, to keep the mood light. 'Organizing family days at a regiment based at Limbo Toto?'

He scowled at the sheet of flimsy paper. 'No decision yet,' he said with a sigh. 'This is just to say that they haven't forgotten me.'

Even though I hate deferred decisions I felt a lot happier. 'We could always go on holiday.'

'Holiday?' he queried as though I had uttered a word in a foreign language.

'Yes, you know, one of those things where you put clothes in a suitcase and go to the station and —'

'Ingrid!'

'All right then, seriously. Instead of providing us with enough kindling for the Aga for the next three thousand years, why don't you put a few ideas into motion? In the

2

time available you could set yourself up as a private security consultant.'

He sat down on the large chunk of wood he used as a chopping block. 'One can hardly put that kind of thing into operation in a few weeks. And I can't see them allowing me to carry on kicking my heels on full pay for longer than that.'

I left him to think it over and went indoors to make coffee. When I took him out a mugful he was swearing under his breath, trying to get a large splinter out of his finger.

'I looked in my diary,' I said, Patrick in my wake as we returned to the cottage for the first aid box and a needle. 'You're owed quite a lot of leave anyway, never mind that they can't make up their minds what to do with you.'

This soldier of mine sat down, gave me his hand and gazed determinedly out of the window. Having recovered as fully as it is possible from appalling injuries sustained during the Falklands War, and sundry other bullet wounds and buffetings since — coming through all this trauma with courage and retaining a bouyant sense of humour — he still finds himself unable to watch a splinter being removed from his finger.

'There's no disgrace,' I said.

'The press thought so.'

'Since when have you worried what the papers say?'

I went upstairs to fetch the reading lamp from my desk for it was a dull morning and the windows of our home are quite small. There had been a few letters to *The Times* too, mostly supportive and, interestingly, not from people whom Patrick knows. One reader had suggested that, as the gunned-down crook in question had been a murderer, racketeer, black-mailer and Satanist, to name but a few of his interests, then why hadn't Gillard been awarded a medal? I had a feeling that a good proportion of the population would agree with this sentiment.

'Can you see it though?' Patrick said, mind on anything but splinters. 'A brass plate on a door somewhere in the West End? "Gillard and Co, Security Advisors." I'd immediately be inundated with dowagers wanting to know how to protect their diamonds and lap dogs.'

3

'You'd employ others to deal with that side of the business,' I told him, probing with the needle. 'And just do the assignments that interested you.'

'That might not bring in much money.'

'Patrick, we aren't *poor*. I should get the publication advance for *Echoes of Murder* this year.' I added, mischieviously, 'I didn't think you were one of those men who hates living on his wife's earnings.'

'I'm not,' he said with the ghost of a smile.

'Personally, I'm still rooting for the holiday. You did promise we could have a break after that business with Terry was over.'

'Where would you like to go?' he asked, utterly without enthusiasm.

'How about a second honeymoon?' I suggested, purely on impulse but liking the idea immediately. 'It's odd, isn't it?' I went on, grinning as his head swivelled and he stared at me. 'How a man's attention can be instantly won?'

'Actually it would be our third,' Patrick said, an unreadable expression on his face.

Patrick and I have been married twice. The first time for ten years after which I divorced him, our relationship having not so much broken down as crashed. We were apart for four during which time I married an old school friend, Peter, now a policeman. He was killed by gunmen in Plymouth. Shortly after this Patrick came back into my life, still recovering from his injuries and endeavouring to cope with having to make a fresh start in life. He had been recruited by Colonel Richard Daws into D12, a new department set up within MI5 to counter foreign interference to the security services. Patrick had been ordered to find a female working partner as much of the job would involve socialising. The only woman he could face working with at that time was, frankly, one who would not want to go to bed with him, the injuries having left in their wake a crushing sexual inferiority complex. All my anger and resentment towards him, a leftover from the stormy ten years together, had evaporated in the face of such a plea for help. And, together, we had solved his problems.

Now it seemed that we were going to have to make another fresh start.

4

'Yes,' I said. 'But second time round we came straight back here. There wasn't time to go anywhere as we were in the middle of a job.'

'So in other words you feel like jetting to a Greek island and indulging in unremitting lust.'

'Something like that.' I bent over the needle so he could not see my smile.

'Where did we go the first time?'

'Can't you remember?'

'Ow!'

'Sorry. It was Torquay for the first week and then the rest of the time in London. Don't you remember that awful hotel near Euston Station where the couple on the floor above bonked all night and you said it put you off your stroke?'

'Only because it made me laugh,' he protested. 'The springs of their bed sounded like a trampoline.'

'Lovely,' I murmured.

'Lovely? What do you mean, lovely?'

I am not often flummoxed. 'I − I − er − just mean the idea of a honeymoon is lovely,' I replied lamely.

The grey eyes bored into mine. 'No, you didn't.' His look became foxy. 'You coming over all broody again or something?'

No, you do not tell the man you really love that he has been undertaking heavy gardening in order to forget his worries and has therefore been too tired for lovemaking. Not directly, that is. 'Ever thought of us having another baby?' I asked.

'Justin was a bit of a miracle.'

'I know. But only because you were still getting over being blown up.'

'I haven't grown a new set of balls though,' he retorted, never one to be coy about the war-damaged zones.

Just then our child and his nanny, Dawn, returned from a trip to the village Post Office and store. Justin, who is nearly two years old, succeeding in tripping down the step from the porch into the dining room and putting his teeth through his bottom lip. Several minutes, howls of pain and quite a lot of blood later, peace was restored, the small patient sitting on

5

the older one's knee, still sniffing but slurping on a chocolate ice lolly.

'And Ingrid tells me she wants another one,' Patrick announced portentously into the comparative calm.

'Why not?' said Dawn, straightfaced.

'Hadn't we better get this splinter out?' Patrick said to me, regarding the piece of kitchen paper I had hurriedly wrapped around the offending digit.

'It's out,' I told him. 'When you said "Ow". Just put some TCP on it.'

He pulled off the paper and dabbed busily. 'Oh. Right. Thanks.'

'What about this baby then?' Dawn prompted.

'I'll go on a course of multi-vitamin tablets,' Patrick said. He got up and gave Justin to me. The front door closed behind him.

'Did I say the wrong thing?' Dawn wanted to know, looking worried.

During the next few days the words 'second honeymoon' were not mentioned, neither was an increase in the size of the Gillard family. But following a trip to the dentist in Tavistock Patrick came home with a pile of holiday brochures and left them, in off-hand fashion, on the dresser. I glanced through several but, in a mental whirl after looking at a myriad photographs of blue skies and golden beaches, was no nearer my holiday. And, in truth, I had a lot of work to do.

Modest success with a few romantic thrillers had become something more with the dramatisation for television of one of them, *Barefoot Upon Thorns*. Then a rough outline for a novel – entitled *A Man Called Céleste* had been taken to the States by Patrick – who in between all his other activities is my agent – and the film rights sold. Thereafter all had not gone so well from the writer's point of view. The shooting script had been forwarded for my approval and it was so appalling that I had refused to have anything further to do with the production unless I was permitted to rewrite it myself. After Patrick had fired a couple of broadsides across the Atlantic this was agreed. The task had been far more difficult and taken far longer than I had envisaged and had entailed the burning of much midnight oil. I had finished this in the summer but so far had not had time to accept an invitation to watch the commencement of filming. The reason for this was that my London publishers, Thorpe and Gittenburg, were agitating for the delivery of a long-promised novel, *Echoes of Murder*. The work was completed in rough and I was just over half way through the final draft. The real problem was that even when you have a live-in nanny to look after your child and a local girl who comes in three mornings a week to do the most bothersome housework, when you have a husband at home things just don't get done.

'This is bloody impossible,' I said to my typewriter that night. 'When we were *both* working for D12 I used to have more time for writing.'

There was a faint mew at my feet and my cat Pirate looked at me from the wastepaper basket where she had curled up for warmth.

'You're right,' I said to her. 'It's October and we haven't put the central heating on yet. It's freezing up here.'

Pirate, who is not allowed on the Aga because she has been known to sample things from the cooking pots thereon when no one is looking, went back to sleep, fur bushy in protest.

'All that sunshine,' I said, addressing the typewriter again. 'All those sandy beaches and blue skies.'

I mentally battened myself into concentration and worked for two hours.

'I didn't bring you coffee because I thought it would stop you working,' Patrick said when I went downstairs at just after ten. He had a cup by his elbow, together with a tot of whisky.

'Is that the real thing or instant?' I enquired grumpily.

'The real McCoy, of course. You can't drink instant with single malt.'

Very grumpily I said I didn't know about things like that, adding that the house was like a fridge and that Pirate had hibernated.

'Diddums,' observed my husband mildly and went away.

7

He returned with fresh coffee, some rather battered chocolates he had discovered in a paper bag at the back of a kitchen drawer and a tot of Drambuie, which I adore. Then he brought logs and firelighters and soon a bright fire was burning in the inglenook fireplace.

'Better?'

'Sorry to be such a misery.'

Patrick sat by my side on the settee. 'I checked on Justin. I knew he went to bed with Teddy bears but not a saucepan and two wooden spoons.'

'It's the latest craze,' I explained. 'Helping with the cooking. At least, that's what Dawn says. I think he just likes banging them all together.'

Patrick chuckled. 'I'm told I had a phase of refusing to go to bed unless it was with a certain turnip tucked into a certain woolly hat.'

'Perhaps it reflects your taste in women.'

He gazed at me, eyes dancing with suppressed mirth.

'Shall we try it tonight?' I asked. 'The woolly hat, I mean.'

He thought about it for a moment. 'Oh, I don't know ... you'd look quite fetching in a turnip too.'

'We seem to keep returning to this subject,' I said when we both stopped giggling.

He kissed me on the cheek without comment and for a while we drank our coffee in silence.

'Patrick, despite what I said, I can't really spare the time to go on holiday,' I said at last into the quietness.

'How long will it take you to finish the book?'

'At least a month at this rate.'

'You'd get far more done if I wasn't at home,' he said candidly.

'That's a fact of life. I'd rather you were here.'

'I could push off for a bit. Go fishing or something.'

'No. It irks me when I can't do as much as I want to but my writing shouldn't come between us.'

'I don't particularly want to go anywhere alone. How about having a short break and you taking the typewriter along?'

'But you can't. Not to an hotel.'

'We could rent a cottage in the country.'

8

'Patrick, we already *have* a cottage in the country!'

'No, somewhere quite different. Scotland? Somewhere really remote.' He held his whisky up to the firelight, admiring its colour. 'You know, I've always wanted to look round a distillery.'

'It's October. Scotland will be all damp and misty.'

'To hell with being practical! Let's just pack up and go. While you write, I'll go out and tramp the heather.'

'Looking for distilleries?'

'Yes. And clans. And haggis. That kind of thing.'

Later, when we were getting ready for bed, Patrick said, 'It's all very well for me to *talk* of another career, I've spent nearly all my working life in the army. In a way it's a closed world. I know nothing of industry or commerce. Don't you think I might be ... well ... a bit too stupid to do anything else?'

'For Heaven's sake!' I exploded. 'So it wasn't you who took *A Man Called Céleste* to the States and flogged it without any previous experience of such matters? I reckon they were so bemused by your style, they'd have bought *me* as well to star in it.'

This appeared to cheer him up somewhat and he bounced into bed. 'So we're making babies then.'

'I only asked you how you felt about it.'

'It's not just the doing of it, though. It's afterwards.'

'Me being on the wrong side of thirty-five you mean?'

'It gets more of a risk when you're older.'

'There were no problems at all with Justin.'

He gave me a wry look. 'I've a feeling that's why you want a holiday. To liven the old stud up a bit. And to have another sprog might make the said bloke feel more cheerful and not such a failure.'

'I get very annoyed when you *dissect* my thoughts, D12-style,' I informed him.

He smiled at me, not looking at all contrite.

'Do you still get pain?' I asked. 'When we ...'

'Sometimes,' he replied. 'But that's not why I haven't been making love to you very often lately.'

There couldn't be someone else, he simply isn't the sort of man to have affairs.

9

'I thought,' Patrick went on, 'that if we were to try for another baby, and if this wasn't to entail yours truly having to go and have various treatments to boost the necessary, then ...' Unusually for him, he floundered to a halt.

I stared at him. 'You mean you've been holding back to sort of ...'

He grinned at me when I too stopped speaking. 'Yes, absolutely. Manufacture a few more of the whatsits and therefore – '

'But I'd never for one minute suggest that you went to have treatment,' I interrupted. 'You've been in hospital far too much over the years as it is.'

The grin became a brave one.

I said, 'I couldn't bear the thought of you – '

'With wires attached to my – '

'Wires!' I shrieked.

'Giving one sort of little shocks in the – '

'You're out of your skull!' I shouted. 'They don't do that. Perhaps hormone treatment but not – '

'Injections,' Patrick interposed in strangled tones. 'Right in the the ...' His breath hissed through his teeth in graphic fashion. Then he could keep it up no longer and flopped over to howl with laughter into a pillow. I hit him with another pillow and then we both laughed until we cried.

'I forgot the woolly hat,' I said a while later.

'I'll manage without it this time,' he said softly into my ear.

When things were getting businesslike the phone rang.

'That *might* be my mother,' I said.

'She's the only person we know who rings at this time of night,' Patrick agreed resignedly.

It was. The call was a long one while I had to listen to the latest in a long series of petty resentments in an otherwise empty life. One is just expected to commiserate, nothing else will do. And all the while I was thinking of a hard, lean, masculine body and its promise of languid pleasures.

'Well, dear, I expect you're just off to bed,' my mother finished cheerily, the poison unloaded on to someone else. She had not asked how we were, not even after Justin.

'It *is* after midnight,' I was stung into saying.

10

'You once said you didn't mind what time I rang,' she said, bridling. 'Before you married that Patrick again you used to think about me.'

I gazed dumbly at the receiver. She had hung up.

As I went up the stairs I actually began to wonder if it had not been a blessing that my father had died in his forties and not had to endure what his wife has now become.

Patrick was sound asleep.

I sat on the bed gently and looked at him. It sounds daft but I love him even more when he is asleep. He was lying flat on his back, arms flung wide, lips slightly parted, his face artless as a child's. In repose, the brilliant grey eyes closed, there is no hint of the man who can reduce other men — strong men — to tears with his voice alone.

Life has not been kind to him.

Chapter One

The next morning I received the impression that Dawn was about to seize a bull by the horns. Sure enough . . .

'Would it be all right . . .' she began, being careful, I felt, to address neither Patrick nor me directly.

'Spit it out,' Patrick said, glancing up from toast, coffee and newspaper. 'I know — you want to start a weird sect and can you use the garage for meetings? Yes, of course. As long as you sweep out the bodies by the following morning. No?'

'Worse than that,' said Dawn.

'Worse! A year's salary in advance? Permission to marry a Cornishman? Yes to the first, most certainly no to the second.'

Here he broke off because I had kicked his left ankle hard. Kicking the right one would have been a complete waste of time.

'While you're away,' Dawn continued, blushing, the reason for my under the table violence, 'can Terry come for the weekends?'

'Of course,' Patrick answered without hesitation. 'He's always welcome here.'

'Is he really welcome *now*?' asked Dawn, a defiant tilt to her chin.

Patrick folded up the newspaper carefully in preparation for doing the crossword. 'Just because he's been given my job, doesn't mean I no longer speak to him.'

'I don't want there to be any awkwardness, that's all.'

He smiled at her. 'Verily, Miss Clark. I promise you there

will be no awkwardness.' He patted a chair next to him.
'Have some breakfast with us this morning instead of your
usual three slices of carrot and a glass of water. Justin's still
asleep.'

Dawn, who is always dieting, hesitated for a moment and
then sat down.

'Coffee?' Patrick enquired, a hand hovering over the
pot.

'Please — just black.'

Winningly, he went on, 'A slice of toast can do no *lasting*
harm.'

'I'll do it,' I offered. 'I want some too.'

'If you're quite sure you don't mind being left to hold the
fort while we're away,' Patrick was saying when I returned,
'Ingrid and I'll come to some kind of decision about having
a short break. It means you won't have your usual days off so
I was thinking along the lines of paying you double time for
those and then your having time off in lieu when we return.'

'There's really no need to be so generous,' said Dawn,
going pink again. 'You know I love living here. It hardly
seems like work. And with my mother living so close by I
can take Justin over to her for a couple of days. She welcomes
the company, and from the fuss she makes of Justin anyone
would think he was mine.'

She's really in love with Terry, I realised all at once,
watching her. They had known one another for a while now
and before Patrick had resigned Terry had been a frequent
visitor. One of the reasons for his absence, of course, was that
he had until very recently been on sick leave, the kidnapping
and ill-treatment almost being the cause of a youthful demise.
But youth being resilient and Terry's mother a wonderful
cook had gone towards his making a rapid and complete
recovery. I wondered if Dawn was about to set her cap at
him in a determined manner and hoped that Terry would
not take advantage of her. He might be well-educated, have
impeccable manners and be a person to be trusted with the
Crown Jewels, but he lacked none of the usual inclinations
of his sex. And I speak from experience.

It seemed unwise to say anything about this to Patrick,
there was no point in inviting awkwardness.

'Shall we take the high road then?' he said after break-fast.

'What? Just go? Without making any arrangements?'

'I'm sure it won't be too difficult to find somewhere to stay for a couple of weeks. Not at this time of the year.'

'We could put the car on the train.'

'Too right. I've no intention of driving that far.'

All at once the idea appealed to me enormously. The prospect of being footloose and fancy free, possibly staying in several places if we did not succeed in finding a permanent base, was beguiling.

'Tomorrow?' I suggested.

'If you like.'

We should have known better than to make plans. Half an hour later the phone rang. It was Colonel Daws, Patrick's boss when he worked for D12.

'Daws wants to talk to us,' Patrick reported, putting his head round the door of my writing room. 'Tomorrow.'

'I hope you told him we wouldn't be here.'

'Er — no.'

'Patrick!'

'It sounded as though it might be rather important.'

'I suppose we could go and see him and get a train from London.'

'It's not as easy as that. You have to book on the train. Anyway, he's coming here — he has business in Exeter.'

I glowered.

'I don't suppose he's going to offer to give me my job back,' Patrick said quietly, putting the reason for my scowl into words.

'Then why — ?'

'He's not one to waste a body's time.'

I sighed loudly. 'So we go on holiday the day after?'

'Of course. I'm just about to book the tickets.'

But because of a convention at the Gleneagles Hotel the train was fully booked for the next three days. Preferring not to travel over a weekend, Patrick made the arrangements for the following Monday.

Daws arrived very early the next morning. He had inti-mated over the phone that he would come before lunch and

I suppose nine-thirty cannot be described as a departure from this. But all the same I was slightly irritated when he made no apology for his early appearance, not even in joking fashion. I refrained from asking him if he would like breakfast and busied myself making coffee, grimacing when Dawn raised her eyebrows.

The Colonel looks like a soldier. He is tall, carries himself very straight, and progresses as though keeping time to a regimental march. His fine, greying fair hair tends to flop over his forehead and every so often he impatiently scoops it back. Despite his years, around fifty-five, he looks very fit and I imagine that if he was ever required to undertake active service again he would do so with great relish.

I felt, observing both men as I took in the coffee, that Patrick was at this moment the absolute antithesis of his one-time superior. Not having had time to change he was lounging in an ancient pair of jeans and even older sweater, his hair — unruly anyway as it was in dire need of cutting — festooned with a large black cobweb because, once again, he had been chopping kindling in the garage. I bit my lip to repress a quite unwarranted giggle.

'That business of Keeble ...' Daws said, referring to a past assignment.

'Not my pigeon,' Patrick responded. 'Terry worked on that.'

'But I thought you tidied up a few loose ends for him.'

Patrick emphatically shook his head. 'No. Steve Lindley gave him a hand. Wasn't it all about industrial espionage, with the added worry that someone had given away a few defence secrets for good measure?'

'Yes. Unfounded, fortunately.' The Colonel frowned. 'Funny, I was convinced you'd been involved with that job.'

The other quirked an eyebrow, his face openly wearing a 'Surely you haven't driven all the way from Exeter to ask me about *that*?' expression.

'Have you been offered anything yet?' Daws asked in careless fashion.

'I've been *ordered* to stay on leave,' Patrick told him.

It occurred to me that Daws might be bitterly regretting

forcing Patrick to resign. I also had an idea that he was feeling guilty.

The Colonel said, 'Well, I dare say you were due plenty of that. Going away?'

'To Scotland,' I declared, thinking that it was about time Daws stopped ignoring me. After all, I too had worked for D12. There had seemed little point in carrying on when Patrick left.

'Shocking weather they've been having north of the border,' Daws said to me with guileless gaze.

'It'll be a break for us even if it rains every day,' I said.

'Heard anything about a fella called Knox?' Daws asked when I had given him a second cup of coffee and after some rather dusultory conversation, mostly about the weather.

'D'you mean the Knox who's a washing machine tycoon or the guy who lives not a mile from here?' Patrick said, his face so bereft of expression I nearly cheered. I was beginning to see the reason for the visit.

'The latter,' Daws said stolidly.

Patrick cleared his throat. 'Rumoured to be a millionaire, supports local charities. Other than that keeps a low profile.' He smiled, sharklike. 'Why?'

'Any idea how he earns his living?'

'No.'

Daws obviously decided that it was about time he came to the point. 'It's rumoured that dirty money might be involved. He has quite a few friends in high places – Members of Parliament and so forth.'

'And Special Branch are worried about him?'

Daws nodded.

'And someone said to you what about it, and you said to them that as I live not far away I was just the chap to do some checking. The answer's no.'

'If you were thinking of going freelance –' Daws began.

'I'm only *thinking* about it,' Patrick interrupted.

'I can offer the usual arrangements,' said Daws. 'A commensurate fee for a few days' work.'

'No,' Patrick said again, adding, 'Sorry,' as though he did not mean it.

16

'There are no ill-feelings, I hope?' Daws said rather sharply.

'Not at all.'

'I thought you'd − '

Again Patrick butted in: 'Even if I was in the market for work I don't think I'd be prepared to snoop on the neighbours. And looking at it from another point of view, and assuming that this guy isn't boiling up postmen for breakfast every morning, people around here know me as the one-time head of a team involved with the PM's security − an army wallah. They might have read in the papers that I also worked for MI5 and got kicked out of that too. That's OK by me − I can live with it. But I'm not going to camp in the trees outside a neighbour's bedroom window wearing SAS long-johns.'

'As you wish,' Daws said after a short silence.

'Let Special Branch do their own dirty work,' Patrick suggested politely.

'They can't really. One of their top bods is a friend of Knox's.'

'Masons?'

'Yes.'

'Ah,' Patrick said without further comment.

Aware that Daws was not a Mason, I said, 'So that's why D12's been given the job?'

'In a way,' the Colonel replied blandly, not about to let us into all his secrets now we had refused to co-operate.

Why couldn't he just come straight out with it and say he had made a mistake? I thought angrily. Why are such men so stiff and proud? By being so obdurate he was actually hazarding the efficiency of the entire department, and well he knew it. *Had* he come with the idea of offering Patrick his job back but been unable to utter the words, 'I'm sorry'?

After a little more conversation during which Daws again tried gently to quiz Patrick on what he intended to do if the army came up with nothing interesting, and Patrick equally gently fended him off, the Colonel left.

'Do you realise you never once called him sir?' I said, clearing away the coffee things.

Patrick looked up from the crossword and smiled.

'D12 needs you desperately.'

17

'We're both fairly indispensable,' he observed. 'And God above knows I'm the last man to say such a thing if it wasn't true.'

'Terry's showing huge potential but ...'

'That's right, he's not ready yet.'

I did wonder what Daws would have said if Patrick had asked to be reinstated. Perhaps that would have provided the opening a proud man had been hoping for. But it was too late to worry about what might have been.

Daws was quite right about the Scottish weather. The problem was that it moved south, bringing snow and high winds. As we live several hundred feet above sea level, very close to Dartmoor, this meant blizzards with hungry ponies coming into the village looking for something to eat. To try to prevent incursions into the garden − the hinges on the gate in the lane having broken the week before − we bought a couple of bales of hay and scattered the fodder on the verge where the lane joins the village road. By this time I was beginning to think our holiday would never happen.

'You sure you don't fancy the Med?' I asked Patrick on the morning after the big snowfall. We had just come indoors, wet and exhausted after shifting a ton of logs that had been delivered about an hour before the snow started and which had been thoughtfully dumped in front of the garage doors. So we had had to dig the BMW out as well as there had been no choice but to leave it out in the yard all night.

Patrick was warming his hands in front of the Aga. 'I've booked the tickets for Monday now. Trust us to choose the coldest October on record.'

I had given Dawn the weekend off and she had gone to her mother's in Tintagel. When the phone rang just as I was getting Justin ready so he could play in the snow for a while − a bit like trying to get a Whirling Dervish into a flying suit − I thought it must be Dawn saying she could not get back as the roads were blocked.

After a short interval Patrick came upstairs.

'Don't tell me,' I said, seeing the expression on his face.

'The army have changed their mind and are sending you on manoeuvres in Finland.'

'No, it was Larry.'

Larry is Patrick's brother.

'He asked if he could come and see us tomorrow. Something seems to be bothering him so I could hardly refuse.'

'Shirley and the children as well?' I asked with sinking heart.

'No, he's coming on his own.' Patrick leaned on the doorpost, frowning deeply. 'He sounded really worried. Different. I wonder what the hell's the matter?'

Justin bounced towards his father and was given a bear-hug, complete with growling noises.

I said, 'I sometimes wish someone would invent a harmless powder that you could sprinkle on children to calm them down a little.'

'Gnome dust,' Patrick said, squinting at Justin ferociously. 'I'll get some in the Post Office.'

'That reminds me of the American editor who pronounced "nomenclature" as "gnomenclatter",' I recollected happily.

We both forgot about Larry and it was in this silly, carefree mood that we took Justin into the garden and built him a snowman. We had no possible way of knowing that Larry, a person who up until then I had regarded as a somewhat tedious, scruffy schoolteacher with decidedly left-wing political leanings, would present us with the most dangerous assignment we had ever handled.

I suppose that even the following morning I was tending to dismiss Larry's impending visit as of little importance. I had seen neither my brother-in-law nor his wife for several months, a fact that caused me no distress whatsoever as we had nothing in common. Ever since first meeting him I had — rightly or wrongly — regarded him as a bit of a misfit in the Gillard family. Elspeth, his mother, had once startled me greatly by commenting that he was a chip off no one's block. He has smartened himself up a little over the past couple of years, no longer to be seen in frayed jeans and sweater whatever the social occasion. Upon seeing him for the first time sporting slightly too-tight yellow trousers, a matching leather jacket and gold jewellery, Patrick had once been obliged to hide his face in his mother's walk-in larder.

Larry arrived at a little after ten in the family's elderly estate car.

'He's lost weight,' Patrick said from where he was covertly watching from the window.

'Come away! He'll see you,' I scolded. 'And don't go getting him riled. You know you have the same effect on him as throwing petrol on a bonfire.'

'Hi, Ingrid,' said Larry as I let him in. He thrust a heavy carrier bag into my arms. 'Brought a few bits and pieces for the youngster. Ours have grown out of them.'

The bag was full of plastic and wooden bricks and model making blocks, toy cars, tractors and trucks, all in new condition. I thanked Larry in a bemused kind of way and, looking at Patrick, saw that he too was lost for words.

It was not just that the man was considerably slimmer, there were other changes more subtle than the fact that he now wore smart cavalry twill trousers with a fine white wool polo-necked sweater, and that his hair was more stylishly cut than I had ever seen it. There was now a hard edge to him, something indefinable, almost as though at thirty-eight years old he had suddenly come of age and knew it.

Patrick collected his wits and both men shook hands.

'Sorry to descend on you like this,' Larry said when he had seated himself. He held out his arms as Justin ran to him. It came to me rather forcibly that our son ought to see his uncle far more often.

'It's lovely to see you,' I said, knowing it was an inane thing to say.

Larry pulled a wry grimace and shockingly, all at once, I saw how he had *really* changed. Leaner, fitter and somehow more mature, he was now virtually his brother's twin.

'Sorry about the job,' he said. 'Or should I say jobs? You were both involved, weren't you?'

'We were getting a bit old for all the excitement,' Patrick told him with a grin.

Larry said, 'I must admit I always thought you drove a

20

desk in Whitehall somewhere. When I read in the papers about shoot-outs and so forth ...' He whistled. 'It's why I'm here in a way. I need the kind of advice you can obviously give me.'

'Security?' Patrick enquired.

'Yes. We have a bit of a problem at the school.'

'Not a police matter?'

'No, not really. You'll see why when I explain.'

I sat down. I had a premonition that we would not be going to Scotland after all.

'About this time last year a member of staff left,' Larry began. 'A young bloke – only in his mid-twenties. He hadn't been at the school long but while he was with us he started to take the kids on adventure weekends in the Brecon Beacons in south Wales. You know the kind of thing – rock climbing, abseiling, pony trekking, caving. It really took off – fantastically popular. He was the kind of guy who inspired enthusiasm even in lazy kids. Well, the upshot of it was that when Alan left to take a much better paid job, I found myself in charge of what he'd started. If I hadn't taken it over the whole thing would have gone to the wall.'

I could think of nothing intelligent to say for the simple reason that I couldn't imagine Larry doing it.

'It does wonders for difficult children,' he continued, 'and gives a lot of self-confidence to the timid and motivation to those who are academically slow. I *had* to take it over. I couldn't have lived with myself if I hadn't.'

Patrick said, 'I hope you won't think I'm being bloody rude if I say it must have been very difficult for you to begin with.'

'Difficult!' Larry exclaimed. 'It was nigh-on impossible! Alan took me to the area for a whole week literally to show me the ropes. It was a crash course, again literally. I broke a bone in my foot and bruised every square inch of my body. Had to lose weight – get really fit. Wouldn't have been fair on the kids otherwise.'

'I know the feeling,' I said fervently. 'I won't tell you what happened to me the first time I abseiled.'

'I bet you didn't go all the way down upside-down.'

21

'Upside down!' I said in horror. 'What on earth do you abseil off?'

'A railway viaduct,' said Larry with a touch of pride. 'Right down the middle of an arch.'

'So what's the problem?' Patrick asked.

'Everything went swimmingly until a couple of months ago,' Larry said. 'I take a group once a month in the winter – usually older children – and fortnightly in the better weather. I've even had requests from parents to take a group of them too. I'm thinking on that one. No, there's no problem getting numbers. Things started to go wrong when one of the sixth form boys fell during a climbing session.'

'Go on,' Patrick prompted when his brother stopped talking.

'He wasn't badly hurt, thank God,' said Larry. 'Luckily he landed in a bush.'

'No safety rope?' I enquired.

'Yes, of course. That's what made it worse in a way. You see, both ropes had been tampered with.'

'You mean *cut*?' Patrick asked.

'Yes, there was no doubt about it. Nearly new ropes cut most of the way through.'

'And you didn't go to the police?'

Larry leaned forward and spoke in an undertone. 'Look, what would you have done? Some of the boys on that run were, quite frankly, oddballs. One had been in trouble with the police. I thought it might be an inside job – the lad who had fallen wasn't exactly *popular*. In fact, between ourselves, he's a young bastard. But talking to them afterwards – back at the school – I began to think that it might not have been an inside job after all.'

Patrick said, 'You mean, you now think someone had got to your equipment during the night – someone from the area.'

'I now know that *is* the case.'

'Surely you should call in the police,' I said.

Patrick had his eyes fiercely slitted, thinking. 'No, I'm beginning to see this from Larry's point of view. If someone locally doesn't approve of noisy kids all over the landscape, what better way to get rid of them than messing with the kit?

22

When parents get to hear of a couple of little accidents they won't allow their children on the expeds and the thing's stone dead before you can say knife.'

'I think it's a lot bigger than just a selfish native,' Larry said, a quiver in his voice. 'And as you know, I've always accused *you* of melodrama.'

Patrick gave him a good-natured but calculating look. 'Aye, you did too,' he murmured. 'What are your suspicions?'

'I don't know exactly. But things have happened since. We take all the equipment up into the loft of the barn at nights now.'

'Barn?' I queried.

'Where we sleep,' Larry explained. 'No mod-cons on these trips. But the minibus has to stay outside and the tyres have been let down on that a couple of times. And a boulder came at us on a scree we were walking over. I know for a fact that the damn thing hasn't moved in millions of years. But last weekend was the final straw. Someone took a shot at me.'

Placidly, Patrick said, 'Are you sure?'

'As sure as anyone who's had a bullet ricochet off a rock near their head.'

'Had you heard any other shots beforehand?'

'No, there was just the one.'

'Could you see where it came from? Was anyone around or running away afterwards?'

Larry shook his head. 'I didn't even look. I'm not used to being shot at. I just yelled at the kids to get their heads down.'

'And then what happened?'

'After it had been quiet for a few minutes I took a look around. There didn't seem to be anyone around so I mustered the group and we came back down the hill as fast as we could. It crossed my mind at the time that we might have disturbed some poachers.'

'Poachers usually operate at night. Were you still within the boundaries of the park?'

'Yes, just. If the weather's reasonable I take them up Bryn Glas and we have a bit of a picnic lunch. After that had

23

happened I started to wonder about other things I'd noticed but hadn't thought important at the time.'

'Things that made you ask yourself if you were being watched?'

'Yes. It was when we were at the viaduct mostly. We kept seeing a white van – just cruising around the lanes. And sometimes we'd see the glint of something shiny as it caught the light. I wondered if it was binoculars or a telescope that someone had trained on us.'

'Or the telescopic sights of a sniper's rifle,' Patrick mused aloud.

'Who does the barn belong to?' I asked.

'The landlord of a pub. The pub's where we get our meals so it's rather a good arrangement.'

'I take it he knows you've had problems,' Patrick said.

'He couldn't fail but know seeing the barn's right opposite the pub. Yes, he's almost as worried about it as I am – it's a lucrative little sideline for him, especially as the place is pretty remote.'

'As far as you're concerned, is he absolutely above suspicion?'

'Grief, yes! Him and his wife seem to live a hand to mouth existence in the winter. The summer's a bit better but he needs all the trade he can get. And he's a nice guy, goes to quite a lot of trouble in his own way. If he finds out it's one of the kids' birthday his wife makes a cake.'

'Some of this must be filtering through to the parents,' I said. 'Hasn't a lot of damage been done by whoever it is already?'

'There seems to be a conspiracy amongst the kids,' Larry replied with a smile. 'They don't want the weekends to stop so they're keeping mum.'

Patrick said, 'What about the headmaster? Does he know?'

'Of course. I'm not stupid. He told me to call in the police and stop the trips until it's sorted out. Naturally I had to agree to the latter but he was quite happy for me to consult you first.'

'Um,' Patrick said, dreamily looking at the ceiling.

'What do you think?' Larry asked tentatively.

24

'I think – '

'There's a PTA contingency fund that would pay your expenses should you decide to do anything personally.'

'I think,' Patrick said again, 'that there is nothing I should like better than to doss down in a no doubt bug-ridden barn at night and crawl over the frozen hills by day with maniacs taking pot-shots at me.' His gaze snapped back to Larry.

There was a rather pregnant silence until Larry realised that his brother was not being entirely sarcastic. 'You mean you'll – ?' he began delightedly.

'There's no need for you to pay our expenses,' Patrick continued. 'We have our own contingency fund. It's known as Ingrid's royalties.'

I laughed. I don't really know why since I could see that our holiday was as good as dead. Sometimes you have to get your laughs where you can.

'We?' Larry said. 'Surely Ingrid won't want to come. It's pretty primitive. No real facilities for a woman.'

It seemed sensible not to enlighten Larry that besides being able to abseil I can climb, map-read, am quite a good shot with a pistol and, if driven, can kill with a knife. I have also been comprehensively trained on how to live very, very rough.

Patrick obviously thought it a good idea for his brother to find this out slowly too. He said, 'But you take female children, don't you? And you mentioned you'd been asked to take a group of parents. Let's make it look like that, natural. It's no good rolling up with the Mountain and Arctic Warfare Cadre. Yes, to bring Ingrid's a good idea,' he rambled on as though I was anywhere but sitting not four feet from him. 'We've done a bit of camping together so it'll be all right.'

'I'll go and find the Keating's,' I said. 'And chilblain ointment. And the Arctic underwear.'

'The long-johns are in the loft,' said my husband helpfully. 'In a bag under the Christmas decorations.'

He was right too.

'You said you thought it might be something big,' Patrick said after lunch. 'Was that because you were shot at?'

25

'I just had the idea that whoever it was must be well organised,' Larry said. 'Keeping an eye on us, possibly following us around. And messing with our stuff without the dogs at the pub hearing them.'

'One man *could* keep surveillance on a group,' Patrick remarked. 'But I'm inclined to think there must be more than one. And you say there was a white van – did you by any chance get the number?'

'No, it was never that close to us.'

'Were there any objections locally to the school's presence in the area? Any landowners with a grudge against kids ruining their peace and quiet?'

'No. In fact everyone's been most helpful and welcoming. And don't forget, we're not the only people who visit the area.'

'Have you heard if anyone else has had bother?'

'No, but it would probably be worth making a few enquiries.'

'We must be subtle though. Softlee, softlee catchee monkee.'

'You *really* think there's something going on then?' Larry fretted. 'I have a ghastly worry that the business of the rope *was* one of the lads trying to put a few dents in young Matthew, and most of the rest a series of accidents and my imagination.'

Patrick grinned. 'Larry, old son, you have no imagination whatsoever and never have had. It doesn't bother me if the whole thing turns out to be a fluke. Something's got to be done to *prove* that it's either a fluke or it's not. Otherwise the children don't go on exped.'

'I hadn't thought of it like that,' Larry confessed. 'D'you think there ought to be a few more of us to make it look right?'

'Oh, yes, three's not enough.'

'Another couple,' I said. 'Preferably people we know really well and who are reliable enough to be told what's going on.'

'Plus another bloke who's handy with ropes and so forth. I wonder if Steve – ?' A long arm went out to the phone on the dresser and then halted in mid-air. 'No, he's not living

26

at home, is he? He and his wife have separated. I'll have to call him at work tomorrow.'

'How about the Murrays?' I said.

John and Lynne Murray live a matter of yards from the top of our drive. We have known them for years.

'Brilliant!' Patrick exclaimed. 'Ingrid, that really is brilliant. It'll give us a medic too.' He explained to Larry who they were, finishing up by saying, 'John's the local GP. They're outdoor sort of people and I'm sure John once said that they used to do a lot of hillwalking when they lived near Keswick.'

'Can a doctor get away that easily?' Larry asked.

Patrick once again reached for the phone. 'Well, John's father stands in for him when he's away. He's retired now but enjoys keeping his hand in. One can only ask.'

The Murrays were at home and accepted the offer of pre-dinner drinks.

'Have you noticed ...?' said Lynne to no one in particular but with a big wink at me ' ... that when *Patrick* asks us down here for a drink, he usually wants something. When Ingrid asks there are no strings attached.'

Patrick threw himself on his knees before her. 'Madam, it is your fair company alone that I desire.'

'Shall I come back later?' John asked in mock seriousness.

Larry came in and was introduced. When everyone was settled with a drink Lynne said to Patrick. 'Go on, tell us what the strings are. I know there are some and I can't relax until I know the ghastly details.'

'The strings are that you might get shot,' Patrick told her. 'Ice?'

She held out her glass. 'Tonight? How madly exciting.'

'I think the man's serious this time,' John observed.

'We wondered if you'd like to come on a little expedition with us,' Patrick said.

'Ooo, yes!' Lynne cried. 'Count me in.'

Patrick explained, and while he did I studied our would-be team members. Of the two Lynne is slightly older, although she never reminds anyone about it. Both are in their late forties. John has medium height, a stocky build, black crinkly

27

hair that always looks as though he has just plastered it down with water. He's a reserved sort of man. Lynne is anything but reserved, especially when with members of the opposite sex whom she finds attractive. Patrick, for example. She has the sort of figure that used to be described as 'comfortable', loves clothes and always seems to be wearing something new. An untiring and dependable woman, she works hard for several charities, toils endlessly in her immaculate garden, her only real relaxation seemingly that of reading romances. She totters, laden with them, to and from the mobile library every other Thursday.

I should really have mulled over her taste in reading material as I sat quietly listening and watching, drinking white wine. It should have occurred to a writer – who after all studies the human mind – that a woman who reads nothing but love stories might not be able to face life in the raw, might in fact, once removed from her own cosy surroundings, be unrealistic and unreliable. But I did not and therefore I am partly to blame for what happened.

'There's the usual clause, I suppose,' John said, straight-faced. 'That we come at our own risk?'

Patrick said, 'In my experience people on military exercises or even fighting a war are often injured driving vehicles into ditches or sprain their ankles running over rough terrain. Yes, most certainly you come at your own risk. But everything will be done to maximize safety. And I'd like to point out at this stage that we're only going to *find out* if there's a problem. If we discover there is, under no circumstances will either of you be expected to help sort it out.'

'And we won't really have to abseil and crawl through caves getting all muddy,' Lynne said.

'Yes,' Larry said. 'You will.'

She went a bit pale. 'But aren't there spiders in caves?'

'White ones,' Larry replied with a relish I had heard coming from someone else well known to me.

'Oh, *no*,' Lynne moaned and took a large mouthful of her gin and tonic. 'I couldn't. I really couldn't.'

I nudged her and said in a stage whisper, 'But they're only about half an inch across and blind so you end up feeling really sorry for them.'

She placed a hand over mine and implored, 'Ingrid, swear on everything holy to you that they're no more than half an inch across.'

'On her great-aunt Matilda's liberty bodice,' Patrick said.

'Three-quarters of an inch at the absolute most,' I promised.

Lynne shuddered.

It was decided that we would not all travel to the school in Bristol together. Larry, of course, would already be there. We would meet him at the school, from where we would depart in the mini-bus, the following Friday lunchtime, round about twelve-thirty.

'I'll be in touch with you during the week,' Patrick told him. 'And I'll hold another briefing here before we come. Perhaps you'll organise some kind of programme and let me have it.'

'There's still only five of us,' Larry said. 'Five isn't really a group.'

'We can't risk taking any more of what I can only call ordinary folk,' Patrick said. 'I'm going to ask Steve Lindley, a colleague, when I can get hold of him.'

But when he rang first thing on Monday morning he was told that Steve had gone to the States on a ten day mission for Daws.

Then I remembered something. This produced an idea which I immediately rejected. But the idea itself was a good one even though it had major drawbacks. These would not affect me personally so I decided to sound out the person whom they would.

Patrick was in my writing room, having borrowed my desk to write cheques to pay bills.

'You've got that look on your face that denotes I'm required to agree to something I won't like,' he said after glancing up quickly.

'Terry's due to arrive here on Friday night to spend the weekend with Dawn.'

There was quite a long silence.

'Dawn won't be very happy if we whistle him off to Wales,' Patrick said.

29

'No, we'd have to take her too.'

'What about Justin?'

'It's possible her mother might have him. She dotes on him and has already offered if we're ever stuck.'

There was another silence while Patrick sealed an envelope.

'Are Dawn and Terry lovers?' he asked.

'Not until next weekend,' I said. 'I think.'

'And would a mere male be correct in assuming that he would be Dawn's first?'

'That would be a fairly safe assumption.'

'And that Terry doesn't know about it yet, and the whole idea's to lure him eventually to the altar?'

'As usual, your perspicacity is breathtaking.'

'Ingrid, it does *complicate* matters.'

'Not at all,' I declared. 'It's up to them whether they come. And they're not children. Besides, Terry's exactly the sort of person we want. That's if ...'

'That's if he and I can overcome any initial difficulties,' Patrick finished for me. 'Yes, you're absolutely right. But I think we ought to ask Dawn first. She's probably been planning this weekend for ages.'

We found her with Justin in his room, our son perched on his potty. Having an audience never bothers him.

Dawn's reaction to the proposal was exactly as I had expected. She looked bitterly disappointed but said, 'You don't have to ask me along just because you want Terry on the team.'

I found myself praying that Patrick would be tactful. This really was rather a delicate situation.

'I'm not really an outdoor girl,' she continued. 'I'll get in the way and chicken out of doing things.'

'You won't when I'm shouting at you,' Patrick said with a smile.

'I just don't want to be a drag.'

'Honeychild, you could never be a drag,' Patrick said and then astounded the girl by kissing her cheek. 'If you can cope with this little monster you can cope with anything.' As he went down the stairs he called back, 'There's no privacy in a barn though, just carry on as you would have done here.'

30

Dawn had her fingertips on the spot where he had kissed her. 'There's no answer to that is there?' she said to me.

'Don't worry,' I said. 'I intend to remind him it's supposed to be our second honeymoon.'

Chapter Two

During the next few days I wrote like a woman possessed. This meant that I did not answer the phone, made no tea or coffee and prepared no meals until the evening by which time I was cross-eyed from typing. At nine-thirty I went to bed and slept deeply and dreamlessly, not even noticing when Patrick slipped in beside me. This regimen had been put into operation before, when I had a deadline to meet. No deadlines this time, just the realisation that if I intended to carry on being a writer I would have to deliver the goods.

While I was working — and I was in a world of my own, that of *Echoes of Murder* — I was aware of people moving around me, as it were, in their own orbits. Justin, of course, was Dawn's responsibility and other than being on hand to give him a cuddle before he was put to bed I did not have to worry about him. Patrick, I knew, gave him a lot of attention during the day. Patrick also fixed his own breakfast and lunch and could be relied on to produce the odd sandwich for a hungry wife. At least, sustenance arrived on one corner of my desk and I confess that sometimes I was not sure who had put it there, or afterwards, what I had eaten.

By Thursday *Echoes of Murder* was a most satisfying pile of newly typed sheets of A4. It was beginning to look as though even with the weekend break I would finish it some time during the following week. I silently promised that I would take everyone out to dinner as a thank you.

'That was Larry on the phone earlier,' Patrick said as I descended from my eyrie to prepare the dinner. 'Someone burned down the barn last night.'

'Really arson?' I asked.

'Yes, the bloke who owns it, the innkeeper, said when he rang Larry that he could smell paraffin in the ruins. None was ever stored there.'

'So what now?'

'Well, not unnaturally, he called the police. But he was keen that it shouldn't put an end to the trips. A farmer friend has promised the use of another barn. Apparently it has proper locks on the doors.'

'It's proved that Larry was right,' I said, taking fillet steak from the fridge.

'Is there enough steak for Terry too?'

'I thought you said he wasn't coming until tomorrow morning.'

'No, he rang as well. Asked if he could come tonight. Dawn's gone to fetch him from Plymouth station.'

'Patrick, you might have mentioned this while the butcher was open.'

'Sorry, I never gave it a thought.'

I groaned. Yes, I told myself, this man could organize a military expedition to Outer Mongolia. But not an extra guest for dinner.

'Is there any in the freezer?' he asked.

'Yes, but it'll never thaw in time.'

'Bung it in the microwave for a bit.'

'That's beastly cuisine!' I raved. 'You know I *hate* doing anything like that.'

Patrick shrugged. 'Give him mine.'

'Oh, sure. While you have bangers. That'll really put Terry at ease.'

In the end I decided that we'd each have a bit less steak and a lot more sauté potatoes.

Terry arrived with enough kit to suggest that *he* was off on a trip to Outer Mongolia. He and Dawn staggered in with it and the room looked quite full.

'Pump action shotguns?' Patrick said, testing the weight of a large sports bag. 'Machine guns? A small culverin? Ammo for the mortar in pieces in your other luggage?'

'You're very hot and it's yours,' he was told.

'Mine!'

33

'Oh!' said Dawn and I together when the bag was unzipped.

It was indeed a baby cannon, of burnished iron resting on a brass carriage.

Patrick became quite speechless with joy.

'Dad found it in a junk shop in Southport when he and Mum were on holiday,' Terry explained. 'He likes messing around repairing things. It's a starting cannon for yacht races.'

'But he gave it to you,' Patrick said.

'And I looked at it and thought of *you*.'

'Oh, brother,' was all Patrick could say just then.

'It only fires blanks,' Terry added meaningfully.

'Is that why you immediately thought of me?' Patrick asked, one eyebrow quirked.

'No, because you've got Justin now.'

'He didn't mean *that*, Terry!' Dawn burst out in an agony of embarrassment.

'Yes, he did,' Terry declared and Patrick hooted with laughter, causing poor Dawn to scuttle off into the kitchen, cheeks aflame.

'I popped into Tesco's for some more steak,' she said to me when I followed. 'I didn't think there was enough.'

I hugged her. We were all off to a very good start.

It immediately became apparent that, as far as Patrick and Terry were concerned, there would be no problem. Patrick's controversial departure from D12 was not discussed. The circumstances of what we were proposing to do, and the fact that it was to be undertaken during free time, meant that both men were able to slip easily into their previous relationship. Only once was the work of the department mentioned.

'Have you been asked to check up on a guy called Knox?' Patrick asked Terry over dessert.

'No. Why?'

'Daws wanted me to.'

'Never heard the name. He's said nothing to me about it.'

'How very odd,' I commented. 'You don't think – ?'

'Yes, I do think,' Patrick said. 'It sounds as though our Richard was satisfying himself that I wasn't prepared to do dodgy freelance jobs in order to work for him again. In other words, to return to D12 at any price.'

'Some work *is* being contracted out,' Terry said and thereby probably revealed more than he ought to have done. Patrick made no further comment.

At eleven, the Murrays – who had had a dinner date elsewhere – arrived for the briefing. As they sat down, Lynne wearing an off-the-shoulder glittery thing, I suddenly wished they weren't coming with us. I inwardly berated myself for being so churlish. But the feeling stayed. It might have had something to do with the condescending smile Lynne had given Dawn when she discovered she was accompanying us.

'Positively the last impression I want to give,' Patrick began, 'is that this is me playing soldiers for the weekend. Strictly speaking my brother Larry is in charge of this trip and from the point of view of venue, times, and the exact locations for activities he is. But I made it quite clear to him when he was here that he is not responsible for our personal safety beyond the normal call of duty and he agreed, emphasising that he'll take as much care of us as he does the kids. In other words he'll do his utmost in his particular field. Now Larry hasn't been doing this outward bound stuff for very long and there's a hell of a lot of difference between keeping kids in one piece and undertaking the kind of surveillance that I feel past events have justified. The surveillance will be my responsibility. The practical effects of this will be that Larry will issue orders concerning, say, abseiling down a cliff and everyone will obey him, including me. Everybody will obey *me* if I suddenly shout to get your heads down. Is that understood?'

We all agreed to this, Lynne then saying, 'I hope there's no confusion. His voice sounds quite similar to yours.'

'You'll know,' Patrick told her. 'If I shout, you'll know.'

It occurred to me that only two people present have been on the receiving end of Patrick really shouting and how this has the effect of a kick in the pants.

'If we nail the source of this interference we can regard

the trip as a success,' Patrick resumed. 'I do not propose scampering all over Wales after some English hating nutcase – if that's who is the villain. We leave the police to make arrests.'

'They must mean business though,' Terry said, 'Setting fire to the barn like that.'

'It could be an accident,' John pointed out. 'It would only need a cigarette end.'

'The smell of paraffin notwithstanding *everything* could be an accident,' Patrick said.

'Your brother was shot at,' Lynne reminded him.

Terry said, 'D'you reckon he'd be able to tell the difference between an air rifle pellet and a bullet?'

'No,' Patrick replied. 'I don't.'

'So it could be just a prank by some yobbo,' said Lynne.

'I don't think we are talking about anything much more serious than that,' Patrick said. 'Yobbos. Possibly rich yobbos with nothing better to do. It might even have been a .22. The same people might have cut the ropes and burned down the barn. For a laugh. There are some pretty sick folk about.'

'There's the question of range though,' Terry said slowly. 'You have to get quite close to use an air rifle or a .22. Was there sufficient cover? Did Larry see anyone?'

'He said he didn't,' Patrick recalled. 'But he wouldn't have done if they were hiding in a bush and wearing camouflage clothing. We'll need to go to the exact spot and have a look. There's one request I'd like to make to you personally. We're not aiming to look like experts at anything. This is supposed to be a parents' outing. So don't shin up mountains like a mountain goat and abseil down 'em with your usual aplomb.'

'There's no danger of that,' Terry told him. 'The last time you saw me I was in a wheelchair, remember?'

'So you were,' Patrick remarked softly and there was a silence while, I think, the three of us again re-lived the moments in that room in London. To reiterate bald facts – that Terry had been kidnapped and badly treated and that Patrick made no move to stop him killing the one responsbile,

36

Pugh – does not present a true picture. Terry was at a stage where he could have slid into an easy and, by that time, probably longed for death. Barely conscious, he had become aware of our capture in that room set aside by Pugh for black magic rituals and as he said himself afterwards, was not sure what to do. It is a measure of the man that he was able to contemplate doing anything. Patrick, cuffed to his knees by Pugh, ascertained whether Terry was shamming or torpid in fairly typical fashion. He kissed him, a ploy that succeeded in shocking the comatose prisoner awake. Pugh, who had Patrick's revolver, had then pulled the trigger on Terry. The Smith and Wesson had jammed. Twice. The rest was inevitable. Pugh was overpowered, his men disabled and another gun snatched from the floor by Terry. Pugh had died. It had all taken moments. Seconds. How could we ever forget?

'Of course! The kidnap,' Lynne cried. 'I'd forgotten about that. I must say, Terry, you've made a wonderful recovery.'

'I wouldn't have thought you ought to do anything too strenuous,' John said soberly. 'Don't want to push your luck.'

'Absolutely,' Terry agreed. 'I've only been swimming a bit and not running more than five miles a day.'

'A few reminders,' Patrick announced. 'Wear warm clothing. Jeans are banned. They chafe and you'll die of cold in 'em if they get wet. Wool, silk and cotton in several layers. Waterproofs, hats, gloves. Changes of warm socks and long-johns. And as I said, we're supposed to be parents. Terry, Larry and I don't expect anyone to be *clever* at anything. So ladies especially are permitted to scream whilst dangling on ropes.'

'Gee, thanks,' Lynne drawled. 'Do the ladies get a laugh at *your* expense?'

'We'll have our own briefing,' I said, slightly miffed that he hadn't included me among the experts.

It was a very early start the next morning. Justin had to be taken to Dawn's mother in Tintagel. Dawn herself took him as she would not be required to do any further driving.

Patrick would drive the four of us to Bristol — the Murrays were making their own way — and we would leave his car by the caretaker's house at the school. At least, that had been the plan. In practice not all our kit would go in the boot of a single car.

'It's no good, we'll have to take your car as well,' Patrick said, throwing out some of the bags. 'I'll make a start with Terry right now and you wait for Dawn. Do you know where the school is?'

'Of course,' I said.

I was gathering the last few bags together when Dawn drove into the yard.

'D'you know something?' I said as she got out of the car. 'I've just had a look indoors and I can't see it anywhere. Patrick's taken that bloody cannon to Wales with him!'

Pirate always seems to know when we are going away and takes herself off to the neighbour who feeds her for me. At first this elderly lady had been quite adamant that although she was very pleased to feed the animal, cats belonged outside. This was a good arrangement as far as I was concerned. At home Pirate has a box lined with old sweaters in the garage. I am not sure exactly when it was that the tortoiseshell began to wheedle herself into the widow's affections but now, I know, there is a chair with a cushion by the fire and, on very cold nights, a blanket at the bottom of the bed.

We stopped for coffee near Taunton — the timetable was generous to allow for emergencies and refreshments — and then carried on to Bristol, arriving with at least twenty minutes to spare.

As he helped me stow the bags I said to Patrick, 'What did they say at the Army Ordnance Depot?'

He gave me one of his ghastly stock-in-trade death's head smiles. 'They said they didn't have anything to fit. But if I went to a naval place they'd probably have grape and chain shot.'

'Left over from the Battle of Trafalgar, I suppose?'

'Why not? Petty Officers can still get cutlasses if they want a guard of honour for a wedding.'

Sometimes man and wife can talk to one another and be unsure of the presence of leg-pulls.

38

'Only I rang them,' Patrick went on, 'this morning while you were in the shower.'

'You're serious?' I squeaked.

'You know me. I'm always serious. I described it to a gunnery officer who knew his stuff. It's not a starting cannon at all but a very small stern-chaser. They used to be placed at the stern of first-raters. The idea was that you pretended to run away from the enemy and then fired along the length of his ship, bringing down all the rigging of the enemy ship and maiming everyone for'ard.'

'But you need things like gunpowder and stuff like that,' I stuttered.

'Or shotgun cartridges taken apart and so forth.'

'Are you telling me this man gave you some kind of recipe?'

Patrick chuckled. 'No one's going to burn down a barn under *me*.'

Mentally, I wallowed. 'But things like that were hundreds of years ago. It all belongs in the days of Hornblower.'

'Pieces of eight! Pieces of eight!' he cackled.

I gave up. Sometimes men are beyond my understanding.

It was still very cold for the time of year. Larry had had to return home for something he had forgotten and while we waited we stamped our feet to keep warm, standing in the lee of the mini-bus to shelter from the strong northerly wind.

'I thought you were joking when long-johns were mentioned,' Dawn said, shivering.

'So what are you wearing underneath?' Terry sternly demanded.

'You mean, extra?'

'All right, extra.'

'A tee shirt. Another pair of pants.'

Patrick groaned. 'Woman, you'll freeze.'

'I've got two pairs.' I said. 'You can have the others.'

'Combs!' Lynne exclaimed, just back from a walk round the playground. 'Really?'

'Not another one,' Terry said under his breath.

'Combs!' Lynne said again, this time her voice an octave higher.

'Not necessarily,' Patrick informed her heavily. 'The things

39

are available in two separate halves. And I can assure you that this weekend will not be conducive to flitting around in lacy black underpinnings. When you fall into an underground river and we fish you out and strip you in order to get you warm again, you won't be worried about looking seductive, will you?'

Lynne stuck out her bottom lip at him and walked away for a short distance.

'Underground rivers?' Dawn said to me in a whisper.

''fraid so,' I confirmed.

'I think I'll check that with Larry,' Dawn decided as he arrived, full of apologies.

'Water in the caves?' he repeated. 'Oh, yes. Of course. A river no less. You have to make sure it's not going to rain before you enter the underground cave system in case it floods. But you'll get wet because you have to crawl through it − right up to your chin.'

'What, the little kids as well?' Lynne said, appalled.

Larry gave her a scornful look. 'Why not? But they get a shift on. I tell 'em there are crocs in it.'

'It does wonders for their characters,' Patrick informed the gathering at large, his face as sober as a priest's.

Chapter Three

Once across the Severn Bridge it took very little time to reach our destination, too little judging by the set expressions on the faces of a couple of females present. All the while the weather deteriorated until, by the time we were negotiating the narrow lanes near Ystradfellte, it had started to rain, icy rain that soon turned to sleet. Of wooded hills, valleys and mountains we could see nothing. Visibility by this time was down to about fifty yards.

A short while later Larry pulled into the yard behind a very run-down looking pub. On the other side of the yard the blackened roof beams of a barn were open to the sky, still smoking slightly. In the present weather conditions it was the most dismal, depressing place I had ever seen.

'I'll check with Jimmy to see where we've to go,' Larry said.

'Jimmy doesn't sound a very Welsh name,' Lynne said, speaking for the first time in twenty miles.

'He's a Scot,' Larry said, clambering out. 'Shan't be a mo'.'

No one spoke while he was away.

'It's good,' he said when he returned. 'The place he's found for us is only a hundred yards away. I know where he means — it fronts right on to the road.'

It was another barn, the slate roof patched with rusting sheets of corrugated iron, the doors rotting, sagging on their hinges.

'I thought you said it would be secure,' John said to Larry as we all piled out.

Larry gave the offending doors a quick glance. 'Yeah, Jimmy mentioned that. There's a guy coming to do something about it.'

Sometime, I thought. When he has nothing better to do and feels like it. Never.

'We go for our meals to the pub,' Larry was saying. 'And we can use the loos there. But Jimmy does ask that the ladies especially don't book the ... facilities all the time.'

'Aren't there any toilets in the village?' Lynne asked, nostrils flaring.

'No,' Larry said shortly. 'Personally I find it easier to leave off shaving while I'm here.'

'I see,' Lynne said, giving John a 'you dare' look.

We lugged our stuff into the building. It was indescribably filthy. In one corner of the 'downstairs' — the upper area being reached by a ladder with several rungs missing — was an ancient Rayburn solid fuel stove. I opened the door to the firebox wondering if we could get it going to provide a little heat and hot water and then saw that the chimney was badly rusted, now merely a shell of corroded metal.

'At least all the ropes and stuff are okay,' Larry observed. 'They're kept locked away in Jimmy's garage when we're not here.'

'I should check them all the same,' Patrick advised.

'It's not too bad up here,' Terry called from above. He had been stamping about up there testing the strength of the floor, sending cobwebs and dust down on to our heads.

'The mattresses in the other barn were all destroyed in the fire,' Larry said sadly.

'Thank the Lord for that,' Lynne snapped, gingerly climbing the ladder.

'There's plenty of fresh straw to sleep on,' Terry said.

I went up, inwardly agreeing with Lynne about the mattresses.

It was dark, just a little light coming through a small opening with no glass in it. Oddly, there was a door in one end wall. Transverse low roof beams had the effect of dividing the loft into three; a middle part where the ladder was with a floor area some six feet square, and two larger areas at either end of the barn. As my eyes got used to the

42

gloom I could see that, indeed, clean golden straw had been heaped on the floor of these.

'That settles it then,' said Larry happily. 'One end for the ladies, one for the blokes.'

'You sleep where you like,' Lynne retorted. 'We've got a double sleeping bag.'

'Where does the door lead to?' I asked.

'There's a twenty foot drop into a midden,' Terry replied with a laugh. 'I think we'd better regard it as an emergency exit.'

Patrick was looking through the small opening in the wall. 'This is *excellent*,' he said to Terry. 'It's right above the main entrance.'

I knew what he had in mind but thought it best to say nothing.

'I didn't think it would be like this,' Dawn said plaintively when we rejoined her. She had remained below and was staring disbelievingly at the beaten earth floor and rotting sacks and rubbish piled in the corners.

Patrick glanced at Larry, observed that his brother found nothing amiss, gave him a Gilbert and Sullivan salute and said, 'Ingrid, let Dawn have your spare warm layers and the pair of you jog to the pub where she can climb into them. All other members of the party to assemble outside in three minutes with cameras and valuables from kit bags which will be locked in the van. Then we'll all repair to the pub for something hot to eat and drink.'

'It'll be all right,' I said to Dawn as we arrived, slightly out of breath, at the back door of The Dragon.

'John's very aloof,' she said. 'He's hardly spoken. Did he really want to come?'

'Well, Lynne did. But, then again, Lynne ...'

'Has a bit of a crush on ...'

'Umm.'

'It might make it a bit awkward.'

'You always get undercurrents — whoever you're with on outings like this. It's human nature.'

'Ingrid ...'

'Look,' I said. 'If there's one person on this trip who Patrick won't let fall down a hole or get stuck in a cave,

43

it's you. And it's nothing to do with the fact that you're Justin's nanny.'

But she just gave me a wan smile.

Larry, sensibly, brought the mini-bus and parked it where he could keep an eye on it. Lynne and John came with him, something I had not expected. I shared a little of Dawn's misgivings for a moment, but for another reason.

Patrick and Terry were almost right behind them, jogging slowly and chanting a rugby ditty I hoped Dawn couldn't catch the words of. Every few paces they paused and with frenzied oriental cries made violent judo-style lunges at one another that always missed widely.

'I thought this was supposed to be a low-profile thing,' John said to me.

'I reckon that's two ordinary high spirited blokes fooling around, don't you?' I retorted, going inside.

The first thing I noticed in the public bar was a huge fireplace with logs burning brightly. We all made for it and basked in the heat. But the landlord shooed us next door into the saloon bar where the fire was, if anything, larger. Several small tables had been pushed together to make one long one and laid with cutlery and plates.

Jimmy, in fact, was the kind of Scot I would have preferred to call by his full name. He looked like a James and was a quietly spoken, towering Highlander, shyly smiling and with hair like a full-blown marigold. In my mind's eye I could see him on Burn's Night in full regalia and kilt, piping in the haggis.

'What on earth is a man like that doing in *Wales*?' I whispered to Larry.

'No idea,' he said. 'You ask him, Ingrid, I've never had the nerve. Perhaps he doesn't trust the Welsh to serve good beer.'

'There's not much good beer in Scotland,' Patrick remarked. 'As far as I know there's only *one* pub in Glasgow that sells Marston's Pedigree.'

'You won't get that here,' John said, scanning the bar.

'No, but there's Felin Foel.'

'Feelin' foul?' Lynne said, puzzled. 'Or is that how you are afterwards?'

44

There was only one other person in the room, a dour-looking man dressed in country tweeds who had ignored our greetings and left. His black and white collie followed him out, tail down, casting a mournful look at us over its shoulder.

'We've ruined that dog's day,' Terry said, turning his chair round so that it faced the fire.

'Gone to report back, do you think?' Lynne said to Patrick in thrilling tones.

'I *think* he's the local magistrate,' Larry said.

Terry said, 'Just think, no baths until Monday night.'

'There's no need to rub it in,' Lynne said crossly. 'Anyway, I intend to bathe in the river you can hear down the road somewhere.'

'I shouldn't if I were you,' Patrick said. 'Just think of all that slurry going into it and dead sheep.'

At this point Jimmy and a girl I immediately knew not to be his wife brought our meal. It was an old-fashioned high tea; cold ham and beef, salad and bread and butter. There were gallons of hot tea that we fell upon thankfully. We finished with scones served with butter and jam and solid home-made fruit cake.

'Now,' said Larry when this was cleared away, 'walkies.' He pulled a dog-eared map from his pocket.

'Surely we're not going to do anything tonight?' Lynne said.

'Yes,' Larry said. 'Walkies. Nothing strenuous. Only just over five miles.'

'Just to ease us into the activities tomorrow,' Patrick explained. 'Larry, did you have any interference on this walk?'

'No,' his brother replied. 'No problems.'

'In that case I think the situation will be secure enough if Terry and I merely ride shotgun, as it were, and don't keep watch from a distance.'

'It'll be dark soon anyway,' Terry observed.

Larry said, 'I usually split the group into two and as the walk's circular one goes one way and the second the other. Do you want to do it like that? Do you want to do *exactly* what the children do or would you find that all too much of

45

a bore?' It might have been my imagination but he seemed to be addressing Lynne alone with this last question.

She removed her gaze from a poster advertising sheep dog trials. 'What does everyone else want to do?'

Patrick said, 'Personally, I think we ought to stick as closely as possible to what the children do. Eventually we have to go back to that school and say that it's safe to carry on with the trips. If there are *hidden* risks then we must explore all possibilities.'

After a little more discussion everyone agreed with this.

'Fine,' Larry said. 'Okay, you lot, listen. We split into two groups. I suggest that Patrick goes with Dawn and John, Terry with Ingrid and Lynne. As I said just now, the walk is a circuit so if everything goes according to plan you'll pass one another halfway round. The walk's over minor roads and forest tracks. You can't get lost if you use the map I'll give you but as a check I usually drive the road part of the circuit in the bus to make sure that everyone's on course.'

'One question,' John said. 'Patrick, can you walk five miles without suffering discomfort? We don't want this to be an endurance test for you.'

The thought was no doubt basically a kind one and of course John could have no idea of the standard of physical fitness that Patrick has had to regain in order to work for D12. But to remind everyone that his Falklands injuries have resulted in his right leg below the knee now being of man-made construction was less than tactful.

Patrick smiled bleakly. 'Army officers have to present themselves for periodic assessments. Usually I'm allowed to prove that my heart and lungs are still functioning on an exercise bicycle. But since a new medic took over he's apt to send me off with the others on a three mile march at the double with full pack and rifle. After that the stump of my leg does *sometimes* have a couple of blisters.'

Clearly embarrassed for his brother's sake, Larry said, 'There's a questionnaire if you're interested.' He gave Terry and Patrick each a sheet of rumpled paper. 'Sorry they're so creased, I didn't have time to get some new ones done.'

'List the varieties of animals and birds that you see,' Terry read out. 'And trees when you're in the forest.'

46

'The trees we walk into?' Lynne enquired and looked a bit put out when nobody laughed.

Terry said, 'As I have Ingrid in my team, we'll win that bit easily. She knows the names of everything. What's the prize, by the way?'

'Buying the losing team a round of drinks,' Patrick said. 'Let's hit the road.'

Terry said, 'There's just one point I'd like to clear up, Patrick. You said that we're not about to sort this problem out if we discover what it is but let the police make arrests. What action do you propose we take if we're attacked?'

Patrick dug in the pocket of the anorak hanging on his chair and handed over the revolver that Colonel Daws has never asked him to give back. 'That kind of action,' he said.

'What does that leave *you* with?'

'A knife.'

Speaking more quietly Terry said, 'And under *no* circumstances will you and I endeavour to go in hot pursuit of an enemy?'

'Ah,' Patrick murmured. 'Let's just say that we'll have to take into consideration whether we regard the particular abilities of an enemy such that they would represent a direct threat to the safety of unarmed police. If we *do* find that to be the case . . .'

'Quite. And it would take a hell of a time to get people from the Tactical Support Group in the area.'

Outside, Larry called to Lynne, who had set off without waiting for Terry and me, 'Your waterproofs are in the bus. If you don't take them I'll bring a pail of water with me and chuck it all over you.'

'I'll give them to her,' Terry said. 'And read the Riot Act.'

With this on his mind he forgot that we should have a torch each and we only ended up taking one.

'How now, old chum?' said Terry to me after a hundred yards or so.

I took a deep breath of pine-scented air and said, 'I can't get over how quickly you've recovered.'

'Steak and kidney pudding three times a day would sort anyone out.'

47

'I've never forgotten the look on your mother's face when Patrick told her you were alive. She thought about the propriety of hugging a major and then did.'

It was not quite dark so we did not need the torch to see where we were going. The road stretched before us, the wet surface a pale silvery grey in the gloom. It was still cold, an occasional spot of rain hitting our faces.

'Can you see the map all right by the light of the torch?' Lynne asked. She had put on her anorak but was still walking a few yards in front of us.

'I've memorized it,' Terry told her. 'But I'll check now and again.'

'Trees!' I said. 'We've passed quite a lot in the hedges.' I acquired the torch and flashed it around briskly. 'Write down oak, ash and elm.'

'I thought we only had to list the forest ones.'

'Initiative,' I asserted. 'You know D12's motto − "Always be a clever-clogs."'

Very soon we reached Forestry Commission fencing and what light there was was blotted out by tall Sitka spruce growing on both sides of the road.

'Yes,' said Terry. 'I'm brought to mind of a certain splinter I got in myself climbing one of these fences.'

'And I held the torch for the medic,' I said.

'A medic for a splinter!' Lynne said.

'It was about two inches long,' I told her. 'Went right through his trousers into his scrotum.'

'I got my own back though,' Terry said comfortably. 'I was there when she had Justin.'

Lynne stopped dead. 'Really?'

'Really,' Terry said. 'In the ambulance, stuck in a snowstorm. I pulled her pants down.'

Lynne snorted. 'You're having me on.' She went off in front again.

'I hope you're writing all these trees down,' I said. 'Norwegian Spruce, Sitka ditto, Scots Pine. And there's a Mountain Ash over there.'

'What was that?' Lynne said.

'What?' Terry and I said in unison.

'A sort of crackling noise under the trees,' she whispered.

'Sheep,' I said. 'Badgers. Hedgehogs. Anything like that.'

'It sounded quite big.'

'Deer?' Terry suggested. 'Shall I write it down?'

'Only when we actually see it,' I remonstrated.

'You two are like a couple of stupid kids!' Lynne stormed. 'Aren't you forgetting what's happened on these trips so far?'

'Be as little children,' Terry said absent-mindedly. 'Shall we proceed? I'm sure you've frightened whatever it was away.'

We proceeded.

It was quite dark now. Terry switched on the torch every fifteen seconds or so to keep us on a straight course. This was important for the ditches at the side of the road, where there wasn't a stone wall, were quite deep.

'I can hear feet,' said Lynne.

'Feet?' Terry asked.

'Other people's,' Lynne said as though talking to someone slow of brain.

I said, 'It can't be the other team. We haven't been going long enough.'

'Perhaps they ran or took a short cut,' Terry said. 'Perhaps on the other hand it's only some more folk doing the same as us.'

It was a group of teenagers coming from the opposite direction. They greeted us cheerily.

Then Lynne stopped suddenly. 'I can't go any further.'

'There's no need for you to walk in front,' Terry pointed out gently.

I knew without being able to see her clearly that she was near to tears.

'The darkness presses on you,' she said. 'I've never been too good in the dark.'

'You have the torch then,' Terry said, handing it over. 'Use it when you want to.'

'Character building for kids,' she said on a sob and then did cry.

Both Terry and I have hit our own private walls under these sort of conditions and when on training exercises. Sometimes it takes you unawares, a deep down aversion or weakness that you had no idea existed until that moment. Often, as with Terry's splinter — and on that occasion he had cried with pain and mortification — the cure is merely a hot drink and a little sympathy. Some difficulties can only be solved by the person to whom they occur, as when I had had to grit my teeth and kill the rabbit that someone had just handed to me and which was to be our supper. Fear of the dark is different again.

'Lynne, honey,' said Terry, 'we're here to find some bastard who's spoiling the children's trips. Now I'm sure you came along with the best possible motives but — '

I'm not quite sure what Terry was about to say at this point but, at a guess, it would have been a slightly watered down version of the homily Patrick would have delivered. He stopped speaking when we were lit by the headlights of a car that swept around a bend in the road immediately ahead of us. It was travelling faster than the road conditions demanded. The vehicle slowed a little, the idea immediately going through my head that the driver was ascertaining our identity, and then swung straight at us.

It was one of those weird, unearthly moments when everything seems to happen very slowly. In the brilliant glare of the headlights I saw Terry scoop Lynne up as though she was a bag of feathers, leap the ditch, and then the pair of them rolled from sight down a bank and presumably right into the base of the fence. I also jumped, slipped, and underwent a forward roll that pitched me down the slope and into the fence with a force that knocked all the breath out of me.

I lay still.

Tyres screeched to a halt, the engine was cut and someone got out of the car. A man swore.

'Someone's coming!' rapped out another voice. 'Beat it!'

The door was slammed, there was more screeching of tyres and the vehicle roared away. Moments later another car approached from the opposite direction. It did not stop, the beams from its lights stabbing eerily between the trunks of the trees.

'They might come back,' I heard Terry say in muffled fashion. 'Follow the fence and you'll get to the track we're supposed to take. Hurry!'

In the dark — for Lynne had dropped the torch and it had gone out — we groped our way along the fence. I could hear Terry and Lynne ahead of me and had an idea he had a hold of her hand and was pulling her along. It was possible to remember the general terrain from the brief illumination of the car's headlights but we still fell over quite a lot and had our faces whipped by the low branches of trees.

'Okay,' said Terry, and obviously stopped for I ran straight into him and there were a few moments of total confusion.

'Everyone all right?' he asked.

'You landed on me back there,' Lynne gasped.

'Thought it was a bit soft.' His waxed jacket rustled as he turned about. 'I was right. This is the track. We turn right off the road here. Hold on a minute.'

There was a gate. Lynne and I leaned on it.

'The man has cat's eyes,' she said, still puffing for breath.

'Hates carrots too,' I murmured.

She clutched hold of my arm. 'They really meant to knock us down, didn't they? They meant to kill us.'

'One does get that impression,' I agreed.

She released me impatiently. 'It's easy for both of you. And for Patrick. You used to do this all the time. This is just playing around as far as you're concerned.'

'We'll have to make do without the torch,' Terry reported, jogging back, this time along the road. 'They ran over it.'

'I have some matches,' said Lynne, who smoked.

'Splendid. Let's have a quick dekko at the map.'

'Trees,' I said. 'Write, poplar, larch, beech, hawthorn, field maple, holly, alder, elder —'

'Hold on!' Terry protested as the match went out.

'Those men might come back,' Lynne hissed in an agonised whisper.

'Animals and birds?' Terry queried, still crouched over writing on one knee. At least I assumed he was, his voice was quite near the ground.

'A badger,' I offered. 'Two foxes, one with cubs, a stray cow, a pigmy shrew, a water vole with a wooden leg, a barn owl, a Scops owl, a . . .'

'A lammergeyer,' Terry said when I ran out of ideas for a

51

moment, his pencil scratching away in total darkness. 'How do you spell it, scribe?'

I told him, adding, 'Put with foal at foot – that'll really throw 'em.'

'Even I know it's a bloody vulture.'

'All right. Put with fowl at foot.'

Lynne started to giggle. 'You're mad. The pair of you are raving mad.'

'Good, good. Magic,' Terry chortled, leaping up. 'She's laughing. Come on, girls – let's make the forest ring with our frivolity.'

The track was wide enough for the three of us to go abreast, Lynne in the centre with Terry and I gripping her elbows. Like this, actually steadying each other, we could make quite good speed. It was possible *just* to see where we were going for the open sky above our heads was lighter than the pitch blackness beneath the trees. Occasionally we stopped and stood in utter silence, listening.

'Patrick only has a knife if they're attacked,' Lynne said as we moved off again after one of the halts.

'Don't worry,' I soothed. 'He's more dangerous with that than the average man armed with a meat cleaver.'

'Lights!' Terry said. 'Out of sight now! Not a sound.'

We dived into the darkness under the trees and lay still for what seemed to be an hour. Then I heard footsteps. I resisted the urge to look up to see if it was the other members of our group. People have had their heads shot off for doing just that.

The footfalls stopped somewhere very close by. A torch beam flashed through the branches above my head. Then Patrick's voice said, 'I can smell Ingrid's perfume. They must have come this way and taken a different path to us. Either that or ...'

Again the torchlight flashed close to me.

'Round Two to us,' said Terry, scrambling to his feet.

'And Round One?' Patrick queried when we had joined him and the others. 'That's assuming that I grant you the second when you were travelling without lights.'

'Avoiding death by hit-and-run,' I told him. 'They only succeeded in killing the torch.'

'You should have had a torch *each*. Are you saying that someone deliberately . . . ?'

'At least two men in an estate car of some kind,' Terry said. 'Sounded like a Volvo. Yes, it was deliberate all right.'

'They must have known what we looked like,' Lynne said.

'I think we should carry on as though nothing has happened,' Patrick decided. 'If you meet Larry first, then tell him to keep his eyes open. John, perhaps you'd be good enough to let them have your torch.'

I said, 'I'm a bit worried about those youngsters we saw on the road. That car went in the direction they were going.'

'It would be crazy to assume that Larry's school's the only target,' Terry said. 'Yes, I'd prefer to check that they're okay.'

'Then go,' Patrick said. 'Both of you. Take the torch and run back. We'll follow.'

'Has it occurred to you that this is a bit like a Famous Five adventure?' I asked as we ran.

'Chalet School story,' Terry corrected. 'Only co-ed.'

'Complete with Lynne, pain of the dorm,' I giggled. 'Terry, how come you know about Chalet School stories?'

'There's a whole lot at home. You know me. Even as a kid I read anything.'

It was the last time I laughed for a long time.

We found them, a shocked, frantic group huddled at the side of the road around a girl who was lying on the ground. They had covered her with their coats. Another of their number, a boy, was in the ditch, very obviously dead.

'Rory's gone to phone,' mumbled a lad of about eighteen. He stood apart from the others, twisting a plastic-covered map in his hands. He stared glassily at me. 'That car . . . I'll swear it came at us on purpose.'

Chapter Four

Terry ran back a short distance and fired the revolver three times into the air. The pair of us then went to the injured girl. She seemed to be dead.

'Let's try,' Terry said.

He gave her mouth-to-mouth resuscitation, I massaged her heart. We were still working when the others arrived at a run and John and Patrick took over. We had changed over again when the ambulance arrived and as it did so the still form jerked an arm. When Terry moved we could see that her eyes were open. Then she was taken away, together with the dead boy, and we were all left standing in the road, numbed.

By this time Larry was with us. He immediately took all the youngsters to the youth hostel where they were staying and then came back for us. I felt utterly exhausted.

'There's your proof,' Patrick said quietly to his brother.

'So what now?' Larry asked.

'We'll have to discuss it later.'

The discussion took place in the loft of the barn as we had no wish to be overheard. Jimmy had made us some hot chocolate and this had gone a long way to restoring our spirits and keeping out the chill.

'I'd like all your thoughts on this,' Patrick said to open the proceedings. 'Real thoughts please – expletives not deleted.'

'I suppose the police have been called in,' Lynne said.

'Yes,' Larry said. 'An Inspector Jones will speak to us tomorrow.'

'Is the girl alive?' John wanted to know.

'Just,' Patrick replied. 'She was being operated on when I rang.'

I said, 'I feel awful. We should have gone back as soon as the car drove off.'

'I don't think it would have made much difference,' Patrick said. 'The boy was beyond help.'

'It's personal now,' Terry murmured. He had been very quiet since we had returned. 'Not because of us being targets – you get used to being a target in our job. But to drive a car at kids just out for a walk! You can imagine them doing jobs after school or college to pay for a trip like this. I curse my own stupidity in not grabbing the bastards when they came after us. I had the gun, for God's sake.'

'*They* were probably armed,' Patrick pointed out. 'And right then your responsibility was towards Ingrid and Lynne. Which brings me to another point.'

'No passengers,' Lynne said sadly.

'No unnecessary risks to the lives of those with their own families,' Patrick said. '*I* intend to follow this up a little more. It's up to Ingrid and Terry whether they stay with me for the rest of the time. You must agree that we've proved there's a problem. That this has happened so quickly is probably helpful. But the risks aren't going to diminish. I'd never forgive myself if anything happened to either of you.'

'What about me?' said Dawn in a small voice.

I realised with a shock that Patrick had forgotten about her. She was sitting outside the circle of light provided by the camping lamp that Jimmy had lent us.

'I'd like you to go back with John and Lynne,' Patrick said to her. 'We can take you to the station in the morning.'

Dawn didn't argue, just gazed at the floor and dashed away what might have been a tear on her cheek.

'Well, that's settled,' Lynne said happily. 'I know we haven't been much help but perhaps it's better like this. Anyone fancy a nightcap? They don't seem to have heard of licensing hours around here. Are you coming, John?'

Patrick was still gazing at Dawn. 'You go on – we might join you in a minute.'

When they had gone she looked straight at Patrick, very, very offended.

'If I can cope with your son, I can cope with anything,' she reminded him bitterly.

'I'm sorry,' Patrick said softly. 'I handled that very badly.'

'I resent being lumped together with that spineless cow.'

It was Patrick's turn to stare at the floor. 'The last thing I intended to do was even to speak of you in the same breath as that truly spineless cow. I hope you'll believe me when I say that you're so much a part of the family that I didn't think of you for a moment as a separate entity, a person in her own right. There's no justification for my risking your life on a whim.'

'I don't want to be safe and cosy while you're all risking yours.'

I kept my mouth shut. I never interfere with this kind of decision.

'I know you don't,' Patrick said.

'And I'm sure Larry's going to see the weekend through.'

'Absolutely,' said Larry. 'Besides, it's my responsibility.'

There was quite a long silence.

Patrick stood up. 'I can't think straight without a pint of bitter.' He climbed down the ladder. 'I'll ring the hospital while I'm there.'

'Coming, Larry?' I said.

'Oh — er — yes, all right,' he said, a little surprised at my practically bundling him out.

'You've still got the gun?' Patrick shouted up to Terry.

'Yes.'

'If you're besieged, light the fuse on the cannon and *stand well clear*. I'm not quite sure what'll happen.'

'Aye, aye, sir.'

'Death and life, ends and beginnings,' Patrick whispered to me, tucking an arm through mine. 'Tonight I feel very old.'

'What about Dawn?' I enquired when we had almost reached The Dragon.

'Looked at dispassionately . . .'

'Yes?'

'I think Terry will apply himself to the job in hand more thoroughly if she stays.'

'She'd never have forgiven you if you'd sent her back with the other two.'

'Lots of people hate me for saving their lives,' he replied ruefully.

'What happened with Lynne though? Terry and I haven't told any tales.'

'She really flipped when Terry let off those shots. Despite my saying several times that it was one of our pre-arranged signals, she shouted and screamed that we were all going to be killed and generally behaved very badly.'

The news about Claire Brooks, the injured girl, was that she was in intensive care and very poorly. Both her legs were broken and there were serious internal injuries.

'The last thing I want to do is sit in a pub drinking,' I said to Patrick as we came away from the phone. I glanced into the bar. 'I've a feeling that the Murrays are going to drink too much. I don't understand them at all — they're not like this at home.'

'It's one of the reasons they take people apart before they let them in the army,' Patrick murmured. 'But look at it from the point of view that they're doing a wonderful job of making us look an ordinary bunch. Grin and bear a swift pint and then we'll turn in.'

'We can't go back yet, Terry and Dawn might be ...'

My spouse swore with some verve. 'So we go back making a lot of noise, strip stark naked and I make love to you in position 343b. Perhaps they'll feel better then.'

'There's no need to be sarcastic,' I said.

He made a weird braying noise that I took to be dissent and went into the bar.

In the event we stayed in The Dragon for a couple of hours talking to a group of shepherds. We made an enormous amount of noise when we went back to the barn, Lynne and John singing and Larry, who wasn't drunk, tripping over something in the dark and dropping four cans of lemonade he had bought for the following day.

Terry and Dawn were asleep in one another's arms in Terry's sleeping bag, both snoring gently.

'Well, really!' Lynne said when she saw them.

'Shut up,' Patrick said to her peaceably. To me he said, 'I'll keep watch in the minibus.'

It was a long, cold night.

'Claire died at three a.m.,' Patrick said when we met for breakfast.

'I should have reported all this to the police before,' Larry agonised.

'There was no evidence,' I said. 'That's why we're here.'

We ate our meal in absolute silence. Afterwards Larry took John and Lynne to Merthyr. They did not wish us goodbye or good luck and as far as I know none of us so much as waved. They were our friends, I had to keep telling myself, and yet away from Devon they had been unrecognizable as the people we knew.

'How long do we wait for this cop?' Larry asked. We were sitting in the mini-bus, planning our next move.

Patrick said, 'I suggest we leave a message with Jimmy with instructions as to where to find us. Otherwise we might be hanging around here all day. And, speaking personally, I'd rather be doing something.'

'If we're sticking to the usual timetable, this morning is rock-climbing time,' Larry said, spreading his battered map out across the steering wheel. 'This takes place at a disused quarry not very far from here, and for the benefit of those present who have not done this before I'd like to say that although the granite cliff we use is just over seventy feet high it's as easy as walking up steps in places. We're only really interested in teaching novices the rudiments of climbing but a lot about safety and responsibility towards others. Everyone gets to the top and enjoys the view.'

'From a security point of view though?' Terry asked.

'You'll be like flies on the wall,' Larry said. 'Would you rather find somewhere else?'

'Was the only trouble you had concerning climbing just someone cutting the ropes?'

Larry nodded.

'Take us there,' Patrick requested. 'We'll decide when we see the place.' He smiled grimly. 'Therein lies the problem.

To be the bait but not be caught. To be novices but yet outwit them.'

'We're doing it for Claire,' Dawn said, mostly to herself. 'And for the boy whose name we don't even know.'

'Richard,' Larry said, folding the map. 'Their parents are arriving this afternoon.'

It remained cold but clouds that had brought overnight rain had gone. The sun shone hazily in a washed-out looking pale blue sky. It was noticeable that when we arrived at our destination and got out of the mini-bus everyone went off on their own for a short distance, taking deep breaths of fresh air. I think we were all trying to erase memories of the night before.

'This is okay,' Patrick said when I joined him. He gazed out over the wide valley towards distant hills. 'There's no rifle I know of that could operate at that kind of range. While we're on the rock face itself we're as safe as houses. The only snag might be when we're standing on the top.' He turned round to look, shading his eyes from the sun. 'No, it's still okay. There's a wide grassy ledge almost at the top that I've a feeling Larry uses as an anchor point for the ropes.'

'Now we know,' Terry said, approaching. 'This is out of range of everything but guided missiles. That's why they only tampered with the ropes.'

'Would you rather give it a miss then?' Larry said, who had overheard.

'No, I rather fancy having a go at that,' Patrick answered, still looking at the cliff face. 'It's a long time since I did any climbing.'

Larry hefted up a couple of ropes and placed them over his shoulders, bandoleer style. 'You'll have to give me a few minutes to walk up the long way round and secure this lot. Then I'll abseil down and get you fixed up with safety harnesses and all the bits and pieces.'

'We'll start,' Terry told him. 'You can check everything.'

'Once up I shall stay up top,' Patrick said. 'Keep an eye on things.'

I said, 'Would you like me to do that? If anyone's around and sees a woman with binoculars, they'll probably think she's birdwatching.'

59

This arrangement worked very well. I went up first – Larry had spoken the truth, it was extremely easy – and then left the others to it. It transpired that Terry stayed with Dawn on the beginner's pitch and Larry went with Patrick a short distance away to where the climb possessed a few more challenges. But no one relaxed.

With the binoculars I quartered the hillside above the rockface. If I had really been watching birds there would have been nothing to complain about. For a long time a buzzard circled slowly in the sunlight and then dipped a wing and glided further down the valley to find better hunting grounds. I saw a kestrel swoop down on a small rodent of some sort and carry it, still struggling, to a tree. There was no sign of other human intruders in this wild place.

'Hungry?' Patrick enquired, bringing a chocolate bar.

'Thanks. How did you get on?'

He dropped down beside me. 'Frightened myself a couple of times. Having no feeling in one foot makes climbing a bit dodgy. I take it you haven't spotted anything to worry about.'

'Not a thing.'

'I think we'll have lunch and then make for the viaduct Larry mentioned. He said he thought they were watched there, if you remember.'

I snatched up the binoculars. 'Fuzz on the starboard bow.'

'Steady as she goes,' Patrick murmured, having a look for himself. 'Mr Meadows!' he bellowed.

'Sir!' shouted Terry from somewhere out of sight.

'Man the lee braces and run out the starboard battery!' He waited until Terry appeared at the run. 'No real panic. Inspector Jones by the look of it. Let's go down.'

The two of them descended the rock face. Dawn and I helped Larry with the ropes and walked back with him down a steep path at one end of the wide ledge. When we reached the quarry floor the police car had pulled up and a man and a woman had got out and were talking to Patrick and Terry.

'How do I play this?' Larry said to me out of the corner of his mouth.

60

'I'd be inclined to tell the truth about everything but follow Patrick's lead as to *why* we're actually here.'

But Patrick was honest, making no bones about the reason for our presence. This was interesting and might have had a lot to do with the fact that Inspector Jones admitted to catastrophic short-manning due to a 'flu epidemic. There was also the matter of a murder the previous night in Merthyr.

'I'd be surprised if there's any connection,' said the Inspector with a brief smile. She was about thirty-five years of age, attractive in a crisply efficient way, and most certainly not a push-over. 'Oh, this is Sergeant Blake.'

Patrick rapidly made the introductions.

'I cannot give you *official* permission to investigate this,' said Carol Jones. 'I'm not sure that I shouldn't be running you out of the district on a rail.'

'You could phone John Brinkley at the Yard,' Patrick said. 'He's the liaison officer for the department I used to work for in MI5 and for which Mr Meadows still does. I'm sure he'd be happy to tell you that we're not likely to do anything stupid.'

She gazed at him steadily. 'I did read in the papers why you were asked to resign. Was it true?'

'Ouch,' whispered Patrick, thereby answering the question.

'Are you armed?' she enquired.

Patrick produced his flick knife.

'Major, I did not fall off the Christmas tree.'

Smiling like a Botticelli angel, Patrick offered her his revolver. 'I *am* permitted to carry this.'

'Now?' she rapped out.

'No one's asked me for it back.'

'That's not the same though, is it?'

Terry dug in a pocket and produced his ID card. 'If you read the small print on the back you'll see that it allows me to carry a gun. I did, however, leave mine at home.'

Inspector Jones read every single word of the small print and then made Patrick unbuckle his shoulder holster and give it to Terry. From then on she ignored Patrick.

'Did you by any chance get the number of the car that

61

appeared to drive at you last night?' she enquired when Terry and I had recounted the events in detail.

'Not a chance,' he said. 'And it didn't *appear* to do anything – we had to leap for our lives.'

Sergeant Blake was lugubriously writing all this down. 'A stolen Vovlo was found in Brecon in the early hours of this morning. We're running tests on it.'

'What are your movements for the rest of today?' Jones asked.

Larry said, 'We're abseiling off the railway viaduct on the old Merthyr to Brecon line this afternoon. This evening we hope to explore a few caves. I can't tell you exactly which ones until I've looked at the height of the river and listened to the weather forecast.'

'And tomorrow?'

'If everybody's willing we'll walk up Pen y Fan and then go along the ridge to Cribyn, returning by the road that passes the Upper Neuadd and Pentwyn reservoirs.'

I bit my tongue to stop myself smiling. Larry's pronunciation of these Welsh place-names was, to my ears, perfect.

'After which I presume you intend to return home.'

'Yes.'

She turned to Terry. 'I would like to be kept informed of your observations.'

'Plus any bullets that we dig out of ourselves,' Terry answered. 'Of course.'

She gave him a stare that he returned, measure for measure. 'I don't want any repetitions of gangland shoot-outs. If there's any trouble you'll be the first people pulled in.' She turned to leave but then faced us again and said, 'Have you any theories about this?'

'Yes, some leek-troughing nutter's on the loose.' Terry then carried on staring at her until she got in the car with Blake and left. Before they were out of sight Patrick's gun and holster had been thrust back in his hands, angrily, Terry's gaze still on the car.

'My skin is several feet thick,' Patrick said to him.

'I hate cops who throw the book at you and then pick your brain for ideas.'

'There might be some fingerprints in the car,' I said.

62

'If it was the right one,' Terry remarked.

'Lunch?' Larry suggested. 'There's an excellent little pub just down the road.'

'That man you shot was Welsh,' Dawn said dreamily.

'Which man?' Patrick asked.

'Pugh!' Terry exclaimed. 'Harry Pugh. Didn't you say that he was known as Harry the Fuse because he'd once electrocuted a man on purpose?'

'I can't think the fact that we were responsible for the demise of a Welsh crook would upset a Welsh police inspector to the extent that she'd —' Patrick began.

'No, no,' Dawn interrupted, it must be admitted, in her best 'Aren't we being slow today?' nanny tones. 'Pugh might have had friends here and they're getting back at Patrick through Larry.'

It must also be admitted that Dawn does not usually refer to Patrick by his christian name although he has never discouraged her from doing so. I found myself hoping that his skin was thick enough to withstand being steam-rollered for the second time in so many minutes.

'It's an interesting thought,' Patrick observed. 'But that kind of retaliation's expensive. And from what I can gather Pugh didn't have much in the way of friends. He made most of his money by blackmailing the ungodly. But it's worth keeping in mind.'

We lunched on mutton stew and then drove several miles into the hills.

'*That* viaduct?' Dawn wanted to know as we parked at a high point above a steep-sided valley. A river wound its way through sheep-nibbled meadows at the bottom.

'That's the one,' Larry confirmed. He grinned at Patrick. 'And all the army types'll find it a piece of cake — just like coming down from a helicopter.'

'Steadier too,' Patrick observed. 'And far quieter.'

'You mean we're going to descend in the middle of one of the arches?' Dawn said.

'It's far easier,' Larry told her. 'You don't have to worry about your feet.'

Patrick gave me the binoculars. 'Saunter around and do your bird watching thing while we get the gear unloaded.

Larry, didn't you say you thought you might have been snooped on here?'

'Fairly convinced,' he replied.

'Show me where, without pointing.'

'The glints of glass catching the light came from the other side of the valley. Roughly just below where that red car's coming down the road now. The white van I mentioned was parked here one morning when we arrived and went immediately. I saw it later that same morning on this side of the valley and on another occasion parked on the other side — there's a lay-by higher up.'

'It might not have been the same van.'

'I realise that. But I was aware of it on several other occasions, just out of the corner of my eye. That's a bit of a coincidence in a small district like this.'

'Shall I drive round to the other side and have a look?' Terry offered. 'If there's a vantage point they might have left a few clues.'

'Okay,' Patrick agreed.

'And if there's someone who looks a bit dodgy there already?'

'Use your initiative,' Patrick said, borrowing the binoculars for a moment to look at the viaduct itself. 'You *are* head of the department now.'

Terry just smiled.

'Children have no nerves,' Dawn said to me. 'You see them in the swimming pool in Plymouth. Tiny tots going round like beetles on a water butt — right out of their depth.'

'Going over the parapet will be the worst part,' I said. 'Then you'll enjoy it.'

'There's another group arriving,' Patrick said, still with the binoculars. 'Army cadets by the look of them.'

'Is there a big beefy bloke with red hair in charge?' Larry asked.

'Yes, too long, sticking out from under his beret.'

'Then they're sea cadets. If they give him any cheek he throws them in the river.'

'What, not from up here!' Dawn cried.

'No, he holds a little court down on the river bank. I don't approve of those methods personally.'

64

'Nor does the navy,' Patrick muttered. 'God, if I got cheek from cadets I'd know I'd failed.'

'Nothing worth mentioning,' Terry said when he got back. 'But there is a place where you can see that people have walked off the road and down the hill to where a fallen tree makes a sort of natural hiding place.'

I quite like abseiling. But I understood how Dawn felt for the two hundred feet drop looked truly appalling. It's important to concentrate on checking kit, listen to what the instructor, if any, is telling you, and not to look down. When all was ready — for I had volunteered to go first — I climbed up on the parapet, itself about five feet high, and sat astride it, facing Larry, who would belay the safety rope around his own body, keeping it tight. In the event of the main rope breaking this would ensure that there would be no unpleasant snatch as I fell. As one who had been trained to abseil without the benefit of safety ropes — literally being expected to tie a rope to a secure anchor-point and go down it — this was feather-bedding indeed. I clipped myself on then bent forward, swung my right leg over and positioned both feet on a ledge. Then, after a nod to Larry, I leaned back into nothing and walked backwards down the first twenty feet or so of stone. No one, except Larry, was taking any notice of me. It was rather lonely.

Somewhere across the valley a raven croaked and I saw it fly with ponderous wing-beats into a dead tree. I lowered the abseil rope so that I stopped and watched it, also scanning the hillside for other signs of life. Then, in the trees behind the dead one, I saw a flash. I took no chances, lifted the trailing rope and held it out with my right hand. Seconds later I was out into the opening of the huge main arch of the viaduct and going down fast enough for the wind to whistle in my ears.

In the next moment my feet touched the soft turf. I unhitched the rope from my harness and waved to Larry, hoping that either Patrick or Terry would descend next. There seemed no point in panicking over what I had seen for, after all, I might merely have glimpsed the sun shining on a piece of broken glass. Then I remembered the cadets. Were they also at possible risk? Should I shout a warning?

65

All this was going through my mind when I heard Larry shout something to me. And at that moment I was grabbed from behind. I was taken completely unawares, seized in a bone-crushing grip by two men. At least, I thought there were two, I could not see because they yanked a hood of sorts over my head.

This was not the right moment to continue to act Mrs Average Woman in the Street. I yelled at the top of my voice, twisted in the hold they had me in, almost strangling myself in the process, and kicked out. My foot should have connected but it didn't, I simply wasn't quick enough. Desperate now, I threw my weight against one of the men and succeeded in getting him off-balance. But instead of the rather elegant manoeuvre that Patrick had taught me coming to fruition, we all fell in a heap on the ground.

They started to drag me by the feet. I knew the answer to this too, wrenched one ankle free, used the force of my other foot to pull myself up and followed the movement through, both hands bunched into fists in a clubbing motion.

After this everything became very confusing.

I'm told that they let go of me and ran off when they saw Patrick and Terry abseiling down together. Suddenly released, I overbalanced and was suddenly rolling down a steep slope. Having no idea I was so close to the river now it was a ghastly shock to plunge into icy cold water. I floundered out, trying to get the hood off. It was pulled off for me in the end and I found myself looking into a pair of grey eyes even chillier than the water.

'That, Mrs G, was a balls-up.'

I didn't reply.

'You forgot everything you've ever been taught,' Patrick continued.

Terry returned just then at the run, presumably from following my attackers.

'There was a van waiting,' he panted. 'A white one. Over there in a farm track. They got away.'

'Number?' Patrick snapped.

'Didn't get it. Slipped over in the mud.'

Patrick did not comment further, just walked through the arch of the viaduct and went downstream.

66

'Is he going for a pee or does he want us to follow so he can beat our heads with boulders?' Terry wondered aloud.

'Probably going to throw up in disgust at my performance,' I said through chattering teeth.

'*Our* performance,' Terry corrected. 'You'd better run up and down to get warm.'

I commenced jogging in circles in an effort to get dry. It was quite hopeless, of course, and I soon had to desist with a stitch in my side. Right then I would have given just about anything for a hot cup of tea.

'Shouldn't you be giving Dawn a bit of encouragement?' I called to Terry.

He turned slowly. 'She doesn't need any.'

'I'm talking about *abseiling*.'

He knew I was and grinned wickedly.

'Terry, don't you dare take advantage of that girl.'

He shot a glance skywards to see if she was on her way down and then came closer. 'Take advantage of her? Are you crazy? I'll have to marry her if we're to make what she has in mind respectable.'

'And will you?' I challenged.

Again the grin. 'A fellow would be crazy not to.'

I hugged him. 'Has she asked you yet?'

He laughed. 'Yes, but I'm playing hard to get.'

'Not by the look of both of you in your sleeping bag last night.'

An expression of horror came over his face. 'You saw us?'

'Everyone did. But we weren't sneaky. We made a hell of a lot of noise. You were both sound asleep.'

'Is Dawn coming down?' Patrick said, appearing from nowhere.

We both didn't *quite* jump to attention.

'I − er − don't know,' Terry stammered.

'Ask her, would you?'

Terry shouted up and received a reply in the negative from Larry.

'Make her,' I said to Patrick.

In his present mood he did not hesitate. He took her through it, step by step, his voice carrying effortlessly, I

67

knew, up to the track bed above. No one, not even the most recalcitrant cadet — and they all stopped what they were doing to watch — could have disobeyed that voice. There was no cajoling in the tone, no wheedling, not a hint of humour. It was the sort of voice that would get people out of a burning building without panic. So Dawn came down and, because the voice delivered orders without bringing any shame or slur — for that would have resulted, Patrick somehow suggested, if she had stayed above — she thoroughly enjoyed the experience, arriving flushed and breathless in our midst.

There was not a trace of malice or spite in my reason for doing this. I knew that Dawn would have hated herself always for not plucking up courage. No, I rather felt that the balance of power in our group had to be restored. Nicely, as it turned out.

Chapter Five

A respectful trio stood at the base of one of the massive arches of the viaduct peering up at the sea cadets and their leader.

'Might we have a word, Chief?' Terry shouted.

Patrick smothered a laugh. 'Quite superb psychology. Ten to one he's only a PO or he wouldn't have such an inferiority complex.'

I wondered if this neat summing-up was correct. But I had to agree with the conclusion that only someone with a chip on their shoulder would throw boys in a river. Whatever the truth we would soon find out. The subject of our curiosity was abseiling down, demonstrating the very best style. Glancing at Patrick I hoped that he would school his face in time. He did, just.

'Jennings,' announced the navy man, eyeing my soaking wet apparel. 'Did I see you having a spot of bother just now?'

'Ingrid was attacked by two men,' Patrick told him. 'We wondered if you'd had any problems.'

'Problems?' echoed Jennings. 'No, not like that. What was their game, anyway? I can't imagine they intended to make free with the lady in the bushes.' He leered at me.

'Have you had equipment meddled with?' Patrick went on grimly. 'Ropes cut? Tyres let down? That kind of thing.'

'God, yes,' Jennings said without hesitation. 'But that was this lot. And the lot before them too.'

'I see,' Patrick said. 'And do they extend their fun and

games to other groups? My brother's bunch of school kids for example?'

'Are you investigating some kind of other incident?' Jennings asked cautiously.

'Yes, several.'

'Several!' the other said incredulously.

'Incidents like just now. And the business of someone taking a shot at my brother last time out.'

'Oh, now wait a minute – '

'And last night two children were knocked down and killed by a car not all that far from here.'

Jennings slumped down on to a rock. 'But that couldn't have been – '

'No, of course not,' Patrick interrupted again. 'And I don't suppose your problems were as a result of pranks by your boys. Could it be that you thought it might be revenge?'

Terry said, 'It's a question of separating incidents of cut ropes from nasty things being put in your sleeping bag.'

'Oh God,' Jennings said. 'Is some lunatic on the loose?'

Patrick said, 'That's what I'm trying to discover.'

'Are you police?'

'No,' Patrick answered and was no more forthcoming.

'Tell us about the incidents you've experienced,' Terry requested.

'Over several weeks, quite a lot,' Jennings replied. 'As you said, tyres let down, all the climbing harnesses slashed to ribbons, karabiners going missing.'

'And you thought the boys had done it?' Patrick enquired, not keeping the surprise from his voice.

'Some of them are right little criminals,' said Jennings defiantly.

'And it makes them more likely to grow up into law-abiding citizens if they're suspected of everything that goes wrong without any investigations being made? Or do you throw them *all* in the river until someone confesses?' When Jennings stared at him in open hostility, Patrick added, 'People aren't blind, man.'

'I'd like to see you control that lot and others like 'em,' Jennings ground out.

'Let's walk up top,' Patrick said and set off, leaving us

with no choice but to follow. I was quite warm by the time we got there.

By the look of it we were not a moment too soon. Three cadets were fighting, in a heap on the ground, several were pelting one another with ballast from the old track bed and one was walking tightrope-style along the top of the parapet. Jennings opened his mouth to bellow, received a look from Patrick and desisted.

'Get down,' was the polite request to the boy on the wall.

They all stopped what they were doing and looked round. After all, they had heard the same voice not so long before.

'Perhaps you'd all fall into line,' Patrick continued. 'I'd like to talk to you.' He wasn't even giving them his full attention as he said this, seeming to be searching for something in his pockets. Having apparently found it he then looked up and beheld the motionless line of boys before him. 'At ease,' he murmured with a smile.

They all crashed into the 'at ease' position.

Patrick walked a little closer to them. 'That's better, we're not on parade and I don't want to shout. My name's Patrick Gillard and in case you're wondering I'm a major in the Devon and Dorset Regiment. I'm a firm believer in the value of young eyes and quick minds so I'd like your help in investigating a series of serious incidents lately in which the climbing equipment and personal property of groups like this were damaged. And the incidents are getting worse. Last night a hit-and-run driver knocked down and killed two young people who had been staying with friends at the youth hostel. Now, what I should like you to do is relate anything strange that you've seen while you've been in this area. First of all, though, have you yourselves suffered any trouble this trip?'

There was a lot of nudging.

'Shall we all sit down?' Patrick said. 'After all, this isn't an interrogation.'

The effect of this was that he got himself in a small close huddle with them and voices were lowered to the extent that no one outside the circle could hear. He did very little talking after that and a lot of listening, only apparently interrupting to clarify a point or ask a question. There were nine boys in all and I suppose they were about thirteen years old. A few nervously shot glances in Jennings' direction. I hoped that gentleman's ears were burning.

'There you have it,' Terry said quietly, admiring the view. 'Either a man has the power to lead or he hasn't. I can't think why they haven't had him on the telly in recruiting ads.'

After about ten minutes Patrick got to his feet. 'Now, don't mess around just because no one's watching you. Don't ever do that. It's what you do when you're not being watched that really counts. I suggest you all tidy up the gear and get some of the mud off yourselves.' He came over to where Jennings was pretending to look at the scenery. 'What you do, Petty Officer Jennings, is of course your affair. But I really think you ought to report these matters to your CO. Tell him the police are investigating other incidents. To be on the safe side, perhaps you ought to take boys elsewhere until it's sorted out. I'll phone your CO if you like and keep him abreast with developments.'

And, having ascertained the name of this person and the establishment where he served, we went back to the mini-bus where Larry and Dawn were waiting for us.

'Hot tea and dry clothes for Ingrid?' Larry asked, hand on the ignition key.

'Then a talk over what went wrong,' Patrick said.

With me, he meant. I said, 'I take it you intend to report this afternoon's events to Inspector Jones.'

'Terry can do that.'

I whistled tunelessly all the way back to the barn.

'You going to shop him?' Terry wanted to know.

Patrick shook his head. 'No. But if Jennings' boss is switched on, he'll want to know why certain happenings weren't reported before.'

I sat, glowing mutely in Arctic underwear – Patrick's, borrowed – near the fire in the saloon bar of The Dragon. Until you have been very wet and cold, feeling warm and dry is taken for granted. I said, 'I'm all agog. What did the boys tell you?'

'Well, for a start, I got a good description of the men in the white van. The boys are under canvas at Ystradfellte and several of them had seen a van parked by the pub there. Before you say it I do realise that it might not be the same one. But the two men who use the vehicle look shifty, according to the lads. Not *scruffy* and shifty but quite well-dressed. Designer jeans, as one boy put it. Now, that makes me feel uneasy.'

'Quite,' Terry said. 'One can understand them being out of work labourers doing a bit of poaching and so forth to keep body and soul together, but well-dressed suspects always make me think of organized crime.'

'You must bear in mind youthful imagination,' Dawn said.

'And last night's crime was carried out by two men in a stolen Volvo,' Larry observed.

'We don't *know* that the Volvo was involved,' Patrick said. 'Not yet. And if someone intended to go out killing people with a car, they wouldn't use the one in which they carry out legitimate business.'

'It shouldn't be too difficult to find out who they are,' Terry said. 'Even if it's only to eliminate them from our inquires, as the police say.' He brightened. 'We could go to the pub in Ystradfellte right now and see if they're there.'

Patrick sighed. 'I know what's going through your mind. How many times do I have to tell you that apprehending and pulverizing small fry only frightens the top men away for a while?'

'But they might talk.'

'They also might be the local plumber and his mate,' Patrick retorted. 'No, we'll let the police deal with it.'

'Did you find out anything else?' Dawn asked.

Patrick gave her his mug for a refill. 'Two boys admitted burying the karabiners because they were terrified at the prospect of abseiling and climbing. Another said he'd put a slug in Jennings' coffee. And another very thoughtful looking lad – so articulate he'll probably be an admiral one day – told me that when they went up Bryn Glas, he and a chum of his went through a fence into the yard of a derelict farmhouse and – '

'Bryn Glas!' Larry exclaimed. 'That was where I was shot at.'

'I thought you said that was the place. He said he saw a wire stretched across an open doorway. He wouldn't have seen it, he said, but for the sun suddenly coming out and shining on it. Then Jennings shouted at them to come out. When I asked him if he thought it might be a trip wire, he said it was the right height from the floor to be one. I told him under no circumstances was he to go anywhere near the place again.'

'But do you *believe* him?' Dawn said. 'I can imagine a boy making up all kinds of yarns to impress you.'

'It's not a question of belief although, as a matter of fact, I do believe he recounted exactly what he saw. But pieces of wire can be left in outbuildings. People can also fix them across doorways by way of a sick joke. They can also be booby traps. I propose we find out tomorrow.'

'And tonight?' Larry said. 'Do you still think we ought to go into the caves?'

'What happened to you in the caves?'

'Nothing. Absolutely uneventful.'

'Then let's have a free vote.' He looked straight across at me. 'Do you want to get wet again?'

I gazed steadily back.

'Sorry,' Patrick said softly.

'I'm wearing your Norway long-johns,' I pointed out.

'And your price for removing them before you go underground?'

'There's no price. I shall merely put them on again afterwards.'

Patrick *did* join in the laughter.

Dawn said, 'But you are hoping that someone'll try to interfere with what we're doing so you can get a bit more information.'

'Oh, yes,' Patrick said. 'With a bit of luck we'll nab somebody on the job. But I must make it quite clear that I'm not risking getting silted up in a cave and rusting like the Iron Man. I'll provide armed back-up at exits and entrances.'

'You were such a good swimmer too.' Larry said sadly.

'I still am,' Patrick informed him. 'But for recreational

purposes I leave the tin bit behind and do twenty knots with the lid of the laundry basket strapped to my right knee.'

We were all grinning over this when the door opened and two couples entered. One did not have to be very astute to realise that they were Claire and Richard's parents. Sadness and mourning flowed in with them together with the cold air from outside.

'They said you were in here,' one of the men began falteringly. 'We just want to thank you for ...'

'Please sit down,' I said. 'I'll ask Jimmy to make some more tea.'

'But we don't want to intrude,' the younger of the women said. Shockingly, in her haggard state she resembled her daughter as we had seen her, dying in the road.

'You're not,' Patrick assured her. 'In fact your presence is a very positive help to the situation.'

They did not understand but came in and we made room for them by the fire. As I had hoped, the positive and homely actions of laying out clean cups and saucers and pouring tea steadied them remarkably. They had, of course, just come from the mortuary.

Nothing was said for a long time. The women drank a little tea and then wept quietly, their husbands holding their hands, only releasing them occasionally to wipe away their own tears. And the cheap cuckoo-clock on the wall ticked away the minutes and the log fire crackled and at last Claire's mother looked up to see that Patrick was watching her gravely.

'What did you mean just now?' she asked. 'When you said our presence helped?'

'This afternoon,' he said, 'I was talking to a sea cadet who, had the sun not come out and shone on a piece of wire stretched across a doorway, might have walked into a booby-trapped building. There might be a connection between that and what happened to your children. There's no time to lose.'

'Are you investigating this?' her husband asked sharply.

'Unofficially, yes. And I'm afraid that my remark was born out of selfishness − your presence is a spur to me to get on with the job in hand.'

'But you don't really need an incentive,' said the wife, kindly.

'No, encouragement,' he said with a smile. 'I've a feeling that this is a very difficult case indeed.'

Richard's father said, 'By that do you mean it's more than just a drunk hit-and-run driver?'

'Yes, I do. A lot more.'

'And you're here because it's too big for the police to handle?'

'I'm here only because my brother asked me to look into occurrences which took place when he was in the district with a school party.'

'Can't we call in someone better?' Richard's mother burst out. 'What about the SAS? They're good at handling difficult things, aren't they?'

'Hush now, Linda,' admonished her husband.

'I won't be hushed,' she stormed. 'My son's dead and this man says it might be part of a plot. Perhaps Richard was killed by terrorists who want this part of the country to themselves. Perhaps there's a whole gang of them here waiting to do something awful and they don't want anyone snooping on them.'

'But, darling, they wouldn't draw attention to themselves by —'

'How would I know?' Linda sobbed. 'How can anyone know with people like that? Who's to say that one of them hasn't gone off his head?'

I nudged Terry and said quietly, 'What's the latest up-date on psychopaths on the loose?'

'Do you mean *international* ones?'

'Yes, people who don't turn a hair at blowing airliners out of the sky.'

'I'd have to phone Daws.'

'That's a very interesting thought,' Patrick murmured. 'It reminds me of something I was reading in a report the other day. I'll tell you later.' He turned to the parents. 'Would you mind if I ask a few questions?'

'Say away,' said Richard's father.

'Was this the first time your son had been here?'

'Yes.'

76

'And Claire,' said her mother.

'So it's no use my asking if they'd experienced any trouble before.'

'Something usually goes wrong on these trips,' Claire's father observed. 'Either they can't find somewhere to stay or someone loses their rucksack. But I know what you mean.'

'And the group had only just arrived?'

'That's right. It was their first evening.'

Claire's mother put a hand over Patrick's as it rested on the table. 'I must know this or it will haunt me always. When you found her ... was she suffering terribly?'

'She was unconscious,' Patrick told her. 'We attempted resuscitation and heart massage and as the ambulance arrived she opened her eyes and moved an arm. But she could feel nothing. She didn't know what was happening.' He took her hand in his. 'That is the truth — we had a doctor with us and he said we could have done nothing more.'

'Thank you,' she whispered and wept.

'And our boy was killed instantly,' Richard's father said. 'You know, I think that if someone pointed out the people who did this, I could kill them with my bare hands. I suppose that as you're an off-duty policeman or whatever, you'd frown upon that.'

Patrick said, 'Killing with bare hands is only easy when you've been trained to do so. The only advice I have for you is to leave justice to the experts.'

'Justice!' the man scoffed. 'If they're caught, they'll go to prison for a couple of years or so.'

'Rob!' said his wife. 'It's not this gentleman's fault.'

'No, but I'm sure he represents so-called law and order.'

Someone quickly changed the subject and the one who had lost his job because of the shooting of an unsavoury crook sat passively listening. Very shortly, and after thanking us again for our help, the foursome left. They had to plan funerals and try to pick up the threads of their lives again.

'To the caves,' Larry announced, relief in his tone.

'I want to talk to Jimmy first,' Patrick said. 'It won't take long.'

Jimmy wouldn't take any money for the extra teas when Patrick and I ran him to earth in the kitchen.

'No, no,' he insisted. 'Not when they came to take home the bodies of their dead weans. That wouldn't be right at all.'

Patrick leaned on a freezer. 'Jimmy, has anyone threatened you in connection with letting groups use your barn?'

'No,' he said shortly.

'It *was* burned down.'

'I know that, don't I?'

'You said yourself that it was arson.'

'Maybe I spoke a bit hastily.'

'You told my brother you could smell paraffin in the ruins.'

Jimmy grabbed a tea towel and savagely rammed it on a hook. 'You're not from the police.'

'No, but I'm trying to find out who killed two *children*.'

Jimmy was silent.

'I'd also like to ask you about two men who drive a white van and hang around Ystradfellte.'

'Now see here ...' Jimmy began furiously.

'Two men who this afternoon tried to grab Ingrid for reasons no one is sure of. They were wearing some kind of balaclava helmets so we couldn't see their faces. But I've an idea you know who they are. They might even be the same ones who threatened to put you out of business.'

'There's no one threatening me,' Jimmy said, pounding the top of the freezer at each word.

Patrick pushed himself upright. 'No, perhaps I'm mistaken. After all, when your ancestors were calling the tune in the Great Glen they wouldn't have kowtowed to a couple of Welsh runts, would they?'

I really feared for a moment that Jimmy might lay hands on him. And the outcome was open to question. He was at least six feet four inches tall and with hands like small York hams.

'Get out of my kitchen, Englishman,' he growled.

'I will, when you've told me the truth.'

'I've nothing else to say to you.'

'So you're going to let it go on? People getting shot at, kids run over? And there's another point I'd like to make. Why didn't you try to put us off when the barn was burnt down instead of finding us some whereelse to sleep?'

I had witnessed others being questioned in this fashion. The pattern of response is familiar, progressing through denial, feigned puzzlement, to anger and even the threat of violence. Patrick never retreats in order to ensure personal safety because this means that the same point must be reached and passed again. When threatened by those he regards as basically innocent, he tends to exude what I can only describe as saintly vulnerability. Few will take advantage of it.

Jimmy turned his back on us and groaned, '*He* hadn't been here then.'

'Who?'

'I don't know his name. He's not the sort of man you ask questions of.'

'Did he come with the men in the white van?'

'No, I think they're only dogsbodies.'

'When did he come?'

'Yesterday afternoon, before you arrived.'

'For what purpose?'

'To amuse himself,' Jimmy answered tautly.

Patrick listens closely to the way people speak. 'Would you say he was mad?'

Slowly, the Scotsman faced us. 'Aye, and not crazy in the way that he ought just to be locked up. Mad like Hitler or that evil bastard in Romania. Enjoying himself. He picked up one of my kitchen knives and enjoyed holding it against my throat.'

'What did he look like?'

Clearly, such was his fear, it troubled Jimmy even to think about it. 'Not very tall,' he said. 'Dark like you but with straight hair. Very dark eyes with a crazy light in them. Smartly dressed.'

Further questioning elicited no more information. Jimmy knew neither where the man came from nor the real purpose of the visit. As to the men in the van he thought they lived in Merthyr or thereabouts and worked on an estate. In the bar one evening they had hinted that there were far too many visitors in the area and Wales should be for the Welsh. Jimmy had assumed them to belong to a Welsh nationalist group. He thought they might have set fire to the barn.

'Sons of Olwen,' Patrick said reflectively as we went in the direction of the barn to get ready. 'I wonder.'

I said, 'It's a nationalist group that's been suspected of setting fire to English holiday cottages, but would they go as far as this? Murder?'

'Perhaps we'll find out if Jimmy does as he promised and reports it all to the police.'

'I get the impression that you're quite happy to hand over that line of inquiry to La Jones and follow a few ideas of your own.'

'Don't rush me. I'm working on it.'

It was nearly dark. This part of the lane went quite steeply downhill between high banks surmounted by hedges. Questioning a sudden and inexplicable feeling of alarm I realised that nothing further had been said about my narrow escape by the viaduct. Another thing was that when it comes to matters of self-defence neither Patrick, nor Terry for that matter, has ever made things easy because I am a woman. If you make a mistake you are re-trained. Pronto.

I was walking into an ambush. For my ultimate own good, of course.

It was important not to allow him to think that I knew. So I carried on walking, relaxed, even though he had dropped back slightly. I rehearsed in my mind what I was going to do if they made it a re-run of earlier events.

They did. All at once I heard a rustling sound and I was grabbed by the two of them with not a whit of charity, iron fingers sinking into already bruised flesh. The pain made me angry but I controlled it, putting all my energy into getting rid of them. I did too, quite stylishly come to think of it, the pair going into the bilges of the lane in highly satisfactory fashion. Afterwards there was silence but for the rather distressing sound of someone parting company with their tea.

Chapter Six

The entrance to the caves was only a quarter of a mile away, within easy walking distance.

'We'll have a longer walk back,' Larry informed us as we trudged along. 'You come out somewhere else. But it's not far – just keep with me.'

'Does Patrick know that?' I asked him. 'He's going to mount guard.'

'Where is he?'

'I thought you told him where the entrance was.'

'Yes, I did. But he didn't make me a party to his plans.'

'Then he'll meet us there. Otherwise he won't know whether we've gone in.'

'I imagined he'd be an invisible part of the landscape,' Larry said, probably grinning into the night as he spoke. 'Dawn, you're very quiet.'

Dawn, upon whose nerve concerning caves and the visiting thereof three double brandies had apparently had no effect whatsoever, said, 'I'm not one of those people who keep yacking for the sake of it.'

Terry said, 'Short of diverting the river I can't see what those jokers can do to us once we're down there.'

For the sake of everyone's peace of mind I refrained from talking about modern methods of guerrilla warfare and the ease with which small things like hand grenades can be carried. We must all have kept our thoughts to ourselves until we reached our destination for the only conversation was about the weather.

We all wore miner's helmets with a light at the front, the

81

power provided by batteries fastened to leather belts around our waists. The batteries measured about ten inches by six by two and were very heavy. Our clothing was the oldest we possessed topped with ancient, damp and slightly smelly overalls that Larry had produced from Jimmy's garage.

I had not expected there would be a car park at the entrance to the caves and said as much to Larry.

'Lots of visitors,' he said, gazing around looking for Patrick. 'It's the beginning of a rambler's trail that leads to some pretty impressive waterfalls. We go in the other direction though. Where the hell is he?'

'Trees have ears,' Terry said. 'I suggest we go to the cave entrance itself.'

I took Larry's arm. 'We don't want people to know someone else is with us.'

'Er − no. Sorry.'

The moon came out fleetingly from behind patchy, scudding cloud, giving us a glimpse of a steep path that plunged into a gulley. It was flanked by bushes but on the right hand side the vegetation clung to the edge of a precipitous river bank. In the depths below water the colour of cold tea swirled between rocks and then disappeared into the side of the hill. No one falling in here would ever been seen alive again. I began to wonder if we had misjudged the situation.

'Switch your lights on,' Larry ordered. 'You need to see exactly where you're going from here.'

We rounded a curve in the path, still descending steeply, and after a little while again heard water. Then we saw it, trickling gently in a wide river bed.

'It's confusing,' Larry said. 'The river you saw just now is called Nant Cwm-Moel. This is Nant y Wem. They meet underground.'

Those who had not seen it before stopped and gazed speechlessly at the sheer size of the cave entrance. I had expected to have to wriggle into a small hole in the ground. A mountain soared above us, invisible in the darkness. One could only guess at its size as the scale of the doorway that led to its heart also defeated our pitiful beams. In the river bed and at least the size of a small cottage was a single block of stone that had at one time fallen from the cathedral of rock above.

'There's a German tourist under that,' said Larry, plunging off happily into the shallow water. 'Don't make too much noise in case you fetch some more down.'

'Couldn't they have got him out?' Dawn asked. 'I mean, to give him a proper funeral.'

'I don't suppose a crane big enough could get down here,' Larry said.

We tiptoed past.

'There's not even a memorial tablet,' Terry said, looking around. He intoned, sepulchral style, 'Here lies Fritz, smashed to bits.'

'Terry, you're horrible,' Dawn hissed.

'So is Larry,' I lamented. 'It's not true.'

A small pebble bounced off Larry's helmet with a clang. One got the impression it had started its journey at the top of the block of stone.

'Are you feeling better now?' I called up.

'Yes, thank you,' said Patrick's voice.

'Nasty to get butted in the stomach when you've just had your tea,' Terry observed.

'Are we going to get this over with?' Dawn enquired.

Addressing the rock Larry said, 'We won't be coming out this way. If you go back to the car park and follow the sign posts for White Horse Falls for about five hundred yards you'll see a steep path going off to the left. That will take you quite quickly to a grassy glade. The cave you'll see right in front of you is the one we'll emerge from.'

'Roger,' said Patrick. 'How long will you be?'

'About an hour and a half. Perhaps slightly more. If the water stays as low as this I'll show them the Cavern of Jewels. We might be just over two hours if that happens.'

We all splashed into the shallow water of the Nant y Wem. The river bed at this point was at least ten yards wide. It narrowed slightly as we went into the cave entrance, the water becoming a little deeper. But we all wore boots and the shingle underfoot made walking very easy. There were several large oblong boulders that looked like sea lions asleep in the water. After we had passed them the opening suddenly became a lot smaller, the flow of water now faster and halfway up our boots. Soon we were walking in single file

83

and there was the occasional clang and exclamation as one or other of us hit our helmets on the rock above our heads. Then we had to bend as we walked. Another few yards and the roof became very low indeed.

'Crawl,' Larry instructed. 'It's only a few yards and then it opens up again.' And with that he plunged out of sight like a dog going down a rabbit hole.

'It's six inches deep,' I heard Dawn say somewhere behind me.

Terry said, 'You have to think of it from the point of view that sometimes it's a foot deep, and count yourself lucky.'

I didn't wait to hear any more, just followed Larry.

We all ended up on a sort of sloping sandy beach, the river burbling merrily somewhere away to the left and going from sight. It was quite easy to think for a moment that we were indeed on a beach somewhere at night and not underground.

Larry said, 'You'll be pleased to know that that's where we part company with the Nant y Wem. You'll cross the Nant Cwm-Moel on the way out but from now until then it's dry. I think, Dawn, that I'd like you to be directly behind me, and then Ingrid, with Terry bringing up the rear.' He shone his light into a cleft right at ground level. 'Now, we're going to crawl into that. It's a tight fit and your heads will be right on the ground. But again, it's only a few yards. Those with large backsides make sure your batteries stay at the side or you might get jammed. And for God's sake leave enough room between you so you don't get kicked in the face by the person in front.'

'Follow *exactly* in Larry's path,' I said to Dawn. 'He's far broader across the shoulders than you are.'

It was nevertheless a very tight fit and I came to the conclusion when literally worming my way through, millions of tons of stone above me, that nothing would ever induce me to go caving again. The feeling was not dispelled when I emerged on the other side and floundered into thick, black mud.

'Is this your idea of dry?' I complained as we were waiting for Terry to appear.

'And if I listed all the discomforts beforehand?' Larry queried crossly.

84

'Sorry,' I said. 'Tell me about the Cavern of Jewels.'

'It's only quartz crystals,' he said. 'But our lights will make a pretty glitter.'

There was a lot of huffing and puffing and Terry fought his way out. We waited for him not to notice the mud either and he didn't, making a satisfactory squelching sound as he flopped into it. I was amused to note that he saw that Dawn was watching him and refrained from swearing.

The next hundred yards or so were almost like a man-made tunnel and we walked in single file, mostly upright. The only event was when Larry turned to make sure that three lights were in his wake and went straight into an inverted dome of rock on the roof, momentarily stunning himself. After a short pause to enable him to recover, we carried on.

'Down through here,' he informed us, indicating a hole in the floor some two feet across. 'Keep your arms above your head as you go down and just let yourself go — there's only about an eighteen inch drop.'

'That's for a man just over six feet in height,' I said into Dawn's ear. 'Add a bit for us.'

But there was no problem. He steadied us as we descended.

This lower tunnel was far smaller and we soon had to crawl again. We came out in a long gallery lined with stalactites and stalagmites on either side, an open space down the middle, so that it was like travelling down the inside of a crocodile's mouth. This soon gave way to a precipitous slope that we had to slither down on our behinds. Then there was another tunnel with boulders on the floor that we had to climb over and around. This came to a dead stop, the way ahead reached by going up through a hole in the roof. We found ourselves in a cave that was so large our lights could not reach the top.

I had just seen my first spider when I thought I heard sounds behind us, down below the hole we had just clambered through. I looked at Terry but he had already wriggled back to the hole on his stomach and, having switched off his light, was listening intently.

'What is it?' Dawn whispered.

Terry laid a finger to his lips.

The spider, only a small one, was making good its escape from unwelcome vibrations. It headed in the direction of

85

what I had thought to be a pale-coloured wall. I looked more closely and saw that it was indeed one wall of the cave but the paleness was a pall of spiders. Thousands upon thousands of them moving like a field of corn in a stiff breeze. Waves of spiders. I must have uttered some kind of sound of horror for all the others looked at me. Dawn then noticed them too and shrieked. Deep underground, in a world of no echoes, the shriek brought its own brand of horror, heard as a dead, flat sound like something that had come from a tomb.

'I've got to get out of here!' she yelled wildly.

Before anyone could move or say anything there was a subterranean burst of laughter. But instead of having the effect − as it was probably designed to − of frightening Dawn further, the opposite happened. She clapped both hands over her mouth, eyes like saucers, her body apparently turned to stone. Dawn cannot *stand* being laughed at. In the next moment Terry had reached her, prised her hands away from her face and was giving her the most lustful kiss I had seen in years.

'Take no notice,' Larry said quietly, obviously thinking of bona fide cavers rather than anyone with malice aforethought as far as we were concerned.

'Fifteen, love,' I said when the pair had sundered. 'Shall we move on?'

Whoever it was followed us. But not closely, we were given no more than a hint of their presence. For all we knew they *were* bona fide cavers and had merely been amused by Dawn's outburst. Then I saw that Terry had Patrick's gun. Far from being a comforting sight, it made me very worried indeed.

'So Patrick has only his knife?' I whispered when we paused to wriggle one by one through a narrow part.

Terry nodded. 'He insisted I bring this.'

We came to a long tunnel that looked for all the world like part of the London underground. The only difference − other than obvious ones like lack of rails, cables, etc − was the presence of two ledges about half way up on each side. they were narrow and sloped slightly towards the empty space in the middle of the tunnel. The bottom of this was indeterminate, the impression being that it was bottomless, an abyss. We would have to inch our way along one or other of the ledges.

Larry stopped. 'The left hand one's a little wider,' he said. 'Don't slide off — no one's ever been able to discover how deep the hole is in the middle.'

Even the left hand ledge was only wide enough for us to inch our way along on our stomachs, locomotion being provided by fingers and toes. It was unbelievably slow and tiring. Our heavy batteries tended to drag us towards the edge where the yawning blackness seemed only inches away.

'They're right behind us,' I said to Terry, somehow contriving to speak to him under my right armpit. I felt his helmet hit my boots and there was a muttered expletive.

When we were about halfway along the ledge — this realised afterwards as at the time no one but Larry knew how far it was to the end — there was another laugh somewhere to the rear. The sound was very nasty indeed in the confined space. A minute or so later, all of us tired to the point of exhaustion, it happened again. A laugh, no talking, just a laugh.

'Bastards,' I heard Terry say quietly. I looked round. He had halted, turning his body round as much as he was able, his head actually hanging over the drop. 'Well, I'm damned,' he muttered. Then he slid off the ledge.

I didn't have hysterics for immediately there was a heavy thump as he hit bottom. I peered over and he was on all fours *on* the bottom. About four feet below.

'It's just as well there's three of us here to take care of any trouble,' Terry said in quite a loud voice, addressing the darkness behind us.

'Some women and who else?' a man called back.

'Smith, Wesson and me,' Terry drawled.

There was silence and then I distinctly heard whispering. Then silence again, followed by scraping sounds that faded away.

'They're going,' Terry breathed.

I manoeuvred myself to the lip of the edge and slid off, landing, like Terry, on all fours. 'You got that from *Dirty Harry*,' I said, almost loving him right then.

'So what?'

'Who are you talking to?' Dawn said, apparently in reverse on the ledge above us. 'Good grief!' she exclaimed as she looked over. 'But it's far easier down there than ... You wait until I get hold of Larry.'

'Someone speak my name?' he trumpeted from ahead, clearly in ignorance of what had been going on.

Terry and I helped Dawn down on to the narrow sandy path that we were standing on and the three of us marched up to where he was waiting for us.

'You cheated,' he said.

'Children are smaller,' Dawn informed him heatedly. 'They'd find that *much* easier. Larry, that really was one of the worst moments of my life.'

He dug in a pocket and took out several Mars Bars, one of which he waggled under her nose. 'They don't hate me when I get the sweeties out either,' he said when she snatched it and then laughed at herself.

All at once I felt weak at the knees. I sat on a boulder to eat the chocolate, saying through a mouthful, 'I'm really glad Lynne and John went home. They'd have hated this.'

'We're hating it,' Dawn said.

'Breathtaking honesty,' Terry observed. 'Yes, sweet maid, but the point is we're coping.'

I said, 'D'you reckon those men got past Patrick?'

'Dunno. Larry, are there any other ways in?'

'Several.'

'So it wasn't a lot of use him watching that one was it?' Terry said sharply.

'Do you think I should have said that to him and made him feel useless?'

'It's probably more important for him to keep an eye on where we're coming out anyway,' Dawn said.

No one at the time, I think, realised the wisdom of this remark.

'D'you want to see the Cavern of Jewels or not?' Larry said.

Terry looked at his watch.

'We're well on time,' Larry told him.

'Is it far?'

'No, just a short detour from right here.'

88

'Okay,' we all said.

The short detour turned out to be a mud slid a mere two yards from where we were standing. It was also very steep and the landing area at the bottom slippery so we got very dirty and those who did not enjoy helter-skelters arrived extremely breathless and out of sorts. I'm sure we all decided to make the detour because we did not want to offend Larry who, without a doubt, wanted to show us the cavern. But it did not change my mind about the undesirability of caving. We dutifully admired clusters of muddy looking crystals in the roof and other phenomena including a rather dreary yellow stalagmite said to be a petrified witch. Frankly, I could not wait to get back into the fresh air, whatever awaited us there.

Getting out of the cavern proved to be harder than getting in and entailed a climb up an almost sheer rock wall. But there were hand-holds together with ropes that had been placed for the novice. We stumbled over the rim of this and then followed a path of sorts for a few minutes. All the time the sound of running water became louder.

'You'll be out in ten minutes,' Larry said, having to shout over the noise when we came to a halt on the edge of yet another precipice. 'Just follow me carefully. It looks far worse than it is. When we reach the bottom we cross the river and then go up the other side.'

It was possible that we had all forgiven him for the business of the 'bottomless pit' in the tunnel, but after about ten minutes and when we were still gingerly picking our way down the horrendous and almost vertical descent, there was a generally disenchanted air.

'I feel about a hundred,' I said to Terry when we'd reached bottom and were surveying the turbulent waters of the Nant Cwm-Moel as they thundered over huge rocks and into the depths below.

'This way!' Larry bellowed, leading the way upstream.

We made the crossing, holding hands, up to our waists in the raging current. Everyone but Terry lost their footing on the slippery rocks, Dawn and I actually together, the men hauling us back to our feet. Then Larry went right under and it was Terry who prevented utter disaster by succeeding in keeping hold of both women while getting Larry by the hood of his anorak and yanking him bodily out of the water.

Then began the long climb up the other side. When we got to the top we all sank down wearily.

'Don't usually do that route,' Larry confessed when he'd got his breath back. 'So far I've stuck to an easier one with the kids that's farther up-stream. Thought this might be okay for the older boys. It isn't really, is it?'

'If the water was lower and you were all roped up,' Terry said. He did not add that he himself had had quite a lot of experience of such things and he thought Larry crazy.

'Yeah,' Larry agreed. 'When Alan brought me this way we were roped up, come to think of it.'

I was literally staggering with exhaustion by the time we saw light ahead of us, a serene full moon that was shining directly down the tunnel and into our eyes. Soon we could switch off our helmet lights. They only confused matters. Blessed fresh air fanned into our hot muddy faces.

'I'm so glad to see the moon again,' Dawn said to me. We were walking side by side, Terry still concentrating on watching our backs. 'Didn't you think that Cavern of Jewels was romantic?'

'No,' I replied. 'I didn't. I thought it was horribly over-rated.'

'Perhaps you're not a very romantic person,' she said.

This shook me slightly for I write novels slanted towards romance. However, if one applied a little of what I could only think of as Gillard deduction ...

'Dawn,' I whispered, 'did Terry by any chance ask you to marry him when you were in the cavern?' My wording, I felt, was tactful.

Her face in the moonlight was ecstatic so I had my answer. Come to think of it, she probably hadn't even noticed the ducking in the river.

'Please don't say anything,' she urged. 'We want it to be a surprise.'

I could hardly tell her that the one-time jewel in the crown of D12 and his wife had been following events closely. Love really is blind.

Larry stopped and turned round to face us. 'I suppose we

90

ought to exercise a little caution on the way out. No good Patrick watching out for us if we blunder out making a hell of a row. I suggest we keep to the left as we emerge into the open — there's quite a large overhang there so folk won't be able to roll rocks down on to our heads.'

'I fancy a rock on the head right now,' Terry said. 'It'll save the expense of getting drunk.' Then he laughed at the enraged expression worn by his wife-to-be, pecked her cheek and cautiously went ahead of us into the open.

To me it was like reaching Heaven to walk on grass again. I wanted to run down the slope before me into the little glade but instead caught hold of Dawn's hand and drew her well into the safety of the rock overhang. Tree roots hung down from it with ivy and long festoons of dripping moss.

Silence. I could not even hear my companions breathing.

In the centre of the glade was a tree. From its size and shape I guessed it to be a young oak. In the daylight I imagined it looked most attractive but in the cold gleam of moonlight, and with a strange, long shape hanging from one of the lower branches, it was unbelievably sinister.

Then, nearby, a fox yapped.

It was answered by another, this time the eldritch scream of a vixen. But these were not real foxes. The sound that followed this was not real either. It was a sound to drown out all others. Peals of manical, quavering laughter. Dreadful falsetto wails of utterly humourless, mindless laughter. Then silence before a long drawn-out tremulous *ha-oo-oo*.

Another silence.

Then the laughter burst out again. It beat on our ears like the end of the world being celebrated by a giant demon goblin.

When the wails ceased I thought my imagination was working overtime. For the branches of a large rhododendron bush on the far side of the glade were waving around wildly. Then three shapes ran off up the slope and disappeared.

'What on earth was that?' Dawn asked in an agonised squeak.

'A Great Northern Diver,' I told her, adding, 'it's a bird.'

The bird in question then strolled into the centre of the

glade and leaned his back against the tree, apparently somewhat amused.

'You know what those things are called in North America, don't you?' I said, going to meet him.

'No, what?'

'Common Loons.'

'I let down the tyres of their van,' Patrick said when I was at his side. He was examining the object that had been tied to the tree like a hanging man. It was a scarecrow.

'I thought you might have grabbed one of them,' I said.

'Let the police do that. They'll have the van too.'

It was a bad mistake.

Chapter Seven

'So what happened, exactly?' I asked.

We had changed into the last of our dry clothing and had persuaded Jimmy to make us some mulled wine. Once started he had become quite enthusiastic and had tipped in quite a lot of other things as well, whether to prevent us asking him any further questions, I'm not sure. Whatever the reason, it was remarkably good.

Patrick said, 'They arranged a little surprise for you on the way out. Whether they intended to have another go at grabbing someone I'm not sure. I think the fox's bark was a signal and someone added the second as an embellishment to get you all really twitchy.'

'Of course if we'd bolted back into the cave we might just have run into the jokers who had been following us and who *might* have been briefed to chuck us in the river,' Terry pointed out. 'Only we'd asked them to go away,' he finished with a grin.

'Did you see the three men arrive?' I asked Patrick.

'Yes, they got there soon after I did. Somehow I don't think they were quite sober. I could hear them giggling as they tried to fix up the scarecrow because its head kept falling off.'

'Doesn't it strike you that two elements seem to be in existence here?' I said. 'The hit-and-run and rifle mob and another that plays silly pranks, slightly drunk.'

'I think,' Patrick said, 'that although there's truth in that, the real state of affairs is one gang with a leader who is utterly ruthless and does all the big jobs himself — probably the man who came here to see Jimmy. Under him are people who haven't the same murderous slant to their minds and play it silly.'

'That suggests to me that he isn't the leader,' Terry said.

'Remember what Richard's mother said?' I enquired. 'I know she was upset but the idea that there's a bunch of gangsters around here not wanting people snooping on them isn't such a crazy one. And, as she said, one of them might have gone off his rocker. Terry, you said you were going to phone Daws.'

Terry shook his head. 'I can't. I've just remembered that he's not spending the weekend at his London flat but at home in the country.'

'And no one knows where *that* is,' Patrick said. 'At least, the Prime Minister does and one or two other people. All we could do is leave a message for him. But it's hardly worth it if Terry's going back to work on Monday morning.'

'You were going to tell us about something that you read in a report the other day,' Terry reminded him.

'Was I?' Patrick took another mouthful of mulled wine. 'Oh, yes. It was about a ski-school that someone had set up in Austria. Only it was really a school for terrorists. It was Linda saying something along those lines that made me think of it.'

'How come you get to read confidential MI6 reports?' Terry wanted to know.

'Brinkley sent it to me.'

'What the hell for?'

Patrick looked a little surprised. 'He wondered if I could add anything to it from cases we've dealt with in the department.'

'I see,' Terry said distantly.

Patrick got to his feet. 'The Common Loon retires to bed.'

'I thought that was super,' Dawn enthused. 'Where did you hear those birds?'

'Canada. Ingrid and I got lost in the wilds once.'

We were all preparing to leave when Inspector Jones arrived. She was on her own — although I suppose someone might have been waiting for her outside in a car — and not in

94

uniform. Without the severe hat she looked quite different. She was also very tired.

'A drink?' Patrick enquired solicitously. 'There's hot toddy if you don't mind waiting for it to be reheated.'

'Doesn't this place *ever* close?' she said, sinking into a chair.

'Yes, but we're sort of residents,' Patrick told her. Without waiting for her to say anything else he snatched up the saucepan that had the rest of the mulled wine in it and took it into the kitchen. When he returned it was with a single steaming tumbler full. He placed this in front of her, disappeared through the kitchen door again and came back with a plate upon which there was a chunk of veal, ham and egg pie, several slices of thick bread and butter and a dollop of pickle for luck. He put this before her and went for a knife and fork, napkin and a cruet.

'Is this to make me feel a cow for the way I spoke to you this morning?' she asked. A woman of direct manner, obviously.

'No, it's because you're hungry,' said Patrick.

She picked up the knife and fork, trying not to smile. 'And how do you know that?'

'I'm an expert at *everything*.'

She laughed then and set to hungrily.

'Any news on the Volvo?' Terry asked.

'Yes, good news. There are traces of blood on the radiator grille and three human hairs caught in one of the windscreen wipers. Tests are being done to see if they belong to either of the victims.'

'Fingerprints?' Patrick asked.

Carol Jones shook her head. 'Only the rightful owner's. They must have worn gloves.'

'I take it you've come to see Jimmy. What he has to say is pretty interesting.'

'Do you think it's the truth?'

'He has no reason to lie, surely.'

'It occurred to me that he might be involved. After all, he's in the best position to know exactly what the movements of these groups are.'

'Only the ones that call at the pub,' Terry pointed out.

95

'And that would not include youngsters staying at the youth hostel.'

Jones gave him a scornful look. 'I simply can't believe that you never called at a country pub when you were a teenager and pretended you were over eighteen so you could have a pint of shandy. Of course they come here.'

Not at all disconcerted Terry said, 'So you think our Jimmy might have invented a sinister stranger to remove any suspicion from himself.'

'It's possible.'

'For what ends, though?' Patrick asked. 'He'd be killing his own business.'

'It depends on what's in it for him from other sources, doesn't it?' said the Inspector with an enigmatic smile.

'I do believe you have a lead,' Patrick said quietly.

She shook her head. 'No leads. Just hunches. We've had warnings that drugs might be coming through the area.'

'That doesn't explain attacks on innocent tourists.'

'It might if two gangs were involved and were trying to scare one another off.'

Patrick pulled a face and fell silent, manifestly not at all impressed with this theory.

'Thanks for the meal,' said Carol Jones when she had finished. 'Is mine host in the back?'

'Watching football,' Patrick told her. He glanced at his watch. 'It's probably finished now so you're quite safe.'

She gave him a twisted sort of smile and went into the kitchen.

'Take their football very seriously do the Scots,' Patrick said. 'In my opinion she would have been in extreme danger if she'd interrupted Match of the Day.'

'Not football – fitba,' I corrected. 'You have to get the pronunciation right.'

'I shouldn't be in *this* game,' Larry said, suddenly shoving his chair back and standing up. 'You're all as cool as cucumbers and my nerves are in shreds. I wish we hadn't come. We seem to have triggered off all sorts of appalling happenings. I can't get it out of my head that we were responsible for the deaths of those kids – just by being here.'

'Larry . . .' Patrick began, also rising.

96

'I'm going to turn in,' his brother said. 'No, please don't say any more. I know you're going to accuse me of being hysterical.' He headed for the door.

'We must stay together,' Patrick said. 'If you'll just hang on a sec, we'll all come.'

But Larry blundered out.

'Can you spare a moment, Major?' said Inspector Jones, putting her head round the door.

'Get after him, would you?' Patrick said to Terry.

'I'll go too,' I said.

Dawn also jumped up and the three of us went after Larry.

It was well after midnight by now and had just started to rain. But warmer though, a lot warmer. Ahead of us it was just possible to make out Larry, walking quickly with his anorak flung across a shoulder. We ran to catch up with him.

The entrance to the barn was in very deep shadow. We were just about to enter when there was a loud clatter from within. We all stopped dead and then were almost bowled over by a sheep that came bustling, panic-stricken, from within.

And at that moment someone opened fire on us with a rifle.

At such times I always notice small details. We all threw ourselves flat — bullets zinging all around us and ricochetting off the stone walls of the barn — but one of my main impressions was of feeling droplets of water hit my face from the wet fleece of the sheep as it tore past us and ran off, its small hooves pattering up the lane.

The rifle fired again, a bullet whanging off the ground near my head. I didn't wait for another but rolled, crawled, and then rolled again into the shelter of the barn. Terry and Dawn piled in after me and we stationed ourselves on each side of the gaping doors.

'He's on the high ground facing us,' Terry said. 'Out of range of a hand-gun.'

'Where's Larry?' I cried, having assumed that like us he had bolted for cover.

'Larry!' Terry yelled.

97

'He's over there,' Dawn said, peering out. 'Look. By the cattle trough along the wall.'

Terry hauled her back in. 'Larry! Get in here!'

Another shot banged off somewhere close by.

I risked looking out and saw the still shape almost beneath the metal drinking trough. Then it moved and I heard a groan.

'He's hit!' I said.

Before anyone could stop her, Dawn ran out. Terry swore vividly and emptied Patrick's gun in the rough direction of our attacker. The shots must have been sufficient to put the gunman off for we heard nothing more of him, Patrick arriving then at the run with Inspector Jones just behind him.

Larry was dragged in with no ceremony. When further helping hands were laid on him with a view to ascertaining his injuries he emerged from his torpor and panicked. He sat up with a hoarse cry and waved his arms around, trying to fend us off. Then he collapsed.

'He's going to die,' Dawn babbled. 'I know he's going to die.'

Patrick had reloaded his revolver and now thrust it at me with orders to watch the door. I crouched by the opening, not daring to turn round. Why is it that at such times the eyes play tricks on one and the very hedges seem to dance?

'A *light*, for God's sake,' Patrick said.

'I'll call an ambulance,' Terry offered a couple of seconds later.

'No, I'll go,' Carol Jones said. 'There's a radio in my car.' And she had gone before anyone could speak.

'Is he dead?' Dawn whispered.

'No, he's fainted,' Patrick told her. 'Go upstairs and get a couple of sleeping bags. We must keep him warm.'

'So much for having a doctor with us,' I said.

Patrick grunted. 'There's a lot of blood,' he muttered, mostly to himself. 'In my experience ... yes, there you are, it came out under his arm. With a bit of luck it was at the end of its range and only rattled a few ribs instead of penetrating his chest.'

After this there was silence behind me for quite a while.

Dawn had brought the sleeping bags and Larry was wrapped in them as closely as possible in the circumstances as Patrick was pressing a pad made of a torn shirt to his side in an effort to staunch the bleeding.

I eased my cramped limbs a little and shifted to a slightly more comfortable position, all the while concentrating on the job in hand. My finger tightened on the trigger as a grey shape came out of the gloom. It was a sheep, perhaps the same one as before. Was it coming back because someone was walking down the lane towards us?

'Everything all right?' Patrick said quietly, probably having noticed me suddenly tense.

'I'm not sure,' I answered.

There was movement behind me and then he was by my side, removing the gun from my fingers. The sheep stood a few feet in front of us, swivelling its ears nervously. I could hear nothing untoward. But a breeze had sprung up and was sighing through the trees on each side of the lane, blotting out all other small sounds.

'I should have gone with her,' said Terry.

'That might have made it more dangerous for both of you if they have nightsights and know who she is,' Patrick said. He threw a handful of small stones on the ground in front of the sheep and it trotted off.

'Is he going to die?' I asked. 'He's not as tough as you are.'

'It'll be because of shock and loss of blood if he does. The wound isn't all that serious.'

It seemed to be a very long time before the ambulance arrived, even though when I looked at my watch afterwards it had only been fifteen minutes since we had left The Dragon. Patrick went in the ambulance with Larry, to ride shotgun, as he put it. The rest of us went with the Inspector to the police station where we had to make statements. There seemed little point in returning to sleep afterwards so we sat around in the police canteen, drinking coffee and dozing until dawn. There was still no news of Larry.

'I don't believe this,' I said as we all tumbled out of the mini-bus, bleary-eyed, having gone back to the barn to collect our possessions.

99

We all stood, aghast, staring at the bonfire that was still smouldering at the side of the barn. All our things; clothes, rucksacks, the climbing gear, everything, had been burnt. The only item to escape was Patrick's cannon, that he had hidden under old sacks, still in the loft.

At the hospital we were told that Larry was in no danger and was just coming round from the anaesthetic. Patrick was still with him but his presence was superfluous as police protection had been provided. This was in the shape of a large armed constable who refused to let me through into the private ward until I had proved that I was Patrick's wife. Terry and Dawn were not permitted to enter on the grounds that four visitors were too many.

I tiptoed in and, amazingly, got a weak thumbs-up sign from Larry. He then laid a finger to his lips in case I had not noticed Patrick sprawled asleep in a chair, his tall, rangy frame contorted into what appeared to be an uncomfortable position. But the delicate-looking fingers were still curled around the gun in his lap. It would be unwise to awaken him with a sudden shake.

Silently drawing up a spare chair I sat down by Larry's side and took the hand that wasn't host to drip tubes and kissed it. There had been several moments the previous night when I thought he might die.

'They found the slug in the ground by the barn,' he whispered. 'Went right through without hitting anything important.'

'Patrick thought it had.'

He grimaced. 'Don't remember much. Did I make a fool of myself?'

'Of course not.'

With a sideways look at his brother, he said, 'Patrick's always thought me a bit of a wally. We fought like cat and dog when we were boys. He always won. But I got my own back when I could.' He laughed a little but stopped, wincing. 'It's just as well you grow up, isn't it?'

I smiled, mostly because he seemed to be conveniently forgetting that they had been at one another's throats, to my knowledge, unceasingly until about six months previously.

100

And I was also recollecting being told of an incident of long ago when Larry had got his own back to the extent of almost breaking up his parents' marriage, John Gillard having taken a belt to Patrick after Larry had told tales, knowing that they were probably untrue. Elspeth, their mother, has always vigorously championed her eldest son − and still does − and was outraged that he had been given no chance to explain. So serious had been the row that it had taken the gift of a racing bike from the bishop to the young injured party to smooth matters over. It occurred to me that Larry − frankly a toady even into his youth − might have upset other people as well.

'It makes you think,' he was saying. 'Getting shot, I mean. I'll be a bit more sympathetic towards him now. Shirley always reckons it was mostly his own fault that he was injured in the Falklands. You know − *Boys' Own* stuff. He was always a terrific show-off when he was a lad.'

'It was an accident,' I said.

Larry stared at me. 'You mean one of our own boys . . .'

'No. They'd taken a prisoner. He managed to get free and grab a grenade. But he only meant to warn his own people with it. It hit a rock and bounced into the shepherd's hut where Patrick had his undercover unit's headquarters. As you know, Patrick's legs were badly injured. The sergeant with him only suffered a broken arm because he was blown into a wall.'

'I wish someone had told me that before,' Larry said after a silence.

'Perhaps you never asked.'

'You don't have to stay,' he said after another silence. 'No one does. We'll have to leave it all in the hands of the police now.'

I agreed. Then I said, 'Larry, someone burned all our stuff while we were at the police station last night.'

'Not the bus,' he gasped. 'Please God, not the bus.'

'No, no,' I assured him. 'That was with us at Merthyr. But I'm afraid all your ropes and harnesses have gone. And whatever you had in the barn.'

'The bastards,' he said through his teeth. Then, 'Does Shirley know?'

'About you, you mean? Yes, the police got in touch with her. They asked me for the number.'

'So did I,' Patrick said, moving slowly and stiffly into a sitting position, and trying to get a crick out of his neck. 'While you were in the operating theatre.'

'How did she take it?' Larry asked.

'She was bloody offensive,' Patrick replied, thus reminding me that while all might be sweetness and light as far as he and Larry were concerned, the truce was unlikely to extend to Larry's wife.

'Oh dear,' his brother muttered. 'I'm sorry about that.'

'Get some sleep, old son,' Patrick said, getting to his feet. 'And don't worry about it. Don't worry about a thing. I'll get in touch with you again in a few hours and let you know what Ingrid and I are going to do.'

'Go home,' Larry said emphatically. 'Don't hang around here because of me.'

'I'll have to find out what the police are doing first,' Patrick said and we left.

'How much of that did you hear?' I enquired as we walked out to where Terry and Dawn were waiting.

The arm that was around my shoulders gave me a squeeze. 'From when you came in.'

'You were deliberately listening!'

'So I was,' he confessed mildly. 'An utter cad the fellow is.'

'What do you make of it all?'

'I'm not sure yet. But I intend to do as I said – first contact Jones and see what they've found out, if anything. Then we'll go from there.'

'So you do intend to investigate this.'

'I think I might get better results, don't you?'

'But really because no one shoots Patrick Gillard's brother and gets away with it?'

He smiled at me tiredly. 'As of old, Ingrid, you read me like a book.'

Terry drove the mini-bus to a quiet lane and we all slept the sleep of the dead for two hours. Then, still tired and very

102

grumpy, the latter mostly because our leader had woken us with facefuls of cold water from a nearby stream, we made our way to a transport cafe for hot food.

'It's quite, quite amazing what bacon and eggs can do for the human condition,' Terry remarked with feeling, mopping up egg yolk with a chunk of brown bread.

Dawn said, 'Pity it can't do anything with the stubble on your chin.'

I glanced at Patrick. 'How did *you* achieve a shave?'

'At the hospital. They wouldn't let me in to their hyper-clean ward until I'd had a wash. I told them I was a colonel and they said I could have a bath.'

'You didn't!'

He grinned. 'No. Actually the ward sister felt a bit sorry for me.'

'No mean feat that,' Terry commented. 'She looked a right dragon to me.'

Patrick waggled his fork at him. 'No, this was the night sister. *Quite* a different lady.'

Terry jeered raffishly and earned a look that made him laugh outright. Yes, things had changed.

Inspector Jones, we were told, was off-duty but Sergeant Blake would see us. We all trooped obediently into a large, bare office and were kept waiting, standing, for there were no chairs in the room, for ten minutes. When Blake did arrive, scrubbing petulantly with his handkerchief at a soup stain on his tie — no doubt resulting from an early lunch — I instinctively took a step or two away from my husband's side. When Patrick detonates, even those who love him feel that they are standing too close.

Blake gazed at us in his morose kind of way and then around the room and went away again. He returned shortly, not with more chairs but with the request that we go into the office next door. This had several spare chairs. Patrick lifted one of them thoughtfully as if testing its weight and then put it down again with a minute shake of his head and a shrug.

'I understand he's recovering,' Blake said, looking up from rummaging amongst the clutter on a desk in one corner.

'Are you addressing me?' Patrick asked softly.

Blake looked at him with eyes that reminded me of a white rabbit's.

'May we sit down?' Patrick said.

'Of course.' Blake went on rummaging and finally unearthed a ballpoint pen. He seated himself with a bored sounding sigh. 'The Chief's not at all happy that you're carrying firearms.'

'Meaning whom?'

'Chief Inspector Parry. He's not here or you'd have had to see him.'

'Well, being as we've already had this argument with Inspector Jones can't we skip that bit and go on to what you're doing about catching the people who shot my brother?'

'There might be a perfectly logical explanation. Had that occurred to you?'

'Of course there's a perfectly logical explanation,' Patrick exploded. 'No one's talking about aliens from another planet or people raised from the dead going round toting rifles.'

Blake's pale face coloured. 'I mean it might be a case of mistaken identity — as far as last night's shooting's concerned, that is.'

'I'm all ears, Sergeant,' Patrick observed dryly.

'The barn was well known to be used by poachers.'

'So well known that the police hadn't arrested them?'

Blake looked at him with something approaching hatred. 'Not known to us *before*. This is information that is emerging from our questioning of those who live in the locality.'

One black eyebrow quirked. 'And those who live in the locality think that that kind of knowledge gives them the right to take pot-shots at anyone seen in the vicinity of the barn at night.'

Out of the corner of one eye I could see Terry's shoulder's shaking. But I felt not a shred of pity for Blake. He had already met Patrick and should have known better than to treat him with incivility.

'Who does that white van belong to?' Patrick asked.

'Ah,' said Blake, riffling through the papers on the desk again, this time to no avail. 'There is a degree of evidence,' he went on slowly, 'that the business of men trying to grab this lady here . . .' a nod in my direction 'was no more than a stupid prank.'

'Who does the van *belong* to?' Patrick said again.

'A survival school. But there's no need to bother yourselves further with it. A couple of people have been reprimanded. Apparently they did it for a bet.'

'Reprimanded by whom?' I enquired.

'The gentleman who runs the school. The culprits were a couple of lads on a course.'

Patrick said, 'And your exhaustive enquiries have established that these high-spirited youngsters were not responsible for any of the other little mishaps.'

'Quite so,' said Blake.

'And no high-velocity weapons with night-sights are kept on these premises?'

'Only sporting rifles for Mr Griffiths' own use – he's the proprietor.'

'Have these been removed for checking?'

'There was no need. None of them had recently been fired.'

'Were the police at the home of this man Griffiths so soon after the shooting?'

'Yes.'

'From that I take it that he *is* a suspect?'

'Was,' Blake corrected. 'We've eliminated him from our enquiries.'

'I think,' Patrick said, fixing Blake with an unfriendly stare, 'that you've been ordered to get rid of us.'

'The police are perfectly capable of handling this case,' Blake countered.

'Have you discovered who it was who visited the landlord of The Dragon?' I asked. 'He seems to be connected with the men who drove the white van.'

'It's being followed up,' Blake replied woodenly. All at once his temper flared. 'I suggest you all leave the area and go home. As I said, we are perfectly capable of handling this.'

'I think we were only being helpful because Inspector Jones said she was short-staffed,' Terry said.

'Having amateurs poking around is not helpful,' Blake

said. 'And just because you all fancy yourselves an important part of national security, it doesn't mean you can solve crimes. I really must insist on this — leave. If the matter has to be reported to the Chief Constable the consequences will be serious for you. And if — ' Here he seemed to have detected a mulish expression on Terry's face. 'And if Mr Griffiths should ring to tell us that strangers are snooping around his property, there will be warrants out for the arrest of all of you. Immediately.'

Chapter Eight

'He's probably kicking himself for letting that name slip out,' Terry said.

'Yes,' Patrick agreed. 'And that of course was why he lost his temper. Not to worry — we can't stay here with only the clothes we stand up in.'

'So you're not going to strike the Griffiths while he's hot?' Dawn said.

Patrick smiled at her. 'No, trusty and brave woman, we will leave him to cool. And joking apart, I'm quite in awe of the way you ignored personal safety to help my brother.'

'Mentioned in despatches?' she said with a self-conscious grin.

'Definitely,' he told her. 'Shall we go home?'

There were many unanswered questions. I had no doubt in my mind that we would return to try to answer them. But for a few days it would do no harm to leave the police a clear field to make their own investigations. There was a possibility that they would get to the bottom of the trouble, thus bringing the episode to a satisfactory conclusion.

'If anyone's thinking that we've failed,' Patrick said as Terry parked the mini-bus outside the caretaker's house at the school, 'then be of good cheer — we haven't. It was of paramount importance to discover whether there was a problem and it has been proved beyond doubt that there is. The police are looking into it. There is a fair amount of evidence. And lastly — this being the end of my little speech — we have all had a lot of fresh air and exercise and frightened ourselves silly, and that never does anyone any harm.'

'I'd like to look into that survival school,' Terry observed.

'I intend to if the police don't come up with an answer quite soon,' Patrick said.

'If you need a hand ...'

'I'll get on the blower. Thanks.'

We returned to Devon, Terry almost immediately leaving again to catch a train for London. Dawn drove him into Plymouth while I collected Justin from her mother's. We got back almost together to find the master of the house in the kitchen concocting what turned out to be an enormous risotto.

'I didn't know you could cook,' Dawn said, sniffing appreciatively.

'Anyone can cook if they can read,' said Patrick, adding more black pepper.

'We'll have to face John and Lynne again,' I said when we were clearing away, everyone having drunk quite a lot of white wine with the meal.

'Don't you think they'll rather have to face us?' Patrick asked.

'I've a feeling they won't see it like that.'

'Are you coming to Bristol with me tomorrow?'

'I thought you were going to leave it for a few days.'

'Only the Wales end. I thought I'd go and have a word with Larry's colleagues.'

'Surely you don't suspect any of them.'

'I'm thinking of it from the point of view that it was *Larry* who was shot. They tried once and failed and then had a second go. I admit I might be way off-beam but if there's anything personal in it, the school might provide a few answers.'

'But the children were killed as well. And the cadets had had trouble.'

'I'm not saying that anyone at the school is directly involved. But there might be a lead.'

'I'll come with you if I don't have to meet Shirley.'

'Heaven forfend either of us do.' Patrick muttered.

In the event the lady got there before us and we had the misfortune to come face to face with her near the main entrance of the school. She unleashed upon Patrick a fairly incoherent tirade of abuse of an intensely personal nature and when he just stood there, soaking it all up like blotting paper, with no expression on his face whatsoever, screamed at him that she knew perfectly well that Justin wasn't his child as the injuries he had sustained in the Falklands had rendered him sterile. Patrick's only reaction to this was to hold my arm more tightly and to wish her good morning. She went, red of visage, glaring at various people who had come to windows to see what all the noise was about.

'Well, we won't have to send *her* a birthday card,' he said.

'Sorry about that,' said a tall, gangling man who had emerged through the entrance doors. 'She's as miffed as hell because her husband's been injured on a school trip.'

'I know,' Patrick said. 'I was there. She's my sister-in-law.'

'Oh, I say,' exclaimed the man. 'I'm Clive Trescott by the way, I take it you want to see Mr Bidwell, the headmaster.'

'Most definitely,' Patrick said.

We were shown along a corridor, asked to wait in an outer office and then bidden to enter a large pleasant room overlooking gardens with a lily pool. Mr Bidwell, Trescott assured us, would not be long and had just gone to give his secretary some letters to type.

'Funny how you always get the same feeling going into a headmaster's room,' said Patrick quietly, gazing out of the window. 'No matter how old you are, you feel guilty.'

'I don't,' I said. 'I never got into trouble at school.'

'We were at the same school for quite a while,' he reminded me with a smile.

'But you didn't notice me until I was fifteen and you were head boy. And where your guilt complex comes from I can't imagine.'

'Perhaps it was because I lured you out on to Dartmoor and seduced you.'

'Rubbish,' I said. 'It was a delightful idea that occurred to us at the same time. Besides, I didn't tell you that I was under age for at least a week.'

'Any regrets?' he asked, turning to look out of the window again.

'Only that we divorced after ten years and I wasn't able to look after you when you came home from the South Atlantic.'

Before he could make any response to this the headmaster came through an inner door. Observing him, I immediately came to the conclusion that he was not looking forward to the interview, probably because Shirley had already ruined his morning. But after he had given us a rapid appraisal – in the way only such people can – I felt that he modified his attitude slightly.

'It's Major, isn't it?' Bidwell said, a hand outstretched. 'Do make yourselves comfortable.' He threw himself into the chair behind his desk and appeared to make a real effort to relax. 'Your brother often speaks of you. How is he, by the way?'

'In military terms, walking wounded,' Patrick told him. 'I reckon he'll be back with you before very long.'

'Oh, it's not serious then?' said Bidwell with great relief. 'I rather got the impression that . . .'

'Say no more,' Patrick said. 'We met her on the way in.'

'She's on the PTA too,' Bidwell grumbled. 'No matter. I'm glad that he's out of danger. Tell me, Major, what do you make of all this?'

'It's difficult to decide whether he was a *planned* target. I wish in hindsight that I'd arranged a flak jacket for him. But that wouldn't necessarily have saved him and we must bear in mind that he might have been hit merely because he was slow in diving for cover. And when we remember what else happened over the weekend, I think it points to the fact that Larry as an individual wasn't a target at all.'

Patrick then went on to give Bidwell a concise account of what had happened.

'Good heavens!' exclaimed the headmaster when Patrick had not been talking very long. 'I heard about some children being hit by a car in the area but never dreamed for a moment that it was deliberate or that there might be a connection. On the news they said something about a stolen car.'

'It looks as though the car might have been stolen for the very purpose of a hit-and-run,' Patrick said.

'Major, this is a very nasty business,' Bidwell commented when he had all the facts. 'And I'm very grateful for your trouble in coming to see me. There's no question of the trips taking place at present. It might be a good idea to stop them altogether. I simply dare not take risks with children's lives.'

'May I make a couple of suggestions?' Patrick said.

'Please do — I need all the advice I can get.'

'Speaking for a moment from my brother's point of view, I think it would be very sad if all his efforts came to an end. I get the impression he's worked hard to make these little expeds a success. Knowing him as I do, I reckon it's the best thing he's ever done. I suggest that when he returns to work and has fully recovered, he carries on but with a change of venue.'

'But where, Major, where? Finding somewhere else suitable might take a long time.'

'I think I can organise something at an army training establishment — certainly in the short term, and possibly for longer. There's a place in Dorset with all the equipment and facilities for climbing, abseiling and canoeing that's set in hundreds of acres of countryside. Plenty of scope for safe adventure.'

'But that would be wonderful,' stammered Bidwell. 'I can't thank — '

'Thank Larry,' Patrick interrupted. 'He's the one who stopped the bullet. The other thing I'd like to do is speak to his colleagues.'

The headmaster studied Patrick closely. 'I hope you haven't any suspicions concerning another member of staff.'

'I've no real theories at all at present. But a little background would be helpful.'

'If you interviewed the staff it would have to be done carefully,' Bidwell said after pondering. 'I don't want people upset. If the word got round that I'd called in my own investigative team ...'

'I can be charm and tact personified,' Patrick asserted with a grin. 'And you must remember that when I worked for MI5, some of the interviews I undertook were *extremely* difficult and sensitive.'

'If the police arrive with the same idea people will feel that they're being thoroughly grilled,' Bidwell pointed out.

'I doubt very much if the police will come here. They seem to be working on a theory that Larry was confused with a local poacher. It's utter poppycock of course and probably only a yarn they spun to get rid of me.'

'Very well,' the headmaster said. 'But I can't ask folk to stay behind after school. That really isn't on. Perhaps something can be arranged during the dinner hour. There's no guarantee that they'll all come — I'm not in a position to impose a three-line whip.'

'I'm most grateful,' Patrick said. 'Are we talking about today?'

'I'll do my best,' Bidwell promised. 'But you must realise that it's very short notice.'

'Will you be present?'

'It might be better if I wasn't. You might find out more.' The headmaster then smiled reflectively. 'No, I won't interfere. If you find out anything interesting that you think I ought to know you can give me a ring at home in the evening. I'll give you the number. That's better than leaving messages with people or notes around the place, isn't it?'

'You'd make a good policeman,' Patrick said as we rose to go. 'Tell me — do you have any ideas of your own on this matter?'

'Only that someone might be trying to get at you through your brother.'

'That had occurred to me. Vengeful nutcases usually write anonymous notes to newspapers. And nothing like that's turned up yet.'

Bidwell wrote down his phone number on a scrap of paper and handed it over. 'Be careful, Major,' he said.

Later, I said, 'Do you think he has his own suspicions but prefers to keep them to himself so as not to cloud your judgement?'

'I'm not sure,' Patrick said. 'He's a shrewd man. I have

an idea that the little warning as we left wasn't anything to do with my chat with the staff but that I might get myself killed trying to deal with the case on my own.'

'He was very careful not to put forward an opinion at all. Not even about Larry.'

'I think that was modesty rather than a desire to be impartial.'

'And he knew that the staff would be a better sounding-board.'

'Yes, quite.'

The headmaster had let us use his own sitting room – a small but pleasant inner sanctum where he spoke to parents in a less formal setting than his office – while he endeavoured to arrange a meeting. He had shown us to it himself and then brought us coffee, saying that he would ring us in half an hour or so with the results of his efforts.

'I'm still worn out,' said Patrick, yawning. He looked across at me, eyes sparkling. 'You still haven't had your holiday or second honeymoon.'

'I'm working on a book about it instead,' I told him. 'This is the opening paragraph: "He tore off her silk blouse and kissed her perfect breasts, his tongue caressing – "'

'Steady on,' Patrick interrupted. 'There might be someone listening.'

'"She lay back on the hot sand and raised her knees. Slowly he entered her and – "'

'Ingrid! We *are* in a school you know.'

'"The powerful thrusts of his body wrung cries of pleasure from her – "'

'For pity's sake, woman!' my husband exclaimed, looking alarmed. 'Do you want me to go to this meeting with a – '

'Tonight,' I intoned, eyes closed. 'You will do this to *me*.'

'Might have a spot of bother finding the hot sand,' he observed sourly.

'Weston-super-Mare?' I suggested, throwing a cushion at him.

He was saved from thinking of a reply by the phone ringing. I did not think it could be the headmaster so soon but it was, saying that he had forgotten an important staff meeting that had already been arranged for the lunch break and would it be all right if he organised something for us the following day? We were very welcome to stay the night at his home. There was no choice but to agree and thank him.

We did indeed spend some time at Weston-super-Mare, walking along the beach sharing a candy floss like a couple of kids. We returned to Bristol for a very good meal in an Italian restaurant near the Law Courts and then went to the cinema. Afterwards we made our way to Filton where James Bidwell and his wife lived. Luckily we always carry an overnight bag in the car.

The Bidwells made us very welcome. Their home was modern and on an attractive estate bordering open country-side. It was one of those houses where the walls are so thin that we could hear Julian's — the younger of the two sons — white mouse trundling round and round in its exercise wheel in the bedroom next to ours for half the night. So, Gillard lovemaking tending to be noisy, there was nothing for it but to kiss each other goodnight and go to sleep.

'I'm not surprised the birthrate's dropping in this country,' I said irritably as we walked around Bristol city centre the following morning, killing time. It had been arranged that we would arrive at the school at noon.

'There's a fairly clean bus-shelter over the road if you're *that* desperate.'

I was not amused. 'I'm merely thinking of a discussion we had at home about having another baby,' I lied. 'It's the right time of the month, that's all.'

Ignoring the fact that we were right outside Marks and Spencer's and the pavement was crowded, Patrick stopped dead. 'Oh, so you don't really fancy me then?'

'Whatever gave you that idea?'

He laughed. '*Touché.*'

To be honest, I thought we were wasting our time talking to Larry's colleagues. Teachers never seem to me to be the stuff of which murderers are made. But every possibility had to be investigated and, right now, Patrick had the time to do it.

114

We arrived to find Clive Trescott waiting for us.

'Consider me as a sort of aide-de-camp,' he said. 'Come this way. We're covening in a room off the staff canteen. There are four apologies,' he went on. 'Two gym teachers are taking lunch-time sports, one's off with a badly cut hand – quite genuine too, he shoved it through the glass side of the fume cupboard in the chemmy lab this morning and had to go to hospital for stitches – and the fourth is Miss Hockney whom I understand twisted her ankle last night. Very nervous sort of woman. I doubt if she was in Wales taking pot-shots at your brother.' He glanced quickly at Patrick. 'Forgive the facetiousness. I always talk too much.'

Patrick chuckled. 'Look, I'm not the Chief of the Defence Staff. Tell me something – is there anyone here who really hates Larry?'

'God, no. He's not the kind of man anyone *hates*, is he? I'm not saying that he doesn't irritate folk now and then. He gets such a bee in his bonnet over things.'

'What kind of things?'

'Oh, the trips with the kids mostly. Thinks everyone ought to be as keen as he is. Goes on about it rather.'

'In other words, bores the pants off people.'

'Since you put it so frankly, yes.'

'He hasn't changed.'

I wondered, as we entered the room, what those inside were expecting. It was possible that – with a view to encourage attendance – the headmaster had hinted that the brother was not a clone of their colleague. On the other hand – and this was more likely – he might have said nothing. For a moment I imagined the 'old' Larry wearing army uniform and the picture thus presented was not far removed from a character in a Gilbert and Sullivan production. The part of me that writes books wriggled in anticipation for human relationships and reactions are meat and drink to me. I was also wondering if someone in that room was responsible for the transformation that Larry appeared to have undergone of late. In other words, a woman.

Carefully observing – careful not to stare, that is – as Clive Trescott made the introductions, I saw surprise and then interest and decided that Bidwell had offered no clues about the visitors. Patrick had apparently decided to play it not as the slightly sinister man from MI5, nor even the efficient militarist with a clipped manner of speech, but as himself — and here I had a quite appalling thought that this is how he presents himself to *me* and no one knows what he's really like — the career soldier and family man whose demeanour, however, does not invite familiarity.

I seated myself in a spare chair by a window and unobtrusively made a note of the names. Reading, as it were, from left to right, the staff of Haswell Comprehensive comprised Messrs. Dawson, Tomkinson, Smith, Dervin, Williams, Green, Hallet-Gardiner, Bobs and Jenkins. There were four ladies, all unaccountably sitting together; Anne O'Malley, Joan Watson, Isobel Parsons and Lorna Templeton. The last of these was the girls' physical education teacher, easily the most attractive. Upon perceiving Patrick she looked a trifle embarrassed and this was noticed by Hallett-Gardiner who grinned wolfishly and nudged his neighbour, Green. I made a note of it.

Patrick selected for himself a plain upright chair, one of several that were obviously from the canteen next door, there being not enough armchairs, and sat down facing the semi-circle of staff, relaxed, smiling and definitely in charge. First of all he gave them a short resumé of events so far, right from the time Larry had asked for help. For those in ignorance of the reasons behind the request he touched on those too. It would be untrue to record that by the time he had finished everyone's mouth was hanging open but nevertheless there was a fair amount of astoundment, as my father used to say.

'So I'm here to ask for your help,' Patrick concluded by saying. 'Any clue, any idea that might throw a little light on this. I realise of course that this school hasn't been the only target for attack. Has anyone had any crazy letters?'

'Blackmail?' said Trescott, shocked.

'That's what I had in mind,' Patrick replied.

'But surely anyone receiving such a letter would have reported it straight away.'

'That would depend on several things — the nature of

116

the letter, the person to whom it was sent and whether that person had anything to hide.'

Joan Watson said, 'So I trust you won't expect any of us to admit we've had such a letter. In public, I mean.'

'No, of course not. I would hope that they would speak to me in private afterwards.'

'Are you part of an official investigation?' Mrs Watson went on coldly. 'Or is this some kind of revenge thing?'

There were a few gasps at the bluntness of this question but I rather got the impression that the gathering had half expected her to take such an attitude. She looked a belligerent sort of woman; grey-haired, her brow creased into a permanent frown.

'You mustn't believe everything you read in the papers,' Patrick said mildly.

She gave him a thin smile. 'Come now, Major. You *were* at the forefront of public attention a couple of years ago when you foiled an attempt to kidnap one of the royal princes. At least, that's what they *might* have intended to do. No one's quite sure because they weren't alive afterwards to be questioned. You shot them both in cold blood.'

'When I was at school,' Patrick said, 'the expression "in cold blood" meant an act performed dispassionately and without heat. Yes, that is how I shot the two men. Lately though, and thanks to the sloppy English of the media, the idea has crept in that "in cold blood" means that those killed were somehow helpless victims, treated abominably cruelly. To put the record straight the first man pointed a replica pistol at the royal car, the second was armed with a knife and attacked the prince directly I had shot his friend – whom I admit I did not question about the authenticity of his weapon beforehand – wrenching open the car door. In fending off the knife I sustained a cut that resulted in a night in hospital and eleven stitches. The prince was sitting nearest the door and his life depended on my behaving in dispassionate and cool fashion. I'm paid to act in cold blood. To answer your first question though, I'm not part of the official investigation but anything I learn of importance I shall report to the police. And, no, I'm not sharpening my teeth to points in order to suck the blood of the people who shot my brother.'

Everyone gave Joan Watson a "You bloody well deserved that" look.

'Will Larry stop taking the children, do you think?' Miss Templeton asked diffidently.

'No,' Patrick said. 'At least, he'll resume when it's safe to do so.'

Anne O'Malley tossed back her long black hair. 'Just so long as he's not put under any pressure to continue. It's enough to make a man lose his nerve a little – getting shot. Just because you found the place for Alan, Lorna, it doesn't mean that Larry has to keep on with it.'

Lorna Templeton flushed. 'I was only asking the Major's opinion. He knows Larry far better than we do.'

'And *did* you tell Alan about the village?' Patrick enquired.

'Yes, I went there with an Outward Bound group a few years ago. I thought the area was perfect for what Alan wanted to do. Larry thinks so too now.'

'So it is,' Patrick said absently. 'Did you ever hear anything about a man called Griffiths?'

She shook her head. 'No.'

'Apparently he runs a survival school.'

'I can't say I ever heard Alan mention the name.'

'Did you hear people talking about a survival school in the area?'

'No.'

'What's the connection?' Mr Dawson asked.

'There's a little evidence already,' Patrick said. 'Does the name Griffiths mean anything to anyone here?'

It did not.

To Lorna again, Patrick said, 'Did Larry tell you when someone first took a shot at him?'

'Yes, it shook him up rather.'

'Yet he waited a whole week before he mentioned it to me.'

'I persuaded him that he ought to get expert help.'

The undertones of this were fascinating, a fact not lost on Mr Hallet-Gardiner who was clearly in anticipation of revealing details and once again nudging Green in the ribs. He was disappointed for Patrick merely went on to ask her about places she had visited with the Outward Bound group.

'I feel that we've let him down,' said Mr Jenkins into a lull in the conversation. He was a quietly spoken man, slightly stooped but not of an age yet when he might be expected to be so. 'Larry mentioned it to me — and that he was worried about things. I can't say that I took him all that seriously. I mean, it all sounds so melodramatic when someone says they were shot at. I should have been more sympathetic, tried to advise him and so forth.'

'You were a gem of understanding compared with others in this room whose names I shall refrain from mentioning,' Anne O'Malley cried. 'One dear colleague I *distinctly* remember made some remark along the lines of "I hope whoever it is doesn't make a cock of it next time". Someone else who isn't present right now remarked that Larry had probably been confused with a scarecrow by someone engaging in target practice.'

Patrick cleared his throat. 'Hardly a day passed when we were boys when I didn't thump him hard. Please don't bother to talk of how he irritates *you*.'

At this point the headmaster came in. 'Your brother's on the phone,' he said to Patrick. 'He wants to talk to you.'

'Nice to have your husband at home and out of danger?' said Hallet-Gardiner to me when Patrick had left the room. He bared his yellow teeth in another grin. 'All cosy in your cottage while you write books, eh?'

'Never believe everything you read in the papers,' I told him with a sugary smile.

'I could have sworn I heard she writes books,' I heard him say as I headed after Patrick, unable to stomach him any longer and sorely tempted to put a bullet in the floor at his feet with the Smith and Wesson that was residing in my handbag for the day.

'Idiot!' Anne O'Malley spat at him. 'Of course she does. That's Ingrid Langley.'

Patrick was still talking to Larry when I reached the headmaster's office, taking my time. But almost immediately he replaced the receiver. His face was tight with suppressed excitement.

'They've got someone,' he said to Mr Bidwell. He swung round and saw me. 'Or more correctly, they've found a body with a note. The man had apparently shot himself and the note was a confession to just about everything that's happened.'

'But that's wonderful,' Bidwell said. 'No, not wonderful,' he corrected himself. 'But the end to all *our* worries.'

'That's what the police will think,' Patrick said. 'That's what I'm sure they're meant to think.'

'What do you mean?' I said.

'They've put a name to the body. From his fingerprints he was a wanted man.'

'Who?'

'Friedrich.'

'What!'

'Yes, precisely.'

'Please explain,' Bidwell begged.

'Anton Friedrich,' Patrick said. 'One of the most wanted men in Europe. To cut a long story short he was a bomber, terrorist and a complete nut-case. Just about every security service in the Western World has been after him for years.'

'But what was he doing in Wales?' asked Bidwell.

'That's the big question,' Patrick replied.

'You don't think ...' I started to say.

'That he really went off his rocker and someone put a bullet in him before he gave their game away? We've heard this before, haven't we? And I keep thinking about that survival school.'

Chapter Nine

'The girl has come to confess all,' Patrick said as we saw Lorna Templeton standing by our car. 'Well, it explains quite a lot anyway.'

'Is it bad news?' she asked, a little breathlessly as though she had been running.

'No. The police have got someone.'

'What? The man who killed the children and shot Larry?'

'Yes, but it might be a bit more complicated than that,' Patrick answered cautiously.

'How is Larry?'

'He can come home in a couple of days' time if someone's there to look after him.'

Her face fell. 'But Shirley works full-time.'

'Then I presume he'll have to stay in hospital for a little longer − until he's stronger.'

'Oh, well.' She turned to go.

'I thought it was half-term in a couple of days.'

'It is.'

'Can't you have him at your place?'

Lorna eyed him narrowly. 'That wouldn't be right, would it?' she said stiffly, and again turned to go.

'He's good in bed, I understand,' Patrick said to her back.

The girl spun round to discover that he was wagging a finger at her.

'You were waiting to talk to us,' he said. 'I wasn't surprised. We were wondering who had wrought the transformation in him.'

'Now I know,' she gasped. '*That's* what he meant when he said you'd always know what made the cat sick.'

Patrick laughed.

'He's terribly unhappy,' Lorna said. 'He's only sticking it for the children's sake.'

'I'm not sure the children should be with a woman who hits the gin bottle a bit too often.'

It was my turn to stare at him.

'I don't ask about that,' said Lorna.

'Does Shirley know about you?'

'No, not unless he's told her. I say, you won't ...'

'Tell Shirley? Heavens, no.'

'I − I thought I ought to be honest with you. And I don't want you to think of me as one of those awful women who break up marriages. We're just close friends.' She blushed. 'Well, perhaps a bit more sometimes. He doesn't seem to have any friends. And deep down he's a very good person − someone you could trust right to the end. No one but me seems to think of him like that.They just treat him as though he's a fool.'

'If we can be of any help ...' Patrick said.

'Thank you but I don't see − '

'Not just empty words on my part,' he interrupted. 'It might be a good idea if he went to our parents for a little while. Mother would love the chance to make a fuss of him. And you could always drive him from South Wales to just outside Bath, couldn't you?'

'Oh!' Lorna said.

Patrick gave her the phone number of the hospital and also that of the Rectory at Hinton Littlemoor and we left. Lorna was still standing in the car-park, looking bemused, as we drove through the entrance gates.

I said, 'Patrick, as you know, I always admire your methods but that was little short of genius. If there's one person who can help Larry sort himself out, it's your mother.'

'The two children already spend most of the school holidays with her.'

'I didn't know Shirley had a drink problem.'

'Nor did I until Larry mentioned it over the phone just now.

He said he thought we ought to know because it explained her behaviour. Mum and Dad have known for some time apparently.'

'Lorna made me feel really guilty,' I said. 'I think I was one of those people who treated Larry as a fool.'

'Likewise,' Patrick sighed. 'And now we have to put that tantalising business from our minds and think about Anton Friedrich.'

'It might be a good idea to ring Terry.'

'Too right. Don't worry, I intend to bring D12 right in on this. Someone like Friedrich wasn't in the Brecon Beacons for his health. We've got to think of things like the Welsh Guards barracks fairly close by, lots of reservoirs that can be bombed to wash entire towns away. Who knows? He might have been hired by a few lunatics who live across the Irish Sea.'

'But who killed him?'

'That worries me even more. *If* the suicide is proved to be phoney – and there's no telling it will – what must be considered first is that there's a cadre of some kind.'

'Isn't it at all possible that he killed himself?'

'Yes, it is. But why in Wales, and why did he kill people and generally create mayhem in a national park? That's the bit that makes no sense. If he'd quietly shot himself in a London flat having blasted a few people off the face of the Earth, it would have fitted. That's my opinion anyway.'

A few miles farther on I said, 'How are you going to play it then?'

'I intend to return to the area undercover. Live in the hills and find out what's going on.'

'Despite telling D12 all you know?'

'Yes. Terry's a grown man now. He can do his own thing. If I bump into him on the top of Pen y Fan it'll merely prove that he was listening when I instructed him for all those years.'

'And your wife?' I enquired in the same practical tones.

He was silent for a moment or two and then said, 'You often have feelings about things. What does your intuition tell you about this?'

'That there'll either be absolutely nothing in it or it'll be the worse thing we've ever tackled.'

123

He smoothly overtook a heavy lorry. 'Ingrid, I'm not trying to prove anything by following this up.'

'No, I think you're trying to stop Terry getting killed.'

The car swerved slightly. When we came to a lay-by round the next bend Patrick pulled into it and stopped. The lorry thundered past but we hardly noticed it, looking at one another.

'Sometimes you're uncanny,' he whispered. 'I don't think I'd realised that myself.'

'I'm not a seventh child of a seventh child,' I said, laughing to dispel the fey mood. 'But I want to be with you. There can be no Holmes without Watson.'

'I've changed my mind slightly,' Patrick said when we got home. 'There's little point in living in the hills to the standard that I'd use in war. That tends to be so effective that you could stay there forever and nothing would happen. No, I think we've got to go well equipped and *prepared* to live rough but otherwise show ourselves discreetly and see what comes our way.'

'Like bullets, you mean?'

He grinned infuriatingly.

It was decided that we would leave first thing the following morning so it was late that night by the time everything was organised for the early departure. We had dinner and then with Justin in bed and Dawn watching a film on TV in her own room, we sat drinking coffee – my favourite blend, Old Blue Sumatra – by the light of just the log fire. Neither of us felt like talking.

'Who the hell's that?' Patrick said when there was a knock at the front door.

'Just wanted to check that you were all right,' John said round the door post, Lynne peering out from behind him. 'Saw you go past in the car.'

'Come in,' I said.

'No, I'm sure you're busy.'

I bundled them both indoors without further ado and Patrick and I swung into what can only be called a damage control exercise. This involved nothing more complicated

124

than pouring alcohol into the pair of them until they felt they could look us in the eye.

'We've come to apologise,' John said at last. 'We were useless to you and behaved like a couple of idiots.'

Patrick said, 'It's a case of one man's meat being another man's poison. If I'd known it was going to be quite so dangerous I'd not have asked you to come. I blame myself entirely. Just thank your lucky stars you came home early.'

He told them what had happened.

'Don't go back,' Lynne pleaded. 'Leave it to the police.'

'I only wish we could help,' John said.

'You can,' Patrick said.

'How?' they both asked together.

'Did I see a brand-new Land-Rover Discovery parked in your drive?'

They agreed that he had.

'Lend it to me for a few days?' said Patrick, beaming.

How could they refuse?

In the early morning light of the next day Dartmoor was all tawny and bronze, the heather winter-brown now, the tors a steely grey after heavy rain in the night. As I watched, leaning on the sill of the open window, taking deep breaths of fresh air, the sun sent the first shaft of brightness over the moor. Bronze turned to gold and granite to silver. Somewhere a curlew called.

'It's a nice day,' Patrick said from behind me.

Too nice.

'Second thoughts?' he queried gently.

'No.'

'But?' he prompted.

Perhaps from someone else I would have resented the probing.

'I'm scared,' I said.

'It's *intelligent* to be scared,' he said, placing a hand on my right shoulder and turning me round to face him. He kissed me. 'And as we've both found out before, the only cure for being scared is to go and get on with it.'

There was one disagreement as we were loading the Discovery, a short, sharp engagement that I lost when I realised that he was taking his confounded cannon again.

'It'll bring me luck,' said he, smiling, albeit warily, at my displeasure.

'Like it did last time,' I rejoined. 'As you know I'm not particularly twitchy about things that go bang but I'm convinced it'll blow us up.'

'It can't. It's not loaded.'

'But I bet there's a companion package somewhere full of cannonballs and gunpowder and jolly ingredients like that.'

'And your food processor to bung it all together with. Of course.'

I conceded defeat.

It was now the third week in October and when we got out of the Discovery at an hotel near Raglan Castle where we had lunch — a last brush with civilised living — a cold north wind reminded me that conditions on these high hills would be those of winter.

We called in to see Larry on the way through Merthyr Tydfil, finding him up and dressed.

'I'm — er — going to stay with Mum and Dad for a few days,' he said. 'You know what Mum's like when one's hit a bad patch. Couldn't disappoint her really.'

'Of course not,' Patrick said, straight-faced. 'It must be your turn too — she's had plenty of practice with me.'

Larry grinned. 'A colleague's driving me over — it saves dragging Shirley all the way up from home. I've a feeling she'll be nagged into staying over the half-term break as well.'

'Why not?' Patrick said stoutly. 'Well, give them our love.'

'Inspector Jones called in yesterday. I think she was trying to pump me about your *plans*.'

'Plans? What plans? If she comes snooping around again, tell her we're here for a well-dressing. No, on second thoughts, don't tell her we're here at all.'

'The police might be keeping an eye open for us,' I said when we were outside.

'Then we'll disappear.'

Disappearing entailed some fairly convoluted driving around country roads until Patrick was sure we were not being tailed by anyone. Then we drove to the Upper Neuadd

126

Reservoir and parked. We had passed the Lower Reservoir on the way, both of these huge areas of water seeming little more than puddles in the gigantic valley surrounded by the peaks of Craig y Fan-Du, Corn Du, Pen y Fan, Cribyn and Fan Big, most of them over two thousand feet high. The lower end of the valley is forested but up here we were above the tree line and in an environment of moorland, scree and ravens.

I said, 'I thought you might have tried to have a look at Friedrich's body.'

'I'd like to have done but that would have announced our presence. Terry can legitimately ask for all the info on the post-mortem. D12 have to keep their files up to date on people like that. I told him I'd give him a ring.'

'Why are we here anyway? It's miles from where Larry was shot at the first time.'

'We're here precisely for the reason that nothing's been known to happen at this spot. I want to examine the remote areas closely. Watch them over a period of days if necessary. To see what moves.'

A couple of hours later we were near the summit of Cribyn.

'Anything interesting?' I enquired after a while.

Patrick focussed the binoculars carefully. 'There are a few other hikers — nobody particularly suspicous looking. No one's keeping an eye on *us* as far as I can see. Have a look yourself.'

The binoculars were very good ones. Details leapt at me; a sheep lying in a hollow, no more than a white dot to the naked eye; a couple of walkers, the woman pausing to re-tie a bootlace; a hare going full tilt across a sheep enclosure bounded by a stone wall.

We saw nothing all that day, nor the next, spending the night in the tiny lightweight tent we had brought with us in a sheltered gully on the slopes of Pen y Fan. Late on that second afternoon we were resting by a waterfall on the Nant Bwrefwr below the summit of Craig Fan-ddu. We had worked our way along the enormous valley, lying for hours in the bracken, watching. Where possible we had kept to the main ridges of the hills so that the valleys on the other side of the peaks could be examined also.

'No sign of Terry,' I said jokingly.

Patrick said, 'I get the impression he has enough to do already. But I must get in touch with him. We should find a phone.'

'Another night under canvas?'

He lowered the binoculars. 'Hell, I've spent so much time looking through these things my eyeballs feel as though they're on stalks. What did you say?'

'Are we in the tent tonight?'

'I don't know yet. Why do you ask?'

I did not answer, shielding my eyes from the bright light in order to look further down the valley. I had seen movement.

'Where?' Patrick asked.

'See the high peak on the other side of the valley? Take a line directly downhill from that – quite a long way down – and you'll see a shepherd's hut.'

'Got it,' he said, having grabbed the binoculars again.

'To the left of the hut there's what looks like a clump of bracken.'

A pause, then, 'Yes, but it's at least a quarter of a mile from the hut.'

'That can't be it.'

'It's the only patch of vegetation that I can see. It's growing in a hollow with a couple of twisted over oak trees. It would be a quarter of a mile if you were over there and walking it.'

'OK, soldier. I thought I saw movement there.'

After another pause he suddenly whistled. 'Grief, woman, you've got good eyes.' He slithered down a little into the grass. 'There's six of them. All in camouflage gear and with bits of bracken in their hats.'

'Soldiers?'

'No, people playing at soldiers.'

'How can you tell?'

'Their kit's not right for any outfit I know of. And they're not all dressed exactly the same. Sort of make do and mend.'

'Are they watching us?'

'I'm not sure yet. Possibly not.' He leaned against me to keep the glasses steady and took a long slow scan down the

128

valley. 'One of them was pointing down here,' he explained. 'Probably indicating the best route – the ground's pretty boggy in places.'

The group walked in a south-easterly direction, towards the road that skirted the Pontsticill Reservoir. They disappeared from sight eventually into a plantation on the hillside above the road.

'Back towards the area around Bryn Glas,' Patrick murmured. 'Where Larry was shot at the first time and where that boy in the Sea Cadets thought he saw a trip wire. Perhaps I haven't been attaching enough importance to that. After Larry was attacked right in the village and there'd been the business of the people near the caves and viaduct, I'd rather ruled that out as being of any significance.' He stood up. 'Let's call it a day. I vote we go back to the bus and drive right out of the area, find an hotel and sleep in a bed tonight. There's no point in living rough for the sake of it. Then we can start afresh tomorrow and find this farmhouse on the slopes of Bryn Glas.'

After consulting the map we soon found a track that led on to the road that would take us back to where we had parked. Neither of us, I think, had realised quite how far we had come across country and it quickly became apparent that we had a long walk in front of us – at least six miles. The first couple of miles were steeply downhill. After a while I noticed that Patrick was limping.

'You stay here with the packs and I'll go and get the car,' I suggested. 'I can run if I'm not loaded.'

'It's only a bloody blister.'

'I know. But there's no point in being in agony.'

'No, I'll deal with it here and now,' he decided. 'I don't want you going off on your own around here.'

The problem was several broken blisters. I let him deal with them, going away for a short distance. Like any man he was furious with himself, and with what he regarded as weakness, and no amount of reasoning on my part would have helped. I could have argued until I was blue in the face that many people in his position would only ever be able to walk for short distances and that he himself can actually dance and run and negotiate an assault course.

But when he caught up with me he was smiling just a little.

I said, 'The news is that there are three men up on the hill above us. One has a radio and the others are carrying rifles. I think I spotted them when they weren't watching us so they might not know they've been seen.'

'In the same kind of clothing as the others?'

'Yes.'

We fell into step. 'I wonder if someone's sending out reconnaissance parties after Friedrich's death in order to ascertain possible police reaction,' Patrick said.

'Where was the body found?'

'That was something Terry was going to find out for me.'

We broke into a jog, not looking behind us or towards the slopes of the hill to our right. Both of us were more than aware that a small guerrilla war could be fought in these valleys and anyone hearing gun-shots would probably assume it to be a shooting party or farmers after foxes.

When the road levelled out we dropped back to a walk. The packs were quite heavy and there was no point in exhausting ourselves. Then, open countryside gave way to forest, a relief. I no longer felt that rifle sights were trained on us.

'There's absolutely no point in leaving the road,' Patrick said. 'For one thing progress is almost impossible in these plantations because of the brash that's left on the ground, and for another we'd be going out of our way.'

'So they'll have to come on to the road if they want to follow us.'

'Yes. Just pray that they aren't in contact with another group up ahead.'

There was no sign of pursuit and I began to feel a little easier. I had been half hoping that we could thumb a lift to the car-park but the only vehicle we had seen so far was an oil tanker going in the opposite direction. For, of course, all holiday traffic would have come to an end by now and there was little human habitation. We passed one house on this section of road, a ruined cottage.

'Don't walk in a straight line,' Patrick said when we came to a long straight stretch of road.

I glanced behind me. 'I can't see a soul.'

'It's not worth taking chances.'

'I wasn't arguing – just making a comment.'

Neither of us spoke again for a couple of miles, frankly saving our breath. We had descended the side of the valley and now the road started to climb again, up towards the Neuadd Reservoirs. Soon, Forestry Commission trees came to an end and we were once again in open moorland. It started to rain.

'Whoa,' said Patrick softly as we rounded a bend. He drew me into the shelter of the trunk of a single ages-old pine.

The head of the valley opened out before us like a vast bowl. The high peaks were now invisible, hidden in cloud that spilled over the ridges and was drifting down. Ahead of us was the dam between the two reservoirs, on the top of this and to one side the car-park where we had left the Land-Rover.

'There's a car parked one on each side of ours,' Patrick said, looking through the glasses. 'Otherwise the car-park is empty but for that old ambulance that's been converted into a camping vehicle. I don't like that at all.'

'No sign of any people?'

'No.'

'Is there anyone in the cars?'

'It's too far away to tell. But even if there is and they're waiting for us to appear, they must be lying flat on the seats.'

'Suppose I go ahead and we see what happens?'

Patrick thought about it. 'Let's get closer first. I'd prefer those vehicles to be in pistol range.'

There was still no sign of pursuit. But we could really only look for this on the road. To have stopped in order to quarter the hillside above would have taken far too long. It *was* possible that the men had not come down to the road but had stayed on the high ground above the tree-line and were now watching us from a couple of hundred feet up the slopes of Fan Big.

'There's a Roman road up there,' Patrick said, his thoughts obviously running along the same lines as my own. 'I've just remembered. Someone could make quite good time along it.'

'Better than us?'

'No, not necessarily – most of our route's been down-hill.'

At any moment I expected to come under attack. But nothing happened. Curlews called, the rain came down more heavily, a cold, cruel wind sending it icily into our faces. Patrick was limping again, his face with a set expression.

The last half a mile was quite steeply uphill. I knew that Patrick was keeping up the fast face purely on willpower by now, biting his lip, a sheen of sweat on his forehead. As we topped a little rise I came to a decision and slipped off my rucksack.

'I'm going to cut across this meadow, climb over the wall and drive over and pick you up.' I set off before he could order otherwise.

It seemed a good idea because the road skirted this field in quite a large curve. As the crow flew the Land-Rover was only a matter of five hundred yards away, hidden behind a clump of trees and the stone wall that bordered the field. I was still half expecting to be shot at and ran fast, jinking. Any hikers observing me would think that I had taken leave of my senses.

I reached the wall and carefully looked over. The three vehicles were directly in front of me across the other side of the car-park. From what I could see of the vehicles flanking ours they looked perfectly ordinary; fluffy mascots in one rear window, holiday stickers in the other. But I have been taught to be careful. It was only at the last minute, before I climbed the wall, that I remembered to check the camping van, parked on its own at the other end of the car-park.

A curtain that had been pulled to one side was suddenly released. The movement was so quick that I thought for a moment I had imagined it.

I ran. I reached the Discovery, checked the right hand vehicle, saw that it was empty and leapt into ours. Someone shouted. My prayer that it would start first time was answered. I reversed out to see, in the mirror, three men running from the van, one with something in his hand, pointing at me. A gun.

I reversed straight at them and saw them run. I braked a few inches from the van, heard a bang and a crash of glass, came all over bloody-minded and let in the clutch again. The old ambulance crunched most satisfactorily into the gully that I was sure I had noticed earlier, actually going from sight. As I howled away across the car-park I heard another bang and a bullet thudded somewhere into the rear of the vehicle. Yes, you *can* dodge bullets in a four wheel drive, I found myself thinking in a silly sort of way, when there were further shots but no apparent damage. I decided I really must tell the manufacturers how splendid it was. The gate into the meadow sort of opened as I got to it and then I was going hell for leather towards Patrick who was running towards me with both rucksacks. Steady, Ingrid, do not kill your husband by knocking him over.

He threw himself aboard while the vehicle was still moving, drew his gun and prepared to repel boarders.

'You can do anything in these things!' I yelled, on an incredible high.

Patrick did not reply, probably closed his eyes in fact as I headed for a broken down part of the wall at the end of the field. We somehow — and looking back, I really don't know how — bounced over. It was a bit like riding to hounds, I actually felt myself airborne for a second or so. There was a surprisingly good landing on a grass verge and then I was swerving across a country lane and away.

'You realise we shall have to buy this vehicle from John and Lynne now,' Patrick said after half a mile. 'They won't want it back with the front all stoved in.'

'Rubbish!' I said. 'Is that all the thanks I get for rescuing you?'

I had a quick kiss bestowed on my cheek.

'Round one to us,' I said. 'Where to now?'

'Somewhere far enough away for a jam butty and a debriefing. Then a long careful think.' He gave me another kiss. 'That was terrific — couldn't have done it better myself.'

Which was as good as being awarded the George Medal.

'Been quaffing that tonic wine for the over-forties?' he added.

There were quite a few visitors to the Brecon Mountain Railway Centre and we felt reasonably safe. We did have a camping stove and provisions with us and had not intended to stop at a public place for refreshment but the sight of a saddle-tank engine in steam was too much for Patrick and he had to stop and gaze at it.

'Never knew you were into this kind of thing,' I said.

'All men like steam engines,' he replied. 'It's nostalgia.'

While Patrick phoned Terry I organised us something to eat in the restaurant. Seating myself after having put the tray on the table I quickly summed up the other customers. There were two retired couples, a family with young children and a man of about thirty-five on his own. He sat engrossed in a railway book and was over-thin, weedy even. I did not think him a potential danger.

'Wait until you hear this,' Patrick said, falling on fish and chips as though he hadn't eaten for a week. 'Friedrich's body was found in a car in a lay-by near Talybont. That's quite a long way east of here if you remember the map. The really interesting thing was the car. It had been bought at a second-hand car dealers in Brecon *the day before.*'

'Bought by whom?'

'A man who gave Friedrich's name but looked nothing like him. The police showed the car salesman a picture of him and he told them that someone else had bought the car. He paid cash, by the way. Now even if Friedrich had asked a friend to make the purchase for him, you're not going to tell me he'd buy a car one day and shoot himself the next.'

'He *was* mentally unstable,' I pointed out.

'Unstable insofar as other people were concerned but pretty careful with his own life up until now.'

'Has there been a post-mortem yet?'

'This morning. He died from a single shot to the head. It was obvious that he'd dropped the gun — it was a Mauser — but there's no knowing whether someone shot him and then

134

tossed the gun in the car. There was one set of clear fingerprints on it, his. Which is a bit odd in a way. You'd think in
the normal state of affairs that his prints would be *smeared*
over it. It looks to me as though the weapon was wiped
and then placed in his hand after he'd been shot and then
dropped on the floor.'

'Anything else?'

'Yes, and I think it's the best yet. His prints weren't on
the steering wheel. Whoever killed him forgot that.'

'So one assumes the police are treating it as murder.'

Patrick nodded, his mouth full. 'And because of who he
was, Special Branch have been called in. Plus a few from the
Anti-Terrorist Branch for good measure. Yes, and wait for
it, John Brinkley is being kept informed. Terry, naturally,
has told Daws.'

'Have they shown the body to Jimmy?'

'Yes, I'd forgotten about that. He identified him as the
man who went to the pub.'

'Can we go home now?'

He grinned with the sort of mad light in his eyes that
always makes my heart beat faster. 'When I've had a look
at this farmhouse on Bryn Glas.'

'Did it occur to you today that those men might know
who we are now and were out to apprehend us?'

'You mean, do they know we're not just a school teacher's
brother and sister-in-law doing a spot of private sleuthing?'

'Yes.'

'That would mean we're talking about a very organised
outfit indeed.'

'Not so long ago you were relating incidents of schools
for terrorists.'

'Don't you want those chips?' he asked, fork already
poised like a harpoon.

I passed them over. 'Patrick, if the police knew exactly
who we are ...'

'The fuzz clapped eyes on us.'

'How do you know who's been watching us? We know for
a fact that people were watching by the viaduct. And any one
of those men who said they were shepherds could have been
spying. You're no longer under cover. The whole country

has seen your picture in the paper.' Admittedly it had been a very bad picture, a photograph taken years ago of Patrick in uniform at the Trooping of the Colour, slightly out of focus, his hair regulation short back and sides, the face beneath the hat extremely youthful and tight with responsibility.

'Why are you looking at me like that?' he said.

'You haven't really changed.' I told him. 'Your hair might be a little grey now and longer than you used to wear it but you're still built like a racing-snake and on this job have displayed much the same demeanour as a hungry reptile.'

'Ingrid, what are you getting at?'

I leaned towards him and spoke more quietly. 'Only that it wouldn't matter if no one had ever seen your photo. Everyone, anyone — the Sea Cadets, Jennings, John and Lynne, Jimmy, the whole word — sees you as a man who means business. For once — and I think this affair has been too close, too personal — you've not played at being Joe Bloke. The professional anonymity hasn't been there. You haven't been a nameless parent on a weekend jaunt. But it's not your fault, this time you couldn't help it.'

'But if you're right it's the same problem as always,' he said after a short silence. 'I become too emotionally involved. That's why Pugh was shot. The fatal flaw of character. What's the cure? Acupuncture? Hypnosis?'

'I'm merely putting a case for leaving well alone now. Initially you said you had no intention of following it up once a problem had been highlighted. Why risk your life?' I was really worried now, he looked at his most stubborn. And the last thing I wanted to do was have a serious argument.

'I've no intention of risking my life. Perhaps that answers both your points.'

'What is Terry going to do?'

'Nothing unless Daws orders him to. His work load won't allow him just to up and come to Wales.'

'I still think you ought to allow the police to sort this out.'

'Ingrid, it isn't a police matter,' he replied angrily. 'Not now.'

From bitter experience of rows we had had in the past, mostly during the first stormy ten years, I knew that by

136

arguing with him further I would only make matters worse. He would become bloody-minded and irrational. But at least I could understand the reasoning behind his stubborness. I was sure that there was no desire on his part to prove anything; that he had been unfairly dismissed, that Terry did not have sufficient experience to deal with such cases. Both of these things were manifestly true. It was also correct to say that Patrick was the only person with the innate ability to deal with the case.

And the whole business, of course, still remained a huge question-mark.

Chapter Ten

Bryn Glas is a hill at the southernmost boundary of the
Brecon Beacons National Park. The lower slopes are partly
arable farmland and pasture, partly woodland. The top of
the hill, on this cold, misty morning, was hidden — by the
mist itself or low cloud, it was impossible to tell.

'It'll lift,' Patrick muttered. 'It always does when you don't
want it to.' He turned to gaze at me. 'Well? Are you coming
or not?'

'I never said I wasn't coming with you,' I replied.

He looked at me for a moment longer and then got out
of the Land-Rover. We locked it and set off up the hill. We
were travelling light this time. There was no intention on our
part to spend the night in the open.

'The survival school was in Yellow Pages,' Patrick said
over his shoulder.

'You're joking!'

He paused so that I could catch up with him. 'So I rang
the number. A woman said that it was closed for the winter.
She didn't ask if I'd like to leave my name and address for
next year's programme.'

'I hope you disguised your voice.'

'Of course. Pure Brum.'

'What address was given?'

'It was all very vague. The actual name is the Cader
Benllyn Adventure Centre. That's deliberately confusing
because Cader Benllyn is a mountain in Snowdonia — a
hell of a way from here. But it was a Merthyr phone number
and I'd bet a penny to a pound that it's somewhere between

138

here and that town, and probably within sight of this hill. Otherwise how would they have known Larry's party was here?'

I had a feeling that we would soon find out. 'How's the leg?' I asked.

'It'll do for a few miles.'

We had left the Land-Rover in a lane halfway up the hill and were soon walking in thick, swirling mist. But before very long a breeze sprang up and the sky became lighter. Then we saw the sun, a pale orb shining through the thinning mist. Then there were glimpses of blue and the mist became rags and tatters of cloud. A little while later only the merest wisps remained in deep, cold hollows.

'Said it would lift,' Patrick said. He stopped to look back across the valley behind us. Directly to the south was Morlais Hill, the stumpy ruins of a castle on the summit.

'That's been a good strategic position since time began,' Patrick said, looking through the binoculars. 'If I was running something clandestine from a house on that hill, the castle's the *first* place I'd set up an observation post.'

'Don't you think this theory that it's a terrorist school just the smallest bit melodramatic?'

'Well, there are several in Eastern Europe, three in Libya alone, four in Central America.'

'We call ours *counter*-terrorism units.'

'Now, now,' he chided. 'You know perfectly well that's all they are.'

'I'm kidding,' I said. 'Could this outfit be one of them?'

'Hardly. Or you and I would know about it. So would Brinkley. No,' he added upon reflection, 'they were too tatty to be official.'

'So what do you make of the castle?'

'There's only about thirty feet of one tower left. But there's rather a vague area to the lee of it that could be something covered with camouflage netting. We'll risk it and continue. I think the thing is to remain alert and watch for anyone coming up the hill towards us.'

After a quarter of an hour or so we reached the ruined farm-house and steading. It stood some fifty yards from the road and was well fenced off, a large notice-board proclaiming:

KEEP OUT, DANGEROUS BUILDING, FALLING MASONRY. Despite the warning the house had been heavily vandalised, graffiti scrawled on the outside walls, no glass in any of the windows.

'Just mind where you're putting your feet,' Patrick said, ducking under the barbed wire fence.

The strong breeze blew through the building, a door in an upstairs room banging. I went into the rear of the house, actually walking on the back door as it lay in a bed of nettles. I had surprised a couple of sheep, which ran off.

Inside, the banging was very loud. It was uncannily even of rhythm, a kind of invisible Devil's Tattoo. It made my skin crawl and I did not want to go any further. I started violently as Patrick appeared, not having heard him enter through the front. He had drawn his gun and now went up the stairs, keeping close to the wall.

'Mind they're not rotten,' I whispered.

'Something's stored up here,' he said, his voice oddly muffled. 'Fodder by the look of it.' He went from view.

I looked through the living-room door. There were water marks on the walls, suggesting that the place flooded in winter; the remains of wallpaper hanging in filthy shreds. Large black cobwebs moved like crazy curtains in the draught, the whole room looked as though it was moving with them as if the house were alive and breathing, watching us.

'Come up here,' Patrick called softly.

'Must I?' I had been about to bolt through the front door.

'Major's orders.'

I went up to find him beckoning to me from the doorway of what must originally have been the master bedroom. Through it I could see several rotten-looking bales of straw stacked at one side of the room, the rest of the floor liberally spread with what looked like a mixture of loose straw and hay. Patrick had brushed some of it to one side.

'There are marks on the floor. Stuff in boxes has been stored up here at some time.'

'They'd have had to be wooden boxes in this damp.'

Judging by the outlines in the dirt on the floor the crates had measured about three feet long and twelve inches wide.

'Guns?' I asked.

'It would have been a bit risky. But if this place was part of a training course it's possible that dummy weapons or even real ones were placed in the crates sometimes.' He held out a short coil of silver-coloured wire. 'Oh, and I found this. It was stretched across the top of the stairs.'

The door was still banging but I no longer paid any heed to it. 'What was it attached to?'

'I haven't looked yet. I just cut it.'

'If it's a booby trap, there might be others.'

'Sure to be.' He patted my arm. 'Courage, wife. Remember your Charge of the Light Brigade yesterday.'

I have never been very good in confined cobwebby places full of nasty surprises.

The wire had been connected to a device bolted to the wall in the bedroom opposite to the one that had been used as a store. At one time the weapon had been a sawn-off shotgun but had been modified further. Patrick unloaded it, allowing the deadly mixture of nails, pieces of broken glass and small pebbles to trickle through his fingers on to the floor.

Across the bathroom doorway was another wire.

'Stay here,' Patrick ordered. He crawled on hands and knees and inspected it carefully. Then he tied one end of the wire from the first booby trap to it and reversed, paying it out as he came. We retreated right back to the top of the stairs and then he yanked on the wire. Nothing happened for a second or two and then a trap door in the ceiling — presumably leading to the loft — swung down and a large piece of concrete crashed on to the landing.

'It's a training area,' said Patrick decidedly. 'These things aren't necessarily intended to kill trespassers. People are instructed on how to set them up. I wonder if they intended to leave them primed?'

'Do you think the devices are connected in some way to a command point and they'll know they've been triggered?'

'It would be a pretty inefficient outfit if they didn't.'

'Someone'll come then?'

'Exciting, isn't it?' he said in a bored sort of voice. 'Let's keep watch in case they do.'

'Surely this is enough evidence to call in the police,'

I said as we crouched by a window in the main bedroom.

'I'm hoping to grab a few of them,' Patrick said, checking
over his revolver.

'What, arrest them?'

'Why not?'

Downstairs, something fell over with a clatter.

'Freeze,' Patrick hissed. 'Looks as though they came down
the mountain instead.'

There was a heart-stopping explosion. The entire building
trembled.

Silence.

Patrick shook the plaster from his hair and then moved,
making no sound, to the head of the stairs.

'Please be careful,' I whispered.

He went from sight and all I could hear was my heart
thudding. Then his head reappeared round the bannisters.

'It was a sheep. Got blown to hell when it trod on a
mine.'

'A mine!'

'Amongst all the rubbish on the kitchen floor. I should
come down if I were you. Watch where you walk.'

Just for a moment I contemplated jumping from an
upstairs window. But the drop was a little too far for one
to be sure of not getting a badly twisted ankle.

'Put your feet where you can see the floor,' Patrick said
from the back door. 'No, not on that piece of cardboard.'

'I can't reach to the next bit of floor,' I said, stupid with
nerves.

'Then bend down and carefully pick it up so you can see
what's beneath it,' was the patient advice. 'That's it. All
right? Come on then.'

I didn't look in the kitchen. But even out of the corner
of my eye I could see blood-soaked wool and sheep's insides
smeared on the walls and ceiling. The rest of the animal had
been blown into a corner out of sight.

'I almost went into the kitchen when I first came in,' I
said when I was out in the sunshine.

Patrick was gazing at the muddy ground surrounding the
house with professional interest. 'I don't *think* they'd be

142

stupid enough to mine the outside,' he muttered. 'Which way did you come in?'

'Over there where the fence is broken and round by the byre. There. You can see my footprints in the mud.'

'Then we'll use them going back.'

Which we did, planting our feet exactly in the footprints. Crawling through the fence, I sighed with relief.

'Tactics,' Patrick said to himself, gazing through the binoculars. 'If I had Terry or Steve with me I wouldn't hesitate to stay and see who turns up. Or even if I had a small squad of ordinary blokes. The problem is not knowing how many will actually come.'

This question was answered almost immediately. While the decision was being made we concealed ourselves behind a stack of felled spruce trunks in a clearing at the side of the road, Patrick peering through a pile of bracken fronds he had placed on the top of it.

'Here they are,' he murmured. He counted eleven and then slid from his perch. 'We get out of here − through the trees and along the line of the hill. Then we can go downhill and make our way to the Land-Rover. If they've left a guard on it we can probably cope with that.'

Progress was very slow and difficult. Years of thinnings lay thickly strewn on the ground. It was also dark. I felt that we were blundering along getting nowhere and making as much noise as a small herd of elephants. It was the worst possible kind of terrain as far as Patrick was concerned and he was soon limping badly.

'Turn right and go downhill now,' he said after a while.

It was very steep and we were soon having to slither for short distances. The going was unbelievably rough where heavy rain had eronded the ground into deep gullies, there being no vegetation beneath the trees to prevent this happening. Almost immediately Patrick tripped, rolled about twenty feet and crashed into a tree.

When I reached him he was semi-conscious, rubbing his head. The first thing I did was to take the Smith and Wesson from his shoulder harness and put it in the pocket of my anorak. The fittest and strongest always carry any weapons.

'I'm not dead,' he said weakly.

I carefully felt his head and could discover no sign of serious injury. I said, 'If I cover us with some of these dead branches and we lie still they won't find us.'

'I didn't mention the dogs,' Patrick said, struggling to rise but forced to sink down again. 'God, I wish everything would stop going round and round.'

'We should have brought a radio.'

'You're absolutely right. That was a bad mistake.'

I made no further recriminations. What was the point?

'I'm a real drawback when things get like this,' Patrick said, succeeding in standing, still very pale. 'In the days before I had a tin leg I could have skipped over the mountain tops and laughed in their faces.'

'But you weren't so good at the thinking bits then.'

'Is that right?'

'Umm.'

We carried on downhill, me with a big handful of the back of Patrick's coat. Very soon we came to a wide path that had been made for the tracked Forestry Commission vehicles. Beggars could not be choosers and we followed it down even though I was fairly sure it would not bring us to where we wanted to go. Dogs were barking somewhere above us on the hill.

It was obvious that Patrick was still feeling very groggy but other than steadying him there was little I could do. Then, when I really thought we were going to make it, three men stepped out of the trees fifty yards ahead of us. They were armed with rifles.

'Comply with everything they say,' Patrick muttered. 'We can have a go at overpowering them when I'm feeling a bit better.'

'Just stop right there,' one of the men called. He seemed to be in charge. Stepping forward he indicated with an impatient jerk of the rifle that we should raise our arms. Patrick was relieved of his knife, I of the gun and the keys to the Land-Rover. They shoved us front of them and we carried on walking downhill.

'No protest?' queried the same man from behind us. 'No "this is a free country and we're just ordinary people out for a walk"?'

144

'I know when I'm wasting my breath,' I said, convinced that Patrick would not respond to such a stupid remark but at the same time wondering if it might be a good idea to attempt to humour our captor by saying something.

After we had covered another few hundred yards he prodded Patrick in the back with the rifle. 'You're not saying much.'

'He fell and hit his head,' I said furiously. 'Leave him alone.'

'I don't talk to erks,' Patrick grated. For this he received a violent shove that sent him sprawling. He stayed down.

'You fool!' I yelled at the man. 'I told you the truth. He fell on the hill and hit his head on a tree. He was knocked right out.'

He threw the keys of the Land-Rover to one of the others. 'Run. Get their bus and bring it up here. We'll be all day otherwise.' He turned to me. 'Go and sit on that tree trunk. And don't try anything stupid.'

'You sound like a B movie,' I told him.

Patrick was moving by this time. The two men grabbed him and dragged him over to where I was. He sat up, his head in his hands.

It became very quiet. A few birds twittered, occasionally there was a rustling sound in the dry, dead branches beneath the trees.

Patrick still had his head in his hands. He leaned towards me and said in an undertone – the two men having walked away a short distance – 'When he comes close I'll go for him. You are *not* to make a grab for the other bloke. Throw yourself over backwards and lie still until it's sorted one way or another.'

The *modus operandi* startled even me. He suddenly uttered two terrible cries, holding his head and then slumped sideways across my lap.

'Patrick!' I screamed. 'Patrick! For God's sake ... Do something!' I shouted at the men. 'This is all your fault.'

The man in charge thrust his rifle into the hands of the other and ran over. He shoved me out of the way and seized Patrick by the front of his coat with the idea, I think, of lying him on the ground. In a blur of movement one of

145

Patrick's hands grabbed an arm while the other administered a stunning blow to the side of the man's head. Both toppled into the long grass.

I did not do as I had been told for the simple reason that everything immediately went wrong. I'm guessing when I say that there was a large stone in the grass upon which Patrick hit his head again – he could not remember what had happened afterwards – but he let go of the man who leapt up and kicked out at him. By this time the other man was running towards us. He was greatly surprised when I tackled him around the knees and went over backwards, the weapons being flung some distance in the process. I was struggling with him when his colleague hefted me up and flung me down by Patrick. He appeared to be semi-conscious, eyes closed.

The Land-Rover appeared shortly afterwards and we were bundled into it. The vehicle was turned round and we set off, bouncing down the hill at great speed. I hung on to Patrick to try to prevent him being flung right off the bench seat he had been laid down on.

At last we came to a main road. After a short distance we turned left and started to ascend a steep track. This went on for quite a way, twisting and turning, and finally ended in a large flat area spread with course granite aggregate like railway ballast. We were hauled out, Patrick left where he had slumped down.

The building before us resembled a large farmhouse; stone walls, a slate roof, extensive well-maintained outbuildings, everything very neat and tidy. There were three stone steps up to the front door, a detail that I only noticed just then because the man who had just left the house ran down them lightly, a large Belgian cattle dog at his heels. He came over and stood looking at us.

His name was Lyndberne. He was wanted in several European countries for murder, bombings and other acts of terrorism.

146

Chapter Eleven

There could be no mistake about this. While working for
D12 Patrick and I had been required to recognise those
criminals known to promote terrorism and had been shown
many photographs of these people, mostly men, in a variety
of disguises. Lyndberne was not utilising a disguise at this
moment; the only real difference to a picture I had seen of
him, taken the previous year, was that his sandy-coloured
hair was quite long, almost down to his shoulders. The pale,
very pale, blue eyes were regarding us in a fashion that told
me that prevarication on our part was out of the question.
He knew exactly who we were.

'Are you the one calling yourself Griffiths?' I asked, wondering who the police had actually spoken to and aware that
there might have been another murder.

'No,' Lyndberne replied, dragging what I can only call
an avid gaze away from Patrick. 'Griffiths lives abroad. I
lease this place from him.' He shrugged disinterestedly. 'It
sometimes suits me if people think that's who I am. What
does it matter?' He swung round to his henchmen. 'Get him
up. Are you just going to leave him down there?'

Patrick was hauled to his feet and discovered to be capable
of standing unaided. There was no shock of recognition when
he beheld Lyndberne, just a slight narrowing of the eyes.
Lyndberne's reaction to this was bizarre in the extreme. He
clapped his hands like an overjoyed child and crowed with
laughter.

'Just like a true professional, eh, Major? Christ, you're
going to show this lot a thing or two.'

And with that we were frog-marched into the house.

In a large living room to the left of the front door were assembled over a dozen men and one woman. They were, I was subsequently informed, the resident staff. When we were inside Patrick shed those holding him, one man yelping with pain, clutching his wrist. Both then had their ears resoundingly boxed, retribution only ceasing when Lyndberne jammed the barrel of a gun into Patrick's chest.

'You were careless,' Lyndberne told the injured parties. 'Serves you right.' He addressed the room at large. 'Gentlemen, allow me to introduce Major Patrick Gillard and his wife Ingrid. They are both late of MI5. Take a good look at him in particular and reflect that even if you train ceaselessly for five years, none of you will attain his standard. Despite the fact that he lost the lower part of his right leg following injuries sustained during the Falklands Conflict he is a formidable foe indeed ... or, should I say, was.'

'My wife is pregnant,' Patrick said.

'No matter,' said the other. 'No matter at all. She will come to no harm. Nor will little Justin at home with his nanny in Devon. Ingrid will lecture my students here, when the new intake arrives in a week's time. She knows as much as you do about the workings of the British security services.'

'Go to hell,' I said.

'But you will,' Lyndberne said to me. 'Otherwise all will not go well for him.' He laughed again in the oddly childlike fashion, chilling in this man. 'Even you, Major, must see the funny side of this. All those assignments, those dangerous missions, the perils of serving your country. And now you have been brought to heel by a stupid little adventure on behalf of your *brother*.'

'Larry's always got me into trouble,' Patrick said lightly. 'As they say, blood's thicker than water. If I'd been a cuckoo I'd have heaved him from the nest.'

I kept my gaze firmly on Lyndberne, hoping that my face gave no reaction to hearing this D12 codeword. "Cuckoo" is a recognition signal with several nuances of meaning. In this case it meant I was to co-operate. At this moment I could see no sense in the order and had a suspicion that

148

Patrick was hoping that by co-operating I would save my own life. But what of his? Lyndberne's next words made me lose all hope.

'You yourselves had hit-lists. You are both on mine and have been for years. But I'm not the sort of man who enjoys killing women. How you die and when, Major, depends on your wife. As far as I'm concerned you're a trophy. I know people in the Middle East who would nail you to their living room wall and ensure that it took a week for you to die. I might do that myself – just for a little while. But perhaps the priest's son would enjoy that? I understand that at one time you were thinking of taking the cloth.' He smiled. Then he gave orders and we were taken away separately.

It was the last I saw of Patrick for a week.

No, that is not quite correct. The same night they brought him to me in the plain cold room in which I had been locked and placed him on the floor for about ten minutes before removing him again. He did not know me and was having convulsions. Electric shock torture. I was told that they would not do *that* to him again if I did as I was told.

After he had been taken away I sat still for a long time just staring at the wall. There was no question of anyone finding us. The reason for this was simple. We were underground. Behind the farmhouse were the workings of an old mine. Directly in front of the entrance a long wooden shed had been erected and used to store equipment used by the survival school, which was a genuine enterprise, taking groups of people every other month throughout the year. During the months in between another type of person altogether was catered for and admitted to the underground complex. These did not enter the country by normal routes but were brought from Cork in Southern Ireland to Tenby in a private launch and then by road, having made their own way to Ireland from all over the world. Some travelled no further than from Northern Ireland.

Lyndberne had given me this information himself when he had released me from the small upstairs bedroom of the house where I had initially been taken. He himself had escorted me to the underground complex; into the wooden shed – the centre filled with tables and chairs used for lectures, the walls

149

lined with cupboards and racks holding climbing equipment, chained-up sporting rifles, waterproof clothing, tents and so forth – and then through the false back of a cupboard and into a well lit tunnel. I heard everything he said and noted everything I saw in great detail. I always can, there is a part of my brain that seems to be able to function entirely without my control, uneffected by emotions or even severe shock.

'More info tomorrow,' Lyndberne had promised, shoving me through a door and locking me in the room I found myself in.

I suppose "cell" would be a better description. Insofar as it had no windows and that I was a prisoner, it *was* a cell. But it was quite large – about twelve feet by ten – and there was a toilet and washbasin behind a curtained-off recess. A single bunk bed took up the rest of that wall and there was a chair and chest of drawers along another. Other than these items the room was bare if one discounted a closed-circuit television camera in a corner above the recess and a framed photograph of Colonel Gadaffi on the wall by the door. This latter concealed, clumsily, it must be said, a microphone.

I absorbed all this information, but as I said, without intention or interest and, after Patrick had been taken away, just sat on the bed staring dully at the wall. I soon discovered that my mind would not tolerate this inactivity.

During training for D12 our relationship had been ignored, by Patrick and me and the instructors. This was important for several reasons. Just because he is my husband it does not mean he stops what he is doing to help me kill and gut a rabbit that is the only food in four days. He does not drop his surveillance of barren countryside because his spouse has forgotten how to use the radio. I do not bind up the small cut on his finger with my handkerchief if I am conducting a surveillance on my own. And if we are captured and interrogated he endeavours to be no more influenced than the next man when all my clothes are stripped off and I am thrown in a river. Any tears and laughter are saved for afterwards.

This was what the training was all *for*, said a small inner voice. The ultimate irony was that we no longer worked for D12. I found myself thinking that this did not matter, surely it was up to anyone of sound mind and limb to try to put a stop to people like Lyndberne.

Over the next few days I was given everything I needed. Meals were brought to me, plain but palatable, soap, a towel, even newspapers. The men who entered my cell refused to speak at all and, despite what he had said, Lyndberne stayed away. The light in the room stayed on all the time. It was impossible to sleep but I managed to cat-nap, fully dressed. I had no intention of removing all my clothes to sleep and washed and dressed again behind the curtain, this part of the room in any case outside the range of the camera.

On the fourth day – and I was praying that my watch would not stop as it also showed the date – two men came in at six-thirty in the morning, one with the usual breakfast of a mug of tea and two thick slices of bread and jam, the other with our luggage out of the Discovery.

'Where did you hire the Land-Rover from?' asked this individual.

'From the garage in Lydtor, Devon,' I replied.

He pulled a pen and a grubby piece of paper from his pocket and wrote it down. 'I'm asking because we know it's not yours and it's got none of the usual hire paperwork.'

'The owner of the garage lent it to us,' I said. 'He's a friend of ours.'

'So it's not a hire vehicle at all then.'

'You're very clever,' I remarked.

He handed me the pen and another piece of paper. 'Write a note to say you're sorry someone else has had to return it. We don't want people getting to think you've disappeared – not just yet, anyway.'

'I will if you tell me what's happening to Patrick.'

'He's alive,' was the sullen response.

'You'll have to do better than that.'

'Write, or he won't be. And don't try and put in any hidden messages.'

I penned a note that could not be faulted.

'And I want some money. For petrol.'

From the purse in my knapsack I gave him twenty pounds.

Round One to the Gillards, I thought when the door had slammed behind them. Precautions are often not needed but this little arrangement between Patrick, John Murray and Bill, the proprietor of the village garage, had paid off. Bill would smile and thank whoever returned John's property and, after letting John know what had happened, would phone a certain London number and leave a message. This, we had felt, would be much safer for John and Lynne. They had, after all, been with us on the first expedition and might be recognised.

The knapsacks had been searched, presumably for weapons, but as far as I could see nothing had been taken. There was no satisfaction in the repossessing of toiletries under such circumstances. I found myself stroking Patrick's scarlet lambswool sweater and a tear trickled down my cheek.

No. This was psychological pressure. This was why the knapsacks had been given to me. Also to make me feel guilty. I put the sweater away. I knew better and I had received my orders. With that very firmly in mind I ate my breakfast and went back to work, the self-appointed task I had started on the first morning. I had started to write it all down.

Right at the beginning I had realised that the episode would make a good novel. So Ingrid Langley's next book would be a true account of the last adventure, names and places changed just a little. It might even be the author's final work but I hoped to leave enough notes for an intelligent editor or another writer to put together. Even the expression "ghost writer" had a certain irony to it.

I had also made notes − on the thick A4 pad I had found in one of the drawers − of the headings of lectures I would deliver to Lyndberne's students if I was so asked. I intended to give them no classified material. And this writer − I had discovered quite early in my career − can be a regrettably glib liar.

I had just started work when Lyndberne came in.

'I'm glad you're busy,' he said. He looked excited and a little flushed and I resolved to be very careful indeed with him.

I said, 'I have the right temperament for solitary confinement.'

'So has he.'

'I want to see him.'

'Not yet.'

'You must give me some kind of proof that he's alive,' I persisted. 'How do I know you're keeping your side of the bargain otherwise?'

'There's no bargain,' said he, surprised.

'But you said he'd show them a thing or two.'

'He doesn't have to be alive for that. We're putting everything that's going on now on video.'

'*What's* going on?' I shouted in his face, throwing caution to the winds. 'What the hell are you doing to him?'

He turned to leave, a hand on the door handle but before he could open the door I said, 'Did you kill Anton Friedrich?'

'Yes. I shot him myself.' This was uttered proudly.

'Because he killed the children?'

'Because he'd become utterly mad. Crazy. He was drawing attention to us.'

'You were employing him as an instructor?'

'No, he had come to see what was on offer. But he was always a risk. He had moments when he thought he was in charge. Killing was fun to him. That's a very dangerous attitude.'

'You're just the same – killing my husband slowly for fun.'

'That is not the case,' he said stiffly.

'All right – torturing him to death, hoping to get information. It amounts to the same.'

'What is torture?' Lyndberne said with an expansive lift of the arms. 'Is it being beaten? To be told that every man on the premises will rape his wife? To have the artificial limb taken away so that he is forced to crawl on the floor? To go naked? To be hungry and thirsty? None of these things? It is a difficult thing to define.'

'Look, I haven't refused to lecture your students,' I said in desperation.

'You told me to go to hell.'

I took a deep breath. 'One sometimes says things in the heat of the moment and without thinking.'

He merely gave me a cold smile and went away.

I went into the toilet recess and cried helplessly, both hands resting on the rim of the basin, tears dripping off my nose. Then I sluiced my face with cold water and sat on the bed for a while. The ghastly images that his words had placed in my mind refused to fade. I was aware that this too was psychological pressure and for all I knew Patrick was being kept in similar conditions to myself, being told the same things about me. I knew that this would be more damaging to his mental stability than it was to mine for when Patrick really loses his temper or comes under extreme provocation he is capable of the unspeakable. Not so his wife, I thought, lifting my head and staring directly into the lens of the television camera. She can be ground down very hard and only tends to become a little weepy.

At two that same afternoon, when a headache had forced me to stop work, the door was unlocked again and the man who normally brought my meals came in.

'You're wanted,' he said. 'No, leave the papers. You won't need those.'

I felt faint with fear that I might be forced to watch Patrick being maltreated. I felt sure he was being kept deep within the mine workings, of which I had seen nothing. My cell was just inside the entrance.

We went outside and into the house, the short walk in the fresh air and sunshine quite wonderful. I wondered how Terry would react when he received Bill's message. All he could do was contact the police and ask for the whereabouts of the survival school. I had a feeling I would be dead before anyone succeeded in smashing their way in to the underground part.

Lyndberne was comfortably seated in the other room at the front of the house, his office. It was like any normal office with filing cabinests, a desk-top computer, shelves with files, a coffee jug on a hotplate. He looked up from reading and told me to sit. Then he said, 'This interview's being recorded for the benefit of the students.'

There was silence for perhaps two minutes and then he tossed the file he had been perusing into a drawer of his desk. 'I thought you'd like a look round,' he said. 'I haven't had time to show you since you arrived.'

It occurred to me that he had either forgotten that he

had already seen me that day or was choosing to ignore the encounter for some reason. This was either to make me feel disoriented or, if the former, worried.

'I thought you were going to kill me,' I said.

'Did I say that?'

'It would be helpful if you put your cards on the table,' I told him.

He frowned. 'It might not have to be like that. You seem a fairly intelligent woman.'

'You have to display a modicum of commonsense to be recruited by MI5.'

'Why were you recruited?'

'As a working partner for Patrick. The job entails quite a lot of socialising and a man on his own stands out.'

'But you've been given quite a lot of intensive training since that has nothing to do with being polite at embassy dinners and so forth. I happen to know that you're a reasonable shot, can map-read to a high standard and of course have recently demonstrated that you can climb and abseil. There's also the matter of the medical training as given to all British special forces.'

I shrugged. 'The rest followed. I don't think anyone realised at the beginning that Patrick was going to regain so much mobility.'

'Ah, yes, the leg,' Lyndberne murmured. 'Does this man mean a lot to you?'

I savagely ground down all emotions. 'If by that you mean, will I do as I'm told in order to save him further suffering, yes. But there are limits to what I'm prepared to do and say. Patrick will understand that.'

'Code words, computer pass-words and that kind of thing? The names of foreign agents?'

'Yes.'

'He's already given me quite a few of those.'

'I don't believe you.' My voice as I said this sounded normal to me but I felt as though I'd been physically struck, such was the shock.

Lyndberne went on to name a couple of M16 operatives who had been directly in touch with D12, liaising with our people on missions abroad. In consular positions, one in a

155

country that could be described as friendly, the other not, the releasing of their names to someone like Lyndberne was very damaging. But I had no way of knowing whether Patrick had been the source of the information.

'Don't worry too much,' he said. 'I have no intention of allowing the trophy to become too tarnished.'

I was beginning to see how this man's mind worked. 'The trophy is to be shown to whom?' I enquired.

'Ah!' he ejaculated. 'You *are* an intelligent woman. In three days' time there's a new intake. Twelve of them. They come from far and wide. Not novices at this game either. There's nothing like giving a good impression, is there? Some proof that the person running the establishment they have chosen to attend is a force to be reckoned with.'

'You sound like a second-rate thriller,' I said disgustedly.

'The writer speaking,' he said with a laugh. 'Yes, I had forgotten for a moment about that side of you.'

'So you intend to parade my husband on a collar and lead.'

'Nothing so crude.' He shot to his feet. 'Now, you're interested in a tour?'

'Please let me see Patrick first.'

He thought about it with every sign of seriousness. 'No,' he decided at last. 'It would serve no purpose.'

For a moment, just a short moment, I mulled over the possibility of killing him with my bare hands. No. I knew how but was simply not strong enough.

'This is Rhona,' said Lyndberne, showing me into a smaller office. 'She answers the phone and does all the paperwork. She also cooks just for the two of us.'

And undertakes night-time duties, I thought, gazing at the sulky-looking black-haired girl. She did not greet me. We just glowered at one another. Lyndberne laughed again and we passed on.

The farmhouse was fitted out to accommodate all those catered for in connection with the advertised business of the survival school up to a maximum of ten. When necessary, extra staff were taken on for cooking and cleaning duties. At no time did the two enterprises mix and those working in the mine complex were never seen by survival school students. Lyndberne told me all this as we crossed from the house towards the shed and the mine entrance.

'It was only completed last year,' he continued. Then he suddenly stopped dead. 'I forgot to ask. I'm puzzled by the cannon.'

'It was a present to Patrick,' I said. 'He regards it as a sort of mascot.'

'I think I'll put it in the outer office. It would look rather good by the desk.' Another few paces he stopped again. 'I assume you don't know much about subversion?'

'It wasn't on the curriculum,' I told him.

'Never mind. You'll just have to lecture them about the subjects you're familiar with. It's a shame in a way, though — this course is concentrating on subversion.'

Ideal knowledge for the overthrowing of the governments of tiny tropical islands, I thought, and the seizure of power thereon together with land and natural assets, businesses and any existing criminal organisations. Opposing factions in politically unstable countries in South America were always in the market-place, offering rich rewards for those with skills in murder, espionage, sabotage and all other mastery of mayhem.

Covertly, I watched him as he walked with quick, short steps towards the long shed. Those strange, jerky, childlike mannerisms. I wondered about Rhona and whether she was part of a deception. Was he homosexual? Over the next few days and when I had learned more about him I discovered this not to be so. He delighted in presenting himself in many forms. Life was a constant rehearsal. It amused him to appear the somewhat fussy entrepreneur. Sometimes, that is. On other occasions, and always to his resident staff, he was humourless, sarcastic and quite ruthless.

There was an immediate transformation when we entered the building. Spread open on a large table were two maps, one of the London Underground, the second of inner London with several areas marked in red. Lyndberne seized them with a roar of rage and started to shout names. I couldn't hear what they were, he was so incoherent with fury. I followed him when he ran into the underground area but when we reached my cell he turned with a snarl

157

and indicated that I was to come no farther. He locked me up.

I did not see anyone again that day — not even the man who brought my meals. So I went hungry, drinking water from the tap and nibbling several small pieces of Kendal Mint Cake I found in Patrick's rucksack. I was finding it increasingly impossible to think clearly and positively. The cell was like a tomb. I could hear nothing, not even people passing outside in the tunnel as the floor had been covered with some kind of sound-deadening matting. Finally I lay down on the bed beneath the thin quilt and tried to sleep. I did sleep, fitfully, but kept having a dream of wandering endlessly in the tunnels, hearing a man screaming and not being able to find where he was.

Quite early the next day, about six forty-five, Lyndberne came into my room. Quickly, and all at once, as if hoping to startle me.

'Are you ready?' he asked as if no time had elapsed since he last spoke to me.

I stood up. He made no move to lead the way but stayed where he was, looking at me.

'The new entrants are due to arrive tomorrow,' he said at last. 'Are you ready to tell them all you know?'

I indicated the notes I had made.

'Some of them might need help with their written English.'

'No doubt,' I responded heavily.

Still he stood there. 'What kind of a man is Gillard?'

At least he was still talking about Patrick in the present tense. I said, 'Surely you know by now.'

This angered him for some reason and he took a couple of quick steps in my direction. 'When I ask questions, I expect answers.'

'I could write a book on the kind of man Patrick is.'

'In a nutshell though.'

'He's complex,' I snapped. 'He can't be put in a nutshell. He's a man of contradictions. Patient yet impatient, bad-tempered and mild, loving and cold, violent and gentle.'

'What was the real reason why he was thrown out of MI5?'

'For the reason that found its way into all the papers. Because he killed a crook. Or rather, failed to prevent one of his men from killing him.'

'Who was it?'

'Harry Pugh.'

'Pugh?' For a moment it seemed that Lyndberne had stopped acting. 'Pugh? That little gutter rat? If one of my men had put a bullet in him, I'd have promoted him.'

'Patrick and you are on opposing sides.'

Again, he bridled. 'Don't play clever with me. You've been mollycoddled so far. Push me and I might give you what I did him to loosen his tongue.'

'Pugh wasn't one of your students then?' I said mildly.

'I'm not interested in people like that. It was true that he had his hooks in half the London underworld but it was a very *grubby* business. Blackmail, wasn't it? He rigged up Satanic orgies and took photos of people biting the heads off chickens and doing illegal things to pretty girls. That's not my scene. Folk like that are dirt — and they ought to be ground into the dirt.' He chuckled. 'Perhaps I'm like your lover boy. It's a bit of a crusade with him, isn't it? He has to take on those he regards as wicked. I've a feeling that's the real reason he was sacked. I bet he's sailed close to the wind before.'

Much later I would remember these words. They could almost have been uttered by a policeman.

We turned left outside the door, walked for twenty yards or so and then came to a checkpoint situated where the tunnel widened considerably. It was manned by two guards. They were not wearing what could be described as a uniform, just soiled camouflage clothing. They acknowledged Lyndberne's appearance with a salute, one of them looking particularly sullen and turning his back on him almost immediately.

'That was the one who left the maps out,' said Lyndberne, taking the centre one of three tunnels and not bothering to lower his voice. 'When you kick their backsides often enough and hard enough and they still don't listen, you have to demote them to sentry duty. I think I shall end

159

up having to shoot him.' He stopped in his tracks in the sudden way he had of doing things. 'You'll be in a room down here from now on. I'll arrange for your stuff to be brought. It'll be better — you won't have to be locked up all the time. Just at night.'

'There's no night and day down here,' I said.

'We *do* operate on a twenty-four hour clock system. But at night they go out for exercises.'

'I've been on the receiving end of some of those,' I told him. 'That's when they steal cars and drive at people out for walks in the country lanes.'

'He's dead,' Lyndberne said through his teeth. 'He paid the price. Those who were stupid enough to go with him on his crazy schemes have all been punished. I had them beaten until they couldn't remember their own mother's names.'

The tunnel sloped very gently downhill. There were doors on either side, some open, some closed, a few offices, some bedrooms, stores, a bathroom. It all seemed to be very well organised. After walking for quite a way and crossing one other tunnel that I guessed connected with the ones on either side, we came to double doors that led into a very large room. It immediately became apparent that what we had entered was actually a cavern. The roof of it was at least fifty feet above our heads and lost in shadow even though the area below was well lit by dozens of spot lamps. And it was vast, about a hundred feet long and seventy wide.

'We can't heat it,' Lyndberne said, seeing that I was shivering with cold in the fierce blasts of fresh air coming from somewhere above. 'In fact it supplies all the ventilation. There's an adit that comes out just below the ruins of the castle. This cave is part of old slate workings, mostly collapsed by now. The tunnels behind us are part of a coal mine. I think both sets of miners accidentally met one day and realised that they'd run out of their respective pickings. This was hundreds of years ago — none of the workings is modern.'

Frankly, my professional interest was kindled by what lay before me. I had seen war-game set-ups before, had actually trained in a very good one in the basement of an outwardly ordinary looking building in London. This was, if anything, better. At the sides of the cavern were stored the packed flat sections of mock-up buildings. Thus, if necessary, a section of a street could be recreated to the fine detail required to rehearse any kind of attack. A kidnapping, bombing, murder, bank raid, anything. Piled on the other side were units made of block-board that seemed to slot together like giant Lego. With these, I assumed, towers or cliffs or any obstacle that had to be scaled could be built.

'We do a lot of active training in here,' said Lyndberne. 'As you can see nothing's set up at the moment but it can be turned into exactly what we want. Our most successful mock-up was when I leased it to someone who wanted to place bombs in an army barracks canteen.' He added, 'He was arrested before he could do the job though − someone grassed on him.'

I wondered why he seemed to find this amusing.

A few men were doing odd jobs, one painting what looked like the front of the set for a shop, a couple of others with carpentry tools undertaking repair work. They worked a little harder when they felt Lyndberne's gaze on them.

'Had to line the sides up to a height of fifteen feet with baffles,' Lyndberne said. 'People were getting hurt from ricochets.'

'You use live ammunition!' I exclaimed.

'The instructors and I do. The trainees sometimes need sharpening up a little. *They* have guns that shoot a red dye.'

We went back to the checkpoint.

'The left-hand tunnel is out of bounds to you,' I was told. 'If you venture down there, I'll not hesitate to kill you.'

Weapon stores, I thought. Possibly an escape route, safes with money, the cell where Patrick was being kept. Everything that I wanted.

'Down here,' Lyndberne informed me, leading the way towards the right hand tunnel, 'is the rest of the accommodation and the lecture rooms. This will be your operating area. You can move freely anywhere here.' He flung open a door. 'Stay here and I'll have your things brought.'

He left me and I found that I was still shivering. No one else seemed to be around so I went the length of the corridor.

There did not seem to be any security cameras here. Perhaps as those who were normally within the area were staff, there was no need. Perhaps I had been promoted.

I stood my ground when a man came hurrying along. He was carrying a bucket and mop. When he skidded to a halt, an appalled look on his face, I realised he had not noticed me until then and that I had startled him.

'Anything wrong?' I asked in friendly fashion.

'No — no, miss. Nothing wrong. Just that twenty-four hours in the day ain't enough to do the work.'

'Short-staffed?' I said, forcing a smile.

'You could say that,' he mumbled.

'Well, I won't keep you,' I said, standing aside. 'Oh, by the way ...'

'Yes, miss?' He was very nervous of me. Perhaps he thought I was a friend of Lyndberne's. Clearly he was not the sort to be told everything that went on.

'How's the prisoner?'

He glanced quickly left and right. 'The army man?'

'Yes.'

'Not too good, miss. But it stands to reason, dunnit? Is that all, miss?'

'Thank you.' I had been wondering if I could trust him with a message for Patrick but abandoned the idea. His very fear would give him away. And how would Lyndberne punish an errant cleaner?

Shortly afterwards someone arrived with my belongings and I was shown into a room. Although, like the other, there were no windows, it was much more pleasant. The walls were pale peach in colour, the furnishings apple green. In a larger recess there was a shower, toilet and hand-basin.

Yes, there were many forms of torture, I reasoned dully as I unpacked my things. One was living in luxury while your husband suffered.

162

Chapter Twelve

By lunchtime the following day the new students had arrived. They were shown straight into the canteen – situated at the end of the far end of Area One, the right hand tunnel – where everyone else had assembled. I too was present. I had received a message early that morning that I was to report for duty at eleven forty-five. I was feeling ill by now and several times had been very sick.

There should have been twelve of them but only eleven turned up, the twelfth having been detained by the police at Frankfurt Airport in order to help them with their enquiries.

I was shocked to discover that I knew who five of these men were. Three worked for terrorist factions in the Middle East. The most important of these, a powerfully built man who for some unfathomable reason was known as The Greek, was Lebanese. The two much younger men with him and reputed to be his nephews were known as Jubeil and Batrun, again probably nicknames. Another, John Murphy, a one-time member of the IRA and, I understand, referred to by his friends as Bally, was wanted in connection with the murder of an RUC policeman on holiday at his wife's family home in Richmond. The fifth was another Irishman whose face was familiar but whose name I could not remember. I had an idea he had escaped from prison.

The remaining six were unknown to me but I was sure Patrick would be able to identify at least half of these. What I did not know just then was that he would soon be able to identify them for himself.

'That one,' said Lyndberne, appearing at my elbow in the sudden, disconcerting way of his.

'The Lebanese?'

'That's right. He's a very important man at home. He has backing from Syria. I'm honoured to have him here.'

'I wouldn't have thought anyone could teach him very much.'

'He's come to learn about Britain.'

'And you're hoping he'll give you a lot of money.'

'I'm in business for money,' Lyndberne said, walking away.

The arrivals had already been checked in so a buffet lunch was served straight away. Afterwards Lyndberne made a short speech of welcome and then went on to outline the first week's activities. I paid no real attention to this, trying to commit every face in the room to memory. Just in case I got out of this nightmare alive.

Lyndberne concluded his speech by telling the students that they would be shown their quarters and have the rest of the day free to find their way around. But they were not permitted to venture outside during daylight hours nor were they to enter Area Three. Just as he reached this point the doors to the canteen swung open and a man was propelled in. I use the word because I received the impression he had been kicked in from the corridor. He staggered and almost fell on top of me.

'Leave him!' Lyndberne bellowed when I jumped up to steady him.

'It's all right,' Patrick said, looking me straight in the eye.

To this day I do not know what prevented me from having hysterics. I became aware, in that instant, that everything that Lyndberne had mentioned had happened to Patrick. And someone had lopped off his hair, roughly, as if with blunt scissors. Most of it was so short now that you could see his scalp, the rest in uneven hanks. He could not walk straight, he hurt too much for that. They had garbed him in shapeless prison-type overalls.

This shambling ruin of a man progressed slowly to the centre of the room where he stopped, facing Lyndberne.

'Turn round,' Lyndberne ordered.

Patrick turned to face the students.

'This is your servant for the duration of your stay, gentlemen, I shall now tell you who he is.'

Lyndberne did so, in some detail, and their eyes widened. Some laughed, most did not. When he had finished giving the information, he said that coffee would be served and sat down. Patrick stayed exactly where he was, in the middle of the room, hands clasped behind his back. He was still there when everyone left the room, Lyndberne calling to me to show the men where I would lecture them. We all filed out. The only person to pause was Murphy, who spat right in Patrick's face.

'You kick a man when he's down, eh?' said The Greek to him when we were outside the door.

'He's filth,' mumbled Murphy.

Once inside the lecture room, I knew I had either to scream, cry or lose my temper. I chose the latter, grabbing the puny Irishman by the neck of his grubby teeshirt and slamming him hard into the wall.

'Now get this!' I yelled at the assembly. 'To set the record straight, that man in there is my husband. So in order to keep what's left of him alive, I'm going to lecture you every morning on the workings of the British security services. And you're going to damn well listen and write essays which I shall mark. And while I'm doing that, no doubt he'll be cleaning your rooms and ironing your shirts and fetching and carrying for you all. How proud you must feel to be in such an establishment.' I did not care if Lyndberne could hear all this over hidden microphones.

I was quite surprised to note that some of them looked a trifle hangdog. And The Greek bent on Murphy a look that promised cold steel between the ribs if he retaliated.

My predictions were entirely accurate. The only way I could stay sane was to take an interest in my task, privately amazed that I seemed to know so much about the subject. All of which, it had to be admitted, could be gleaned from a good library. I gave them nothing secret or sensitive, offering, over the days, the Burgess and Maclean saga, Suez — even though this was hardly of use to them — the structure and workings of MI6 – remembered mostly from a series of articles in *The Times* – the Peter Wright case, rumblings at GCHQ. From there we went to MI5 and weapons issued to the various Police Forces.

My students were oddly diffident, especially the foreigners who, with the exception of The Greek, were far younger than me, little more than boys and of the 'brainwashed since birth' variety. Perhaps it was because they had already paid Lyndberne and I was throwing so many facts at them that they thought if they missed anything they were not getting true value. To spin things out a little I started to correct their grammar and this was instantly resented by the Europeans. I successfully countered this by telling them that if they wished to operate under cover in Britain they would have to learn to express themselves clearly or would be immediately suspect. I'm not sure why they accepted this but they did.

Lyndberne left me alone. He had initially asked to be given an example of their work but after I had let him have a few essays he said he had no time to read them. I felt he had rather more pressing things on his mind.

The Greek sat in on a couple of classes and thereafter did not attend. I got the impression that he was paying for his two protégés and was making sure the instruction was worth the money. Then, after six days had elapsed, he came to the lecture room when the class was over, while I was tidying away.

'I should like my brothers to be instructed in spoken English,' he said. He always referred to them thus but I had assumed this to be like addressing them as 'comrades'.

'Have you mentioned it to Lyndberne?' I enquired.

'Is it necessary?'

'He's an unpredictable and dangerous man. I don't want to upset him.'

He thrust his hands in his pockets and strolled down the room away from me. 'There's an odd situation here. I'm not quite sure what is going on.'

'In what way?'

'Would you tell me if you knew?'

'Probably not,' I admitted. 'But I'm not sure what you mean.'

He smiled, showing perfect teeth. 'The emphasis of this

166

course is supposed to be subversion. Not a lot has been said about it so far.'

I was baffled. 'I'm not in charge. Ask Lyndberne if you've any problems.'

He beamed at me again. 'Please help the little ones improve their spoken English.'

I sat down behind the table I was using as a desk. 'While they beat my husband for not ironing their shirts properly?'

'I doubt if they would dare,' he commented, going out.

I thought about this remark and also about other things I had noticed. For one thing the class were looking a lot tidier than they had on arrival. Most seemed to be shaving every day too. Some of the younger ones, Jubeil, Batrun and another weedy youth from Estonia – probably sponsored by the Russians – were transformed. They no longer slouched around. There was a certain military efficiency about them. Up until now I had assumed this to be as a result of their having been licked into shape. Not so, fool, I told myself, the instructors were all unshaven, foul-mouthed louts.

The first showdown occurred at lunchtime on the eighth day. Someone dropped a pile of dinner plates in the canteen and Patrick was sent for to sweep up the pieces. When he came in with bucket, brush and shovel, I bit the tip of my tongue hard to keep myself under control. The man who has never had a spare ounce of fat on his body was quite literally starving. The smell of hot food hit him like a blow. I think that at that moment I would have rebelled if he had not, again, looked me straight in the eye.

'Are you hungry?' Lyndberne said to him silkily as he passed his table.

A wild thought went through my mind when Patrick stopped and regarded the speaker placidly. Is this what army bullying is all about – to build up resistance? No, came the immediate answer, that was merely cruel narrow minds praying on those who could not fight back. And Patrick was not the sort of man ever to have been bullied. I know for a fact that when he was a junior officer, before he was drafted into special forces, he sought out and put an end to such things.

167

'I asked you a question,' Lyndberne said.

'Yes, I'm hungry,' Patrick replied.

'Sit down, I'll get you something.'

The class made room for him on their long table, someone fetching a chair. This should have warned Lyndberne. Perhaps he did not notice, speaking to the cook. He returned with a large plastic bucket and plonked it on the table before Patrick. The scrap bucket. Then he returned to his own seat, smiling to himself. The four instructors and the rest of the resident staff broke into howls of laughter.

The laughter petered out quite quickly for none of the students was laughing. Dead silence fell on the room. This hush deepened, if this was possible, when Patrick lifted the bucket from the table and put it on the floor so he could see what was in it. His lips were seen to move.

'What did you say?' Lyndberne screamed, leaping up. 'What did that bastard call me? You — that man sitting next to him — what did he say?'

Patrick had fished out a partly gnawed chicken leg covered in what looked like custard and had it half-way to his mouth.

Lyndberne advanced on the man he had addressed, one of The Greek's 'brothers', Jubeil.

'He — he say ...' stammered the youth. 'He say something like, "For what we are about to receive, may God make me grateful."'

Slowly, six of the seated men rose with their loaded dinner plates in their hands. They looked at each other. Then, the one nearest to Patrick, the other Irishman, Regan, placed his own meal in front of him, together with a clean knife and fork, before picking up the scrap bucket. For a moment it seemed that he would up-end it over Lyndberne.

Patrick leaned over to place a hand on his arm. 'No,' he said, and the danger passed.

Lyndberne stalked out of the room and, just then, I had never been more afraid.

The next day, for reasons I was not told about, the timetable was changed so that the students underwent active instruction in the mornings, written in the afternoons. It became apparent that the class was being put through a

fairly punishing regimen. That afternoon they all seemed
to be extremely weary, one or two looking downright ill.
It was a good moment to ask a few questions.

'Your steward,' I said. 'When does he do your rooms?
After breakfast?'

Batrun, who usually regarded himself as spokesman, said,
'Yes, always. But this morning, later. He has more to do
now.'

'Since yesterday?'

'Everything since bloody yesterday,' spat Murphy.

'What do you mean?'

Jubeil piped up. 'This morning we get hell. PT. Unarmed
combat. If we are slow we are tripped, beaten a little. Regan,
he hit with a rifle butt.'

'Regan *was* hit with a rifle butt,' I corrected automatically.

A man whose name was King, and who hardly ever spoke
at all, said. 'Your husband didn't escape either.'

Batrun rounded on him furiously. 'We agreed to say
nothing of that!'

'She has a right to know.' said King.

'We do our own rooms this morning,' Jubeil muttered.
'And the beds. Just as he showed us. As a surprise for
him.'

I said no more. For one thing I could hardly believe my
own ears. These so-called students were all killers, I had to
keep telling myself. Most had already been responsible for
the deaths and maiming of many people. Some had served
prison terms and others certainly would do so. Quite a few
would die in a hail of bullets during pitched battles with
police or soldiers.

'Something funny's going on,' growled Jake from the
back. He resembled an Ethiopian long-distance runner but
with dread-locks. He made no secret of his contempt for the
entire set-up, me included. A long black forefinger stabbed
the air in my direction. 'You hear me, lady? Jake is not a
foolish boy who believes everything he is told. I do not believe
that your man has had any kind of hell pasted out of him. Not
for real. I think he is a bloody good actor. I think he is part
of this outfit. I also think he is in charge. Anyone with eyes

169

in his head can see he is ten of a creep like Lyndberne.'

The denial was on my lips but, perhaps fortuitously, Murphy beat me to it. 'I *know* him,' he shouted at the black man. 'He put my eldest brother in the Maze as a result of working undercover in Belfast.'

'He was thrown out of MI5,' Jake said as though talking to a child. 'If he wanted revenge, what better way than to set up his own business training the likes of us?'

'And the point of the deception?' King snapped.

Jake shrugged. 'You tell me.' A big, crafty grin. 'Perhaps the clever ones who see through it get big contracts.'

'Shall we start?' I asked, thinking about subversion.

That evening Lyndberne sent for me. He was in his own living accommodation in the farmhouse with The Greek and Rhona — whom, I had decided, was the dumbest woman ever to have walked the Earth.

'The department you both worked for — what was it . . . D12?' was Lyndberne's opening remark. 'I'd like to know more about it. You can instruct the students about it tomorrow.'

'It doesn't exist any more,' I said.

'Your husband has indicated the contrary.'

'He can't have done. It was disbanded some time ago after there was a row about the accountability of the security services. Questions were asked in the House.'

Lyndberne smiled. 'Under *pressure* Gillard assures me that is not the case. The department was not disbanded, it merely went deeper into Whitehall and disappeared from the view of everyone but the Prime Minister and a few others. Do you want to see the video recording of your husband telling me all this?'

'No,' I said.

'I want the names of the present operatives and especially of the man who took over Gillard's job. Plus the name of the man at the top.'

'No,' I said again. If there was any information Patrick would withhold, I felt, it was this. And he obviously had withheld it, or Lyndberne would not be asking me.

'You know what'll happen.'

'Yes. But I have some integrity. You don't imagine I'd —'

The Greek interrupted me. 'Let them talk it over,' he suggested to Lyndberne. 'It might save trouble that way.'

'Trouble?' Lyndberne queried.

'The men *like* Gillard.'

The other stared at him as though he was mad.

'Try it,' urged The Greek. 'It can hardly do any harm, can it?'

I was taken down to Area Three — the left-hand tunnel. It was far narrower than the other two and smelt of drains. Water trickled down the walls and along the floor of the passage going in the same direction I was, into a place like a grave. The tunnel went ever downwards for a while and then plunged very steeply, the rock beneath my feet slippery with green slime. Something small skuttled away. A rat.

The man showing me the way counted three doors along in a group of five and unlocked it. I went in alone and it boomed shut behind me.

'Just like a plot for a bad novel, isn't it?' Patrick said. *'The Prisoner of Thingumajig.'*

There was something about him that prevented me from running and taking him in my arms. The restraint that he was holding himself under perhaps. But I went over slowly and sat on the bunk by his side. He gazed at me, eyes brilliant, not quite in command of his lips.

'Straight out of *Vampires at Midnight*,' I agreed.

'I take it there's a reason why you've been brought.'

'Can we talk freely? Is this place bugged?'

'Several varieties. Some in the blanket. A few on the walls. Six legs, fifty legs. All sorts.'

The stench was dreadful, mostly because of a bucket in one corner.

'Has anyone touched you?' he asked.

'No, not yet. But they might. He wants everything about D12.'

Patrick shut his eyes quickly. 'Oh God. I wasn't sure whether they'd given me a shot of truth-drug. Tell him everything he wants to know.'

171

'We always agreed we'd never — '

'Trust me.'

'Are you hurt?'

'It's nothing that I'm going to die of.'

Our eyes met.

'Trust me,' Patrick said again.

It would be gratifying to record that we now spoke of other matters under cover of which we communicated by some kind of sign language in order to plan what we would do next. Reality was that I curled up with him on his damp bunk, put both arms around and hugged him until he was warm. He fell asleep almost immediately.

That night one of the class was killed on an exercise. It was Regan, still presumably too dazed from the blow with the rifle butt to remember about the booby-trap gun in the cottage on Bryn Glas.

I had expected that Lyndberne would summon me as soon as I was brought back from Patrick's cell but this did not happen until the next morning when the whole place was buzzing with the news of Regan's demise. I was told to go to his office in the house and found him, with Brasso and duster, polishing Patrick's cannon. It had been set up on a teak wall unit, also housing a small television set and compact disc player, the cannon facing the desk.

'It looks well here,' he said when he saw me.

I pondered over whether it was wrong to pray that some miracle might occur and the thing would blow him to bits. It didn't seem to follow the approved lines of love and forgiveness but I prayed it anyway.

'About D12,' he said, polishing briskly.

'No,' I said.

The duster paused. 'I was hoping that after your visit to your husband, you'd decide to co-operate.'

I sat down in one of the soft green leather chairs. 'Well, yes, Patrick thinks I ought to tell you everything you want to know.'

'He's a wise man.'

'No. Right now he's half dead with cold and hunger and

you keep giving him a going-over so I reckon he's not thinking too clearly at all.'

Lyndberne's pale blue eyes bulged slightly. 'You're wasting time.'

'No.'

He did not say anything else, just pressed a buzzer on his desk. When a couple of the ever-vigilant staff entered he gave them orders. Then I knew I should have done as Patrick had said and not been fool enough to think I could win. I suppose it was pride then that stopped me from changing my mind. Stupid again.

I lost, and they were in no hurry to listen either.

Chapter Thirteen

There are techniques that can be taught to help overcome the trauma of being subjected to extreme ill-treatment. These do not really reduce the pain but lessen shock and the mental distress associated with torture. In my case this knowledge helped a little but nothing can prepare you for the horror and you are never the same afterwards. Nightmares fade after a while but there are still times when I am back in that room, helpless, in extremis, when I see those two men — two of the instructors — and the way they looked at my nakedness and pressed the buttons that sent the shocks through my body. It was made worse by the awareness of my own stupidity, and also the thought that if Patrick was somehow undermining Lyndberne's authority then no trace of my ordeal must be apparent to the students afterwards. And this, clearly, would be impossible.

Lyndberne's confidence and satisfaction at this time must have been immense — for, after all, he had been summoned by my interrogators to hear the faltering voice give the information and had personally noted it down — so he decided that no better postscript was possible than to put man and wife together as witnesses to one another's misery.

Patrick, I gather, anticipating the worst, clasped me tenderly to himself — I was still unconscious — clinically examined me for serious injury and sign of rape, found neither so wrapped the victim warmly in her bed quilt and then made full use of the shower in her room and the spare clean clothing in his own knapsack. He also ate her lunch when it arrived, brought by someone who had no idea of the true state of affairs. This person, Jubeil, had brought the food on his own initiative, having been told that I was unwell. And of course what Jubeil saw merely strengthened the persistent rumour that what Jake had said was true.

For me, awareness began with the sensation of being held. In an instant the fear that horror was about to start all over again — for of course the newly conscious have no idea for a moment where they are — evaporated. There was no mistaking the touch. He set to work quickly, ruthlessly rolled me out of the quilt, washed me all over with soap and flannel and then, using some skin moisturiser from my bag, proceeded to massage the cramp from my racked muscles. This sounds sexy and languorous. It wasn't. The strong fingers and thumbs dug into the knots in my calf muscles, shoulders, neck and arms, wringing from me moans of pain. But it worked for when he had finished I could stand unaided and was sufficiently mobile to make for the tap to quench a tormenting thirst. I was grabbed and hauled back.

'Think,' he said. 'You ought to know what happens when you drink cold water after that kind of treatment.'

I had forgotten but remembered in an instant his convulsions and wondered if someone had deliberately poured water down his throat. Yes, Lyndberne would do that. Lyndberne, after all, had supervised the interrogation. Lyndberne would have positioned the victim with scientific precision — the thin beam of wood placed behind the knees, the person then forced to crouch, the arms placed behind the beam and then tied at the wrists in front and to the ankles. The beam was then raised so that the one to be questioned was suspended, like a trussed chicken. One was naked, the electrodes placed according to the interrogator's whim.

I wept, memories too vivid. Patrick did not try to stop me, just held me close. This closeness, being of such close accord, was wonderfully comforting.

'It'll get worse before it gets better,' he whispered when I was at peace.

'I gave him all the names,' I croaked.

He got up and methodically began to check the room for hidden microphones. I already knew there were two — one under a bedside table, another behind a small mirror on the wall. He found another tucked behind the waste pipe of the hand basin. They were left in place.

'It was unavoidable,' Patrick said. 'No one could hold out under that.' He smiled at me and then winked. Then he blew me a kiss and went away.

There were only two explanations for this kind of behaviour, I reasoned. One was that my husband had cracked under the strain and was living in some kind of cloud-cuckoo land. The other was that Lyndberne was already a dead man.

The bad dream turned into reality and Lyndberne was in my room, sitting on the edge of the bed staring down at me.

'People came looking for you,' he said.

I said, 'It's to be expected. We just disappeared into thin air.'

'Police were nosing around on the other side of the valley up by Cwm Farm.'

'The ruin? That booby-trapped place?'

He chuckled. 'Might have found a bit more than they bargained for, eh? No, they'd have seen nothing there. I ordered everything to be removed ... just in case.'

'You're playing cat and mouse with us,' I said.

'Not at all. Anyway, they've gone. I watched them get back in their van and drive off. Why should they investigate up there, I wonder?'

'It was where one of your people took a shot at Patrick's brother. Or had you forgotten?'

He nodded slowly. 'Yes, of course. I had forgotten. Now, as far as you're concerned you can carry on teaching The Greek's boys spoken English. He's paying extra for it.'

'And the rest?'

'They're under instruction for a night exercise.' He rose to go, pausing as he opened the door. 'I'm afraid that your husband seems to have had some kind of breakdown. He was found wandering the corridors in tears. So I think I can safely say that he's no longer a threat to me, don't you?'

'Get out,' I said.

He went but did not lock the door as I thought he might.

Later, when I had dressed, there was a furtive knock on

176

the door. It was Jubeil and Batrun, the former carrying what looked like a carrier bag full of books. But the book was only on top.

'Our uncle says to bring your food,' said Batrun. He unwrapped his booty carefully; a cold roast chicken breast, several thick slices of bread and butter and a carton of yoghurt. He had even remembered a paper napkin and a knife and fork. I took this gift to mean that The Greek was not going along with Jake's theory.

'Why aren't you learning tonight with all the others?' I enquired.

'Our uncle says it is too cold here,' said Batrun. 'We might get ill.'

'*Be* ill,' I said in exasperation. 'Are you serious? You've come to a training school for terrorists and he's worried about you catching *cold*?'

'He loves us,' Jubeil said simply.

'And he's not worried about you being hanged, shot, going to prison for the rest of your lives?'

'Oh, no. And he would help us. He would bribe the police. He has much money.'

'He wouldn't be able to bribe the police in *this* country,' I told him, tapping a slim brown arm.

'He says everyone has their price.'

'Do *you*?' I said. 'How much money would you want from Lyndberne to cut my throat?'

Both looked quite shocked for a moment. Then they shook their heads.

'You'd do it if your uncle told you to,' I said severely. 'You know you would.'

'He would not though,' Batrun said, but after chilling hesitation.

'Why not?'

They glanced at one another worriedly and then Jubeil said, 'He has done some things that mean many people want to send him to prison. He put a bomb on a plane — shoots people . . . things like that. But he never would cut a woman's throat. Not unless she had done something terrible to him.'

Like standing him up on a date, I thought bitterly.

177

Later that day I walked fairly tall to the lecture room and listened to my own pupils read extracts from *From Russia with Love*, the only book at my disposal.

When the group returned from their 'mission' – the night sortie deep into the National Park – King, the man who hardly spoke at all, was missing, and the Estonian, whose name was pronounced Harvo but which I had never seen written down, was shaking like a leaf. He was still shaking that afternoon when they mustered for lessons and for one short moment I felt really sorry for him.

It occurred to me that my own position might be difficult. For if most believed Jake's theory that Patrick was really in charge and this was being kept a secret to see which of the more intelligent students would discover the truth, rich rewards for those who did, then they might conceivably blame me for things going wrong. I was not sure what *had* gone wrong, only that King had not returned. So I sat behind my table – this was necessary as I was still feeling very weak – and decided just to let things happen.

Things happened quite quickly. Harvo, sitting with the three men from the Middle East who had so far refused point blank to speak to a woman or give me their names even after I had christened them Shadrach, Meshach and Abed-nego but who had handed in work of the highest quality, jumped to his feet with a cry. He had not gone more than a few yards when he vomited in spectacular fashion, the others scattering with yells of disgust.

This could be classified as an emergency, I concluded, and picked up the receiver of the phone on my table. One dialled 6 for an emergency. Thus, unwittingly, I set the scene for the second showdown.

Lyndberne arrived first. He had with him one of the instructors, Adjit, an Egyptian. Both were armed, Lyndberne with a Beretta, the other with a sub-machine gun.

'What the bloody hell's going on?' Lyndberne roared, looking at me.

I waved distastefully towards the malodorous state of chaos.

'That is the man!' Harvo cried. 'That is the man who shot

178

King. King broke his leg and this wretch shoot him like he was a dog.' Here Harvo's command of English simply was not good enough for the emotion that the moment demanded and he poured invective on Adjit's head in his own language.

Mouth tight, nostrils flaring, Lyndberne came to the phone and issued orders. Then he turned to Adjit. 'Is that true? You said he fell and broke his *neck*.'

But Adjit had his eyes on the Estonian. 'I warned you, you little runt ...'

'Is it *true*?' Lyndberne asked again.

'If that had been war last night,' Adjit said to him, 'he'd have been left behind. But it wasn't and you didn't want him chatting to the police, did you?'

'No,' Lyndberne said. 'I didn't. But as you know, I prefer the truth.' He was delivering a reprimand that I felt was no more than an attempt to placate the students when Patrick came in, carrying a bucket of soapy water and a mop.

'That – that ... *swine* ...' Harvo brawled, obviously ransacking his vocabulary, pointing again at Adjit.

'Did what?' asked Patrick, for he was the one being addressed.

'I'm going to kill him!' Harvo said wildly.

'Did you do that?' Patrick enquired, indicating the mess.

'Yes,' replied Harvo. 'That swine made me with his – '

'Then clean it up,' Patrick said and gave him the mop.

'He killed King,' Harvo told him.

'Leave the administration of justice to the experts,' Patrick told him, and I remembered the last time he had uttered those same words.

'Are you threatening me?' Adjit said to Patrick.

'No, I never make threats,' Patrick said.

I saw Lyndberne wink at his henchman. 'The British soldier knows little or nothing about fighting with knives,' he commented in idle fashion. 'Why don't you show him?'

I found that my fingers were gripping the edge of the table tightly and I made myself put my hands in my lap.

'He's not up to fighting,' Adjit said, eyeing Patrick up and down.

'You don't usually let little things like that bother you,' Murphy drawled.

179

The Egyptian took a flick knife from his pocket and sprang the blade, thoughtfully, looking at the weapon as he did so.

'Don't kill him,' Lyndberne instructed softly.

'Give the man a knife,' Jake said.

Lyndberne turned on him a wide, bland stare. 'There's little point, surely. Have you ever met an Englishman who could use one?'

'I seem to remember you saying you took one off him,' the black man observed.

Lyndberne burst out laughing. 'I thought that was for peeling apples.'

'It is,' Patrick said. 'But it would probably improve your image if you let me have it.'

'Get it,' Lyndberne told Jake. 'Rhona will give it to you. It's in the safe.'

Jake loped towards the door. 'Will they let me through the checkpoint?'

'I'll clear you,' Lyndberne said, 'For pity's sake get a move on – we haven't all day.' He picked up the phone.

Adjit decided not to wait. He walked up to Patrick making small movements in the air with the knife. 'Oh, I forgot,' he said when he was really close. 'You cry when you're under pressure.' He held the blade across Patrick's throat. 'Are you going to cry now, eh?'

I dispassionately tried to sum up Patrick's chances of survival if he lost his temper. I knew that the Egyptian taught both armed and unarmed combat as well as night reconnaissance. He had probably learned many of his techniques as a boy in the back streets of Cairo. It was not difficult to see why Lyndberne regarded a British soldier – and an officer at that – as no more than a toy for such a man.

Patrick raised his right hand slowly, the long delicate-looking fingers placed almost lovingly around the wrist of the hand that was holding the knife. And, slowly, he pushed the hand down. Too late, far too late, Adjit realised exactly the kind of grip he was in. In an explosion of movement he tried to shake the grip off only to apply more leverage in breaking his own wrist. One distinctly heard the bones snap.

Silence but for the breath hissing through the Egyptian's teeth.

Patrick had deftly caught the knife. A kind of incredulous gasp went round the room as he tossed it for the other to catch left-handed.

'Try again,' said that mocking, bored-sounding voice.

I think everyone now had realised that the account of the breakdown was a lie.

With murderous deliberation Adjit narrowed the distance between them. But he looked increasingly nervous, his prey having commenced swaying slightly from side to side, snake-like. The eyes too, ceased to resemble those of a human being. I knew this to be so even though Patrick had his back to me. What Adjit could see were not eyes but mad, living, polished pebbles. Then I saw him tear his gaze from the nightmare vision just before he attacked.

He misjudged it — for this kind of hypnosis really does work — and was again caught as will a fly in the web of a spider.

And at this point I had to cover my eyes. But I still heard the man scream shrilly three times. Then Lyndberne shouted hoarsely to Patrick to stop. The screaming continued. The ghastly sound was still going on when the door opened and Jake returned. I saw this and also the transfer of that thin-bladed, strangely heavy knife. It was thrown in a sweeping sideways motion, strong fingers and wrist providing deadly impetus.

Adjit ceased to scream abruptly and toppled forward from his already crouched-over position, the knife just below his left ear.

'Oh, God,' Lyndberne gasped.

The gift of five vital seconds when Lyndberne could have been over-powered was ignored, wasted. I knew why. I had already been told. I breathed out slowly, my mind suddenly very clear. It would have been possible to have taken Lyndberne, and his gun and used it to capture the others. But that would have left all the staff to contend with, too many for just two to handle. For a while it was useful to Patrick to have the students on his side.

181

Lyndberne had gone, one supposed to find members of staff who could help with the body.

'So it's true,' Jake crowed. 'You really are the boss-man.'

Patrick retrieved his knife. 'We were partners,' he said. 'He tried to take over my share of the business. All you've seen is quite genuine. I *was* a prisoner.' He came over to me and spoke quietly. 'Sorry.'

The apology was because I had been present when quite unspeakable things had been done to the man who was now dead.

'I intend to get a message out,' he said in a whisper. 'This place *is* on the phone after all.'

'Lyndberne's still very dangerous.'

'While he's blinded by his own vanity, we're fairly safe.'

'He might just kill us.'

'No, it's more complicated than that. If he's going to carry on with this enterprise – here or anywhere else – he has to prove that it's successful. He can't gun us down and send the class home. Word would get around that his brain's in his gun barrel. That kind of terrorism isn't relevant today.'

Our lives seemed to depend on Patrick's judgement. For a moment, when Lyndberne burst into the room with three others, all heavily armed, I thought that the reasoning was fatally flawed. He seemed surprised to find Patrick still in the room.

'I told them the truth,' Patrick said. 'How we were partners and you were greedy enough to want it all for yourself. The vote was that they're behind me.'

'I'm not,' Murphy announced in a loud voice. 'I wouldn't believe a word you said while there was breath left in your body.'

Patrick ignored him. 'I told them our bust-up was about Anton Friedrich and they're prepared to forget that you've consorted with people whose mental stability and credentials are highly suspect.'

Handed a face-saving situation on a plate, Lyndberne had no choice but to appear to go along with it. 'Okay, okay,' he said wearily. 'We'll go back to how it was before.

Tomorrow's the last day of the course — perhaps you'd like to organise it?'

'Gladly,' Patrick replied solemnly.

We glanced at one another when Lyndberne had gone again. He still had full control of all communication with the outside world and also all keys to the weapon stores.

Chapter Fourteen

'This is the most bizarre situation,' I said, stating the obvious.

Patrick had moved in to my room and now consigned the last of the three listening devices to a watery grave in the toilet cistern. 'Fascinating,' he agreed. 'I can't ever remember a scenario like this.'

'Well, at least he can't kill us until after tomorrow.'

'One way or another we won't be here after tomorrow.' Patrick sat on the bed and leaned back against the wall. 'Right, what have we got? On the one hand, Lyndberne. He has all weapons and access to communication equipment. He also has on his side the three remaining senior instructors and ten or a dozen general helpers who might or might not be of some use to him if it came to trouble. And what do we have? Ourselves and my knife. There are also nine surviving students, also unarmed.'

'Murphy can't be described as a supporter.'

'No. But they mustn't be put in to a situation where they have to make a life or death decision as far as *I'm* concerned. That would be a mistake for they would instantly take Lyndberne's side if the true facts come out, if you'll excuse the tautology. No, the wizard must wave his wand.'

'All that information you gave him . . .' I said. 'The code words.'

'Out of date. Everything was changed when I left D12; code words, passwords, even some of the agents abroad. There's the rest though, I don't know what I said when they gave me the truth drug. All the names, I expect.'

'*I* gave him those.'

'He probably just wanted to double-check.'

'He could have given us both the truth drug to start with.' I had started to tremble.

'Ah, but there's no satisfaction in that. No screaming or other heart-warming signs of distress.'

'Please don't,' I whispered.

He gazed at me steadily. 'Perhaps for their own good it would be a brave idea to give all security forces trainee operatives a taste of real hell instead of just slapping their faces a few times. Then they'd know that no matter how many degrees you've got, and however steady you are under fire, when folk start suspending you from the ceiling with your backside hanging out and put electrodes the last places you want them then things get very, very distressing indeed.'

'I envy the way you're so resiliant,' I said, sitting down and putting my hands underneath me so he couldn't see how they were shaking. I hadn't intended to even talk about it.

'It's not resiliance,' he insisted. 'It's awareness. We're not talking about weakness or lack of courage but medical fact. Accept it. Say to yourself, "When the human body is restricted and subjected to severe pain and shock, this causes it to cry out and struggle and possibly even to pee all over the floor." Even worse things have been known to happen.'

I gazed into the sombre grey eyes and decided that, yes, indeed there were, in the depths, sparks of humour. I started to laugh, probably slightly crazily and shrilly, and when I stopped, cried a little and then laughed again, but this time softly. 'This was supposed to be our second honeymoon,' I giggled. 'No, I'm really sorry. Go back to what you were saying. The wizard would have to wave his wand.'

'We could escape,' Patrick said after a short silence. 'That would be comparatively easy. But to escape isn't really an option. All these people must end up either behind bars or in plastic body bags. Now what I was proposing to do is this ...' And he outlined an idea that I felt would need a fair amount of wizardry in order to succeed.

For the next fifteen hours I lived, literally, from one moment to the next. Outwardly, all was as normal and I should

185

imagine that this was the impression the students were under for they received tuition according to the time-table and their meals as usual. Patrick stayed with them almost all the time and I saw very little of him.

Adjit had been buried — deeply, one hoped — on the open moorland. I wondered when told of this whether King also lay out there somewhere in an unmarked grave. Regan had apparently been buried on the hill above the booby-trapped cottage.

The Greek imparted this last piece of information when I met him in a corridor. It was not a meeting I enjoyed for he was our greatest danger. It all depended on whom he believed to be speaking the truth. Or so I thought at the time.

'I have been out on the mountains,' he said after telling me this. 'It does not suit me to be underground like a mole. You get used to it, I suppose.'

I realised that I would have to be very careful. 'We're not here all the time,' I pointed out. 'Only when there's a need for security.'

He leaned on the wall, arms folded. 'I wish I had known before that there had been this ... disagreement. Why did you not tell me?'

'You are a friend of Lyndberne. What good would that have done?'

'And how much of the organisation of this business has your husband had a hand in? We all of us admire efficiency. He is efficient. Lyndberne is not.'

'Not much at all. He hasn't been here long. That was one of the reasons for the row.'

'He disagreed with a lot, eh?'

'Yes. About the quality of the training staff and the fact that there was no back-up for the night sorties. We've seen what happened in that connection.' This was straight off the top of my head, but reasonable, I thought.

'I'm still slightly puzzled,' The Greek admitted. 'I've been in this business a long time and I thought I knew men. Gillard does not seem to be the kind of man to turn so thoroughly.'

'He's a bitter man,' I said.

'That first day,' he persevered, 'in the canteen ... that

186

was a man who had been very badly treated. The others say he was playing for sympathy. He was not.'

I said, 'He was being brave and doing as he was told because Lyndberne had told him I would suffer otherwise.'

'*That* bad a quarrel? And now all is forgiven? All is as before? A man bitter enough to turn traitor to his country on account of losing his job is big friends again with a man who threatened to torture his *wife*?'

'There's a lot of money in this game,' I said, heart thudding.

He shook his head slowly. 'Gillard is not a man like that.'

'Then ask him.'

'I will.'

I mulled over what Patrick might say.

As a writer I hope I have avoided being melodramatic. It is however no exaggeration to state that when I awoke from snatches of sleep on that final morning, I really expected the day to be my last. This, I discovered, was a unique feeling. I knew there was a plan in Patrick's mind designed to prevent this coming about but I did not feel very optimistic about it. If it went wrong there would only be two of us against so many.

'Today, you die,' I told myself in the small mirror over the wash-basin. 'Today, someone will shoot you and you'll die.'

It was very hard not to sink into self-pity. I would not see Justin again, not be able to ruffle his glossy black curly hair, so like his father's. There would be no more summer mornings when I would open the bedroom window and hear the River Lyd murmuring in its gorge or be startled by the sudden scream of a buzzard high overhead.

In the absence of orders I wandered down to the canteen for coffee. I could not face the thought of food. I had no idea where Patrick had slept, or if at all. He had gone from my sight the previous evening.

'Good morning,' said Lyndberne politely. 'Won't you join us?'

With him at the table were The Greek and Patrick, the latter

187

consuming with every sign of enjoyment a large plateful of sausages, bacon and eggs. I sat down.

'Seen McFie?' Lyndberne asked me.

'Who's he?' I said.

'One of the instructors. The one with red hair.'

I shook my head. 'I came straight from my room.'

'I can help you with that,' said The Greek smoothly. 'He was taken ill.'

'Ill? What's wrong with him?'

The Greek shrugged. 'I found him in a corridor – collapsed. I took him to his room.'

'Did you get medical help?'

The big man closed his mouth – it had been widely awaiting the arrival of a piece of buttered toast – and frowned. 'There *is* no medical help. That's why people who get hurt are shot.'

Patrick shushed him loudly, casting a worried glance in the direction of the students. 'Careful,' he warned. 'That only applies to them.'

Lyndberne threw his napkin on the table, glaring at the pair of them.

'Anyway,' Patrick went on breezily, 'if he's not in his room now he must have felt better and gone somewhere else. Obviously a doctor would have been a waste of time.'

'He is not somewhere else,' Lyndberne said, each word thudding into the quiet of the room. 'He is nowhere.'

'People can't be nowhere,' Patrick said. 'Perhaps he decided to go home.'

'Was he drunk?' I asked The Greek.

Beaming, he replied, 'Yes, he could have been drunk. This is nothing to worry about, I am sure.'

To Patrick, Lyndberne said, 'Is everything prepared for the last exercise? Are you going to brief them now or in the training area?'

Patrick mopped up the last morsel of egg yolk with a piece of bread, ate it and then said, 'It's all fixed. As a matter of fact I've been up for most of the night working on it. Yes, I'll brief them now.'

'They'll only be permitted to use the dye firing guns,' Lyndberne pointed out when Patrick was halfway to his feet.

'Plus a couple of thunder-flashes to make things realistic?' Patrick wheedled. He added, 'But you'll have to fetch them — you have the only key to the weapon store.'

'Why not?' boomed The Greek. 'I will take responsibility for that if you wish.'

Lyndberne hesitated.

'I hope you trust me,' observed The Greek quietly.

'Of course,' Lyndberne said, handing over a bunch of keys. 'It's the one with the red tally.'

There was an expectant hush as Patrick went over to the students' table. He had no plans or notes. 'Well, gentlemen, this is the end of a rather strange twelve days for you. I hope you'll forgive the teething troubles exacerbated by the difference of opinion between Mr Lyndberne and myself. I've just about forgiven him for locking me up and pasting hell out of me.' Here he turned to Lyndberne with a grin. 'In other words, he's given me a rather large sum of money.'

Lyndberne joined in the laughter. I had a feeling he thought that Patrick was trying to buy time or our lives. I wished I knew what Patrick *was* doing.

'So,' he continued, 'the final day's training. I'm not sure how things have been done in the past but in Army training establishments the last day is usually regarded as something special. This morning I hope that Operation Rook-shoot will live up to my expectations and provide you with a valuable and memorable experience. It must be stressed, however, that there will be no live firing today. You will be issued with the dye emitting pistols with which theoretically to kill your enemy of the moment.'

'Not even blanks?' Jake groaned.

'Blanks don't mean a thing,' Patrick told him. 'But those hit with dye will be regarded as out of the running. Points will be awarded, and those coming through unscathed will be in line for the bottle of whisky Mr Lyndberne's kindly donating.'

I saw Lyndberne start. Then he relaxed and smiled. Leaning over, he whispered in The Greek's ear, causing him to utter a loud belly-laugh.

It was at this moment that the thought came to me that Lyndberne intended to kill everyone. All he had to do was

189

arm himself and his remaining staff and, once the exercise had started, simply pick everyone off. The old mine workings could very easily be sealed for all time. Looked at from a purely practical point of view this was the only way he could safeguard himself; to cut his losses, leave the country and start a new life abroad. And Lyndberne was a totally practical man.

' ... to resemble closely a typical English high street,' Patrick was saying. 'The scenario will involve the assassination of the British Prime Minister. By the way — anyone worked on a plan in connection with that?'

Murphy put up his hand.

'I already knew about you,' Patrick pronounced dismissively. 'Anyone else?'

'It would be good money,' said The Greek wistfully.

Lyndberne said, 'I don't suppose it matters now if I tell you that I was approached myself. I turned it down.'

'I'd be very interested to know why,' Patrick said.

'They were not in possession of the fee.'

The man I referred to as Abed-nego laughed. 'That's the best reason for turning down a job that I know of.'

'Who were they?' The Greek asked.

'A pro-Iranian group,' Lyndberne answered. 'You have to be very careful of people like that — they're all quite crazy.'

'Fanatics,' scoffed The Greek. 'Far better to be like me — free-lance and with no national or religious ideology.'

'Morals are a terrible burden,' Patrick said dreamily and laughed when The Greek looked at him sharply.

The briefing continued in the cavern. It was the first time I had seen it in use and had to admit that the mock-up of the English high street had been imaginatively done, the facades of the "buildings" strongly constructed of plywood and painted like theatre scenery. As I walked round it I saw that a couple even had an "upstairs", platforms behind first-floor windows that were reached by ladders. The whole thing reminded me of sets used by Wild West Shows for shoot-outs. This, of course, was not very far from the truth.

'With a stretch of the imagination, Kensington High Street,' Patrick said, climbing up on to a wooden box so that he could be seen. 'I left out the tube station as that made things a bit complicated. Where there's a gap between the bank and the building society offices, you'll have to imagine a side street. Use it but beware – the PM's security team will have thought of it too. They also might have stationed people in the butcher's shop next door to the bank and in the solicitor's office over the bank. Be aware of the three market stalls too – Special Branch are quite capable of dressing up as market traders.'

There were a few guffaws of laughter at this, the three "stalls" in question – trestle tables loaded with an odd mixture of items – looked as though they were going to collapse at any moment. One had a brave show of pots and pans, presumably from the kitchen, the second merely a few rotten-looking potatoes and a very old cabbage, the third supported what could only be described as a gibbet. From it, hung by their feet, were three dead rooks. They were not freshly dead so I could only assume they had been "borrowed" from outside a gamekeeper's cottage. The implications of this were fascinating.

Patrick said, 'We're assuming that the PM is attending the wedding of a relation. The church, St Mary Abbots, is up the side street. It's a large building and I and my couple of helpers ran out of energy last night so perhaps everyone would grab blocks and build it to the rear of the shops. Make it at least six blocks high and put it right at the back – otherwise there won't be room for any action. Put a ladder on one end so a couple of security people can be placed on the roof.'

They set to with a will, even the two remaining instructors lending a hand. Lyndberne seated himself on a spare block, his face wearing a tolerant, amused expression.

'What part are you taking?' he called to me.

'I'm the Prime Minister,' I shouted back.

'The target?' he observed with a smirk. 'I wish you luck.'

The Greek sauntered up to me, obviously far too important

191

to help with the work. 'What do you think of all this?' he asked.

'Was it your protégés who gave him a hand with it last night?'

'No, I sent them to bed early. We have a long flight ahead of us tonight.'

'Then who ...?' I began to say but quickly stopped speaking.

After smiling broadly he stood watching the activity for a minute or so and then spoke very quietly indeed. 'The Smith and Wesson is in that large black saucepan on the right hand side of the table. I shall go and talk to Lyndberne with my back to you so that you can remove it without him seeing you.'

I gazed at him and realised that he knew the truth. 'You're not on the side of law and order,' I said.

'No. This amuses me. And Lyndberne is a bungler.'

'I hope Rhona didn't see you take the gun.'

'No, again. She is dead. Lyndberne strangled her last night.' And then he too wished me luck.

It appeared that there was a drastic change of plan.

The "church" was completed. As Patrick had said when he had outlined his plan to me, the church built of blocks was all that mattered. From the "tower" — at least thirty feet from the ground — I should be able to climb to the adit above through which fresh air was admitted to the cavern. I would not have long in which to achieve this for if the fire which Patrick intended to start took hold, a lot of smoke would find its way out through the same way. If I did not hurry, I would be overcome and the plan would fail.

It still seemed to me that the plan was no more than a way of saving my own life. This was assuming that it was possible to gain freedom by way of the adit. For all we knew it was sheer. Lyndberne might have had a grating placed over the top to prevent anyone entering from above. And there was every possibility that Patrick would be unable to climb out after me. He had said he would as there was no knowing how long it would take the police to arrive after I had alerted them. I was very afraid that the plan was dependant on too much good luck

192

but it was the only one we had and circumstances forbade any other.

Now, I felt it was imperative that I give Patrick the gun. For one thing he is a far better shot than I, and his would be the rear-guard action.

Hands in the pockets of my trousers, I strolled over to the table with the saucepans on it. I did not turn round to see if The Greek was doing as he had promised. At such times it is better not to look furtive. Seconds later the gun plus quite a lot of ammunition were in the same pockets and I had continued on my way. At any moment I expected to be shot in the back.

Patrick had split the class into four pairs and was at this moment doing something rather complicated with a large tape measure, having laid it on the floor between the rear of the bank and the right hand side of the church. He looked up, saw me and waved me over.

'Your bodyguards,' he said, indicating the two remaining instructors. They were leaning some distance away on a length of the boarding with which the lower part of the cave was lined, looking bored.

I still had my hands in my pockets over my hoard and was praying that no one would notice the sudden bulk. Patrick, aware of the size of his wife's hips and also highly observant, did.

'Where did you get them?' he whispered when I had imparted the information.

'The Greek put them in one of the saucepans.'

'Do you trust him?'

'No.'

'Did you notice whether he was armed?'

'I get the impression he's been carrying a gun in a shoulder harness ever since he arrived.'

'Yes,' Patrick murmured. 'You're confirming my own conclusions.'

'I think you ought to have the gun.'

'No. Keep it. I want you to take out those two over there.' When I did not say anything, he said, 'They're both armed — and not with the dye firing guns either.' He glanced around quickly without turning his head overmuch.

193

'In approximately four minutes' time things are going to start happening. I've a suspicion that Lyndberne is intending to make this entire operation just disappear. The Greek doesn't trust him and will be taking precautions to safeguard himself and Batrun and Jubeil. Anything might happen. Just disable those two clowns over there as soon as they make threatening moves.'

'And then make for the adit?'

'I'll leave that entirely up to you. If things get really bad, save yourself. We owe Justin that.'

'Give me some idea where you'll be.'

'Waving the bloody wand,' he replied without even the trace of a smile.

Just then a large section of the front of the bank fell down. I perceived that this was not planned for Patrick swore vividly. There was a lot of shouting, mostly from Lyndberne, and men ran to secure it back into place. It was while this was being done that I noticed the entry of several of the general helpers, including the cook. They stood just behind where Lyndberne had seated himself, The Greek at his side, positioning themselves in gloomy corners where the light from the huge arc-lamps did not penetrate. I became convinced that they too were carrying guns.

Patrick appeared at the window of the solicitor's office over the bank, apparently checking that all was as it should be.

'Right,' he said, his voice carrying effortlessly to every corner of the cavern. 'May we have the PM with her bodyguards in place, please, near the church? The first pair of would-be assassins have two minutes to work out a plan of action. Go somewhere out of sight to do it. Murphy, you and Jubeil are Special Branch for this round. Hide yourselves in useful places with a view to stopping them.' After a pause he said, 'No, Jubeil, not under the scrap-iron stall. This is for real, not hide and seek.'

Lyndberne had turned slightly in his chair as if to observe what was going on behind him. As I watched he raised his right hand up to shoulder height and kept it there. A signal. Then men stepped from the shadows. Now their guns were not

194

concealed. A couple had semi-automatic Swiss-made pistols, the rest Heckler and Koch sub-machine guns.

I did not see Lyndberne's hand drop for all the lights suddenly went out.

The guns blazed, someone screamed once and then there was three seconds' silence. I know because I found myself counting without knowing why. Then commenced a *son et lumière* of deadly if picturesque nature. Moments after a flare ignited somewhere near the roof of the cave, its intense white light aching to the eyes, the stall loaded with saucepans exploded. It went off with sufficient verve to make standing within twenty feet of it dangerous to say the least. I dropped flat and distinctly heard something whistle over my head. In the next moment it had clanged into the stone several yards away and then clattered to the floor.

In the crazy swaying light of the flare I saw one of the instructors running, gun in hand, towards me. I don't think he could see me lying flat but I was not inclined to keep the thing too sporting and shot him in the leg. His weapon came skating across the floor towards me so I gathered it up and headed for the church.

People were still firing. Virtually on all fours I kept to the sides of the cave, giving the remaining two stalls a wide berth. This was just as well for there were three loud pops as one by one the dead rooks disintegrated, sending a cloud of feathers and rotting flesh into the air. A dreadful stench mingled with the smell of cordite. It was chaos, absolute chaos.

Somewhere, someone laughed.

'You bastard, Gillard!' Lyndberne shouted. He shouted again, orders. I did not catch the exact words. Bullets raked the street mock-up, pieces flying off it in all directions. Then the cabbage on the last stall exploded in a burst of flames. The entire table flared like a torch and in a few seconds it was a bonfire.

I found the last of the instructors, almost fell over him a short distance farther on. He was dead, killed in the hail of bullets.

There was absolutely no chance of climbing up through the adit now for thick black smoke was billowing upwards and swirling around the roof. Not much of it seemed to be escaping, understandable when one remembered that it was the strong down-draught of air that kept the underground area ventilated.

It was odd how I could think about these practical matters when I still expected to be shot at any moment. It was strange too to notice all at once that around me other men were dying. The Irishman, Murphy, lay twitching in a pool of blood, Harvo beside him lying quietly, his eyes on me and filled with boundless terror. I went to him and just as I reached him he died.

The flimsy boarding of the bank was alight by now. Flames engulfed it hungrily, casting a weird glow over a scene that was for all the world like a stage, the flare having just guttered and gone out. Over the crackle of the fire Lyndberne shouted again and bullets smashed and tore into the mock-up.

'No one's left alive,' I muttered to myself. 'It's just me against that lot.'

They were coming towards me, Lyndberne leading the way. Even through the choking smoke and by the light of the fire I could see that he was smiling. I put a bullet into the man just to the rear and side of him and the smile vanished. Feeling quite calm I aimed again and fired and another of his men fell. Lyndberne stopped walking, stretched out a hand and someone placed a weapon in it. But none of his surviving henchmen ran for cover. It was as though he held them under some kind of spell.

Did the man think himself immortal?

It was quite uncanny, then, when a rapid firing weapon of some kind chattered and a neat row of holes appeared in the wall boarding just above Lyndberne's head. This seemed to break the spell as far as his men were concerned for they turned and ran, coughing from the smoke. Slowly, his sub-machine gun held in readiness, Lyndberne began to walk backwards. No further shots were fired in his direction. Soon, he had disappeared into the smoke, the entire episode so strange that I wondered if I had imagined it. Everything was surreal. I couldn't be sure of anything.

It was imperative to escape from the smoke and fumes. All at once I realised that I too was coughing agonisingly, my head feeling as though full of lead. I started to go in the

196

direction that I had last seen Patrick but a sudden belch of flames burst from the bank, forcing me to leap back. Then I fell and dropped one of the guns, tripped by something soft. It was someone's leg. A hand grabbed my arm.

'Help me,' Batrun sobbed. 'Please help me.'

He had been hit at least twice but it was impossible to ascertain how serious the injuries were. There was no time to do anything but get him in a fireman's lift and carry him away. He either passed out or died as I moved him, I did not stop to find out which.

I had not stopped to think, of course. If it had been anyone else and not a slightly built youth, little more than a boy, then my act of mercy would have resulted in my own death. It is a miracle that I found the way out at all. It was only achieved by walking blindly away from the fire until I hit the boarding lining the walls. It was then a matter of groping along until I came to the entrance doors. My only thought was that I was almost certainly a widow.

Somehow, I broke into a run, clutching Batrun and the gun to me. The lights in the tunnel were still on but barely visible in the thick haze of smoke. I probably began to hallucinate a little, imagining myself to be an aircraft coming in to land in fog, following runway lights. I became rather involved with this and forgot everything else, blissfully ignoring the check-point and any need for caution. But nothing happened. It was as if I was alone, the only one left alive. The real shock was running out into bright sunshine and fresh air and hearing a thrush singing in a tree. It was like being re-born.

I discovered that I was on my knees, unable to breathe, unable to stop coughing. I laid Batrun down on his side. His eyes were closed but he seemed to be breathing. There was a lot of blood on his shirt and on his left hand and when I looked more closely I saw that one of his fingers was missing. I left him there. There was no question of my being able to carry him further.

No one was in sight. I approached the rear of the house cautiously but Lyndberne, if indeed he had come this way, had left nobody on guard. I went in through the back door. The kitchen was clean and tidy, quite peculiar after the chaos and mayhem I had just left. The door into the hall was

197

ajar and through the gap came the sound of distant raised voices.

I looked into the narrow dark passage beyond. The voices emanated from the front of the house, probably from Lyndberne's office. After listening for a few moments and hearing only shouted obscenities and recriminations, I turned my attention to the telephone. It was an extension of the one in the office. I had a feeling that when I picked up the receiver the action might cause the bell of the other to make a slight sound.

'Which would draw attention,' I whispered. 'Damn.'

The sensation that you are being watched when there is no firm evidence to support this is quite unnerving. Intuition told me that this was the case. I turned round slowly but could see nothing suspicous. There were no closed-circuit cameras in the room, nor, as far as I could see, spy-holes or one-way mirrors. There were no mirrors at all. I gazed around again and with an appalling shock perceived an eye looking at me through the gap at the hinged end of the door.

I went closer, gun at the ready.

The eye was grey, a darker outline to the gold-flecked iris, black eyelashes.

It winked.

I put a hand around the door and made sure that he wasn't a ghost. The hand was taken and I was drawn into the recess behind the door. Besides Patrick it appeared to house electricity meters and cobwebs.

'Are you hurt?' he breathed.

'No. Are you?'

'Lightly strafed. But nothing actually landed.'

Only afterwards did I see the bullet burn on his shoulder.

'What do we do?'

'Nothing.'

'Nothing?'

'Everything's done.'

'*What* have you done?'

He smiled in unholy fashion.

The voices in the office became louder. Lyndberne must have come right into the hall to stand by the front door for he sounded very close when he said, 'As I said, you'll get your money. But I don't have it here. You'll have to trust me to get in touch with you.'

'Are you telling me that I just get the next flight out and sit on a rock in Brazil waiting to get paid?' yelled a furious voice.

'Yes,' Lyndberne said. 'That's precisely what I'm saying. And if you don't clear out I'll give you the same as I did The Greek.'

There was a lot of muttering.

'Go now,' Lyndberne said. 'There's not much smoke finding its way out but someone might get nosy.'

'And what are you going to do?'

'Destroy the evidence. In other words, save your miserable skins. Go on, clear out, you make me sick.'

'We don't know when there's a flight.'

'We don't know when there's a flight,' Lyndberne mimicked in a whining voice. 'There's a telly over there. Page Oracle, try Ceefax, be your bloody age.' He went out and, judging by the draught, left the front door open.

Patrick pulled our door right back so that it actually pressed us into the recess, holding me tightly with the other arm. Almost instantaneously a bomb went off, the blast slamming into the door and knocking my head into one of the electricity meters. For a moment I was stunned, dust and debris raining down on us over the top of the door. I stared into those unholy grey eyes and saw triumph. But only briefly. Then there was only weariness. Trembling very slightly, he kissed me quickly.

'I think you ought to stay here,' Patrick said, pushing the door away from us cautiously. 'Do you still have the Betsy?'

I gave him the gun. 'I'll come too.'

He did not argue and we went together.

Not a bomb but the cannon.

It lay upside down on the floor, where the recoil had thrown it, smoking gently. Whatever it had been loaded with − nails, nuts and bolts, broken glass − that was where primitive ballistics had ended. Judging by the wires still affixed to it, the charge and firing mechanism had been thoroughly modern and had involved fairly sophisticated electronics. I guessed that as soon as the television had been switched on it had fired.

I shall not describe the carnage in the room. I did not look too closely for there was no wish on my part to remember. Cowardly, I suppose, the desire not to suffer nightmares about the manner of the deaths of others. Suffice to say that it was impossible to tell how many had been in the room. It was manifestly clear though that all had died instantly.

Not Lyndberne, however, he was running in the direction of his car. Then he stopped and I could almost read his mind. Was the car booby-trapped too? Had all the other vehicles been dealt with likewise?

'The last act,' Patrick said and we set off after him.

Chapter Fifteen

The thought uppermost in my mind was that if we became involved with a long drawn-out chase then Lyndberne would get away. Neither Patrick nor I were fit for running. He immediately tried to solve this by putting a shot in the ground at Lyndberne's feet. The result of this was that he set off down the approach road on foot. The next shot whanged off a stone wall, the bullet missing him, probably, by inches. Lyndberne came to a stop, arms flailing as he tried to keep his balance.

'I'm unarmed,' he shouted at us.

'Then surrender,' Patrick called.

'You wouldn't shoot an unarmed man,' he jeered, and carried on running.

'I would if I had a rifle,' Patrick said to me. 'He knows he's out of range now.'

He doesn't often lie.

We had not gone more than a few yards, Lyndberne still in sight, when he ran, literally, into the arms of the police. There seemed to be quite a large contingent of them coming up the hill, some on foot, others in police Range-Rovers.

'That's it,' Patrick said, coming to an abrupt halt.

There were a few silent, sublime moments while we held hands, gazing at one another, glad to be alive and yet hardly able to believe it.

'Terry and Steve are here,' Patrick said. 'Somewhere.'

I said, 'It would have been useful for them to have been in this vicinity.'

'I told them to keep clear of the front of the house. I

201

wasn't sure exactly what would happen when the cannon fired. *If* it fired. The entire window frame might have been blown out.'

I suddenly remembered about Batrun.

He was where I had left him, conscious, and trying to get to his feet. He did not appear to be seriously injured but had lost a lot of blood. We took him into the house and laid him on a sofa in the sitting room. By this time the police were in the house and we were told that several mountain rescue ambulances were on the way, these being the only vehicles likely to be able to ascend the steep track from the main road.

Other than giving us this information no one took any notice of us. Feet tramped, police dogs yelped and tugged at leashes, radios crackled, voices shouted, vehicle doors slammed. Then a plainclothes officer noticed us and we were herded into the kitchen by two very polite but nervous constables. By this time we were both feeling too weak and weary to protest.

'Put the kettle on,' Patrick said to me. 'Please. I'd give anything for a cup of tea.'

'I'm not sure that you should touch ...' began the lone constable who had been left on guard.

'Our fingerprints are all over this place,' Patrick told him. 'For God's sake make yourself useful and find some cups.'

'Until you're interviewed, sir, you're under suspicion,' said the constable archly.

'Of what? Taking this bloody place apart? I'll confess to that right now. If you contact Inspector Jones of Merthyr police she'll tell you I'm allowed to have a cup of tea. The name's Gillard.'

This had the effect of sending the man bolting from the room and returning with a detective sergeant who introduced himself as Glynn Williams.

'Beat it,' Williams growled to his junior colleague.

'Let him make the tea,' Patrick urged. 'Then Ingrid can sit down,' he went on as Williams hesitated, 'And put out two extra cups – I've just heard a voice I recognise.'

In the next instant Terry and Steve were framed in the doorway, of necessity overlapping slightly as both have broad shoulders. They were well daubed with what looked like soot.

'Heaven be praised!' Terry exclaimed. He is not usually given to such utterances. 'And haven't the pair of us been trawling that damned cave for your bodies?' He eyed us up carefully. 'Are you all right? What did the bastards do to you?'

'It was fairly dark in the cavern when we met last night,' Patrick explained to me. 'I was setting up a few incendiary devices when they both came down on ropes from the roof like a turn in a military tattoo. The Greek was helping me and we were being watched over by McFie. He was supposed to be assisting but Lyndberne had actually sent him along to make sure we didn't get up to anything. Fortunately he didn't know a thunderflash from an atom bomb. But when these two turned up I'm afraid we had to tie him up and shove him in a cupboard. I hope he didn't suffocate.'

'It amused him,' I said.

'Who — The Greek? Oh, yes. But I didn't trust him. He'd have turned a gun on me when it was all over.'

'Someone turned a gun on *him*, I think,' Williams said. 'That's if the big foreign-looking man lying dead in an upstairs room is the one you're talking about.' He went out to tell someone to find McFie, Patrick having informed him of the whereabouts of the cupboard.

'What a prize, eh?' Steve said. 'This must be the biggest haul of terrorists since time began. Incidentally, what was that bloody great bang? You told us to keep away from the front of the house but — '

'Go and look in the front room to the right of the front door,' Patrick interrupted.

They both went away for a few moments, returning looking rather pale.

'You did that with the cannon I gave you?' Terry enquired, his voice higher than usual.

Patrick nodded.

'The barrel's split.'

'I'm not surprised. I used Semtex. I thought the whole thing might just blow up.'

'They're ... *pulverised*.'

'I'm glad. One of them was the man who tortured Ingrid.' As he uttered the last words his voice broke and he covered his face quickly with his hands, taking deep breaths.

I put an arm around his shoulders and said, 'Patrick, how on earth did you do it?' I knew it was best to keep him talking.

He made a strange sound, half laugh, half sob. 'You know me. The best burglar in Devon. I already had the key to the weapon store. The Greek lent it to me. Why should he care? He'd already decided that Lyndberne's outfit was a waste of time and money. There was no problem in getting past the checkpoint. On the way out I simply tossed a pebble into one of the tunnels and slipped by when the guard went to check, and sneaked past on the way back when he was reading a paper and scratching his backside.'

'And where was Lyndberne while you were priming the cannon?'

'Having his supper in the kitchen. He'd cooked it himself − Rhona's dead.'

We sat there a long time, drinking tea, sometimes speaking, sometimes not. People came and went; ambulance men, police, a doctor, a photographer, a forensic scientist. Last of all came Inspector Jones.

'Major ...' she began, her expression one of shock.

'It needed cutting,' Patrick said. 'But more important right now is the fact that Mr Meadows will be waving his credentials under your nose and wanting an up to the moment report on your findings. I'm afraid he's wearing his MI5 hat today − even thought strictly speaking this has nothing to do with MI5 at all.'

She quirked an eyebrow at Terry and when he did not immediately speak lifted the lid of the teapot and inspected the contents. Then she found a spare mug and poured herself some refreshment. 'Of the eleven men in the cave,' she began, 'five were dead and six injured, one seriously. Cause of death, as far as one can tell from initial investigations, gunshot wounds and the inhalation of smoke. There was a man dead on a bed upstairs here and another in the front room on a sofa, injured but not seriously. They had both been shot. Please don't ask me how many were in the other front room — I never was very good at jig-saw puzzles. We have in custody one man who was running away and who refuses to talk to us at all plus another three who also seemed to be running away but gave themselves up at the bottom of the track. No, I should re-phrase that. To say they were giving themselves up suggests I think they were guilty of something. *They* say they put themselves under our protection as they only worked here in a menial capacity and the whole place seemed to have gone raving mad. That's a fairly intelligent comment. Major, I'd be *fascinated* to hear what you and your wife have to say.'

'The course was about subversion,' Patrick said. 'That's always been a strong point of mine.'

Giving the statements took hours. There were the added complications of the deaths of King and Regan and where they had been buried. Also of Rhona, of course. It was only discovered afterwards that she had merely fled — Lyndberne, having been unable to admit this to The Greek, had said he had killed her for threatening to leave him and tell the police — and she was found in London working at a branch of a multiple chemist. So far as I know no charges were preferred against her.

The complications were made worse by Lyndberne's silence. Inspector Jones kept him on the premises under guard during which time he refused even to give his name and then had him removed to a place of greater security where he could be questioned further.

'They only have our word for it that he's Lyndberne,' Steve muttered, the four of us still sitting in the kitchen. 'That means telexes and Special Branch and the Anti-terrorist lot and Uncle Tom Cobbly and all.'

Patrick said, 'I've been waiting until there could be some private discussion. There's a problem. During the course of our stay here I gave Lyndberne your names.'

'I did,' I said. 'I'm sure I did.'

For a moment Terry was speechless. Then he said, 'Daws' too?'

'Probably,' Patrick replied. 'But you know what it's like

when you're under truth drug. It's in your mind but you don't know whether you've said it.'

'I wasn't under the influence of drugs,' I assured him. 'I *know* what I said.'

Terry got up abruptly, almost flung himself out of his chair. 'You know what this means, don't you?'

'Yes, it means he has to be put away for a very long time with no contact with the outside world,' Patrick said.

'Are you serious? What it means is that someone's got to shut him up. Now.'

Patrick shook his head. 'D12 was set up with the very idea of preventing that kind of thing happening. MI5 and MI6 have been known to take the law into their own hands before.'

Terry stared at him. 'I can't say that anyone's ever mentioned that side of it to me — you included.'

'Then it must have been just between Daws and me, mustn't it?' Patrick observed quietly. 'The old boy network, the old school tie, Masonic vows, call it what you like, he wanted to get rid of it.'

'But Daws' cover is *blown*. And mine.'

'To my great regret,' Patrick said, just as quietly.

'So you're just going to drive off home saying you're terribly sorry, having wiped the entire department from the map.'

'Steady on, old man,' said Steve. 'You must remember they were — '

'Tortured?' Terry interrupted angrily. 'I've no doubt. But it's odd how no one gave the game away when the Major was in charge.'

'I'm so sorry, Terry,' I said. 'I know we received training but nothing can prepare one for the real thing.'

'Now listen,' Steve shouted at Terry. 'I know you're upset but it seems to me that you're saying things you don't mean. Personally, I don't care a damn if my cover's blown. It's only a job, for God's sake.'

'That's always been your attitude,' said Terry. 'That's why you're not in charge.' He went out, quietly closing the door.

Steve turned to us with a groan. 'I'm really sorry he said

that. I'm sure he'll apologise when he's calmed down.'

Patrick stood up, found that the auspices were favourable for further activity and walked over to the sink. He ran some cold water into it and commenced to splash it over his face and head. Surfacing and finding a towel, he said, 'Whereas my weakness is to let emotion run away with me, Terry is still of a mind that some problems can be solved with a little heavy metal. Unfortunately that's far more dangerous.'

'Where are you going?' Steve asked as Patrick headed for the door.

'To prevent him using all the skills I taught him to put a bullet in Lyndberne.'

'I think you ought to report this to Daws.'

'*You* report it if you've a mind to,' Patrick retorted somewhat bitterly. 'Give him my love.'

'It would help if we knew whether Daws sent them in,' I said.

Patrick said, 'He didn't. When the Discovery was returned to Bill he phoned Terry as arranged. Luckily Terry was in the office at that moment. He grabbed Steve – although they were both supposed to be doing something else – and they came up to Wales. A few questions locally soon pinpointed the survival school and they laid plans accordingly. After several nights' surveillance they came to the conclusion that all was not as it seemed. I gather it was Steve who thought of asking a retired mining engineer about the locality. He actually took them up on the hill above and showed them the series of adits that had at one time been used to pump out water from the workings. One had a very new looking metal grille over the aperture. That night they returned, cut through the grille and climbed in. It was as simple as that.'

'But Daws will know *now*. He'll have heard through the usual channels.'

'Almost certainly. That's why I asked him to meet us here later.'

But other matters had to be attended to first. The unlikely venue for this was the bar of an hotel in Mayfair. It was only thirty hours since we had signed our statements in

Lyndberne's kitchen and as far as I was concerned a world away. Freedom had provided the energy and strength of will to drive home in a borrowed vehicle. There, we had fallen into bed and slept like corpses for twelve hours. Hot baths and a couple of good, light meals had also gone towards instituting a surprisingly high feeling of well-being and enthusiasm for the job in hand.

Up until this moment we had not discussed what had transpired. All I knew of events since was that Patrick had made a lot of phone calls and arranged to meet Terry — and, later, Daws — in the Mace Hotel with a view to our all having dinner. I had already discovered that Lyndberne's fate did not interest me greatly. It was far more important to be alive and free from worry and, most important of all, still with the man I love.

Patrick must have felt my gaze on him for he turned from where he had been keeping watch on the entrance and smiled.

'Your hair's okay,' I said. 'Since I trimmed it up a bit and you've washed it again. It just looks very short. Actually it suits you.'

'The beautiful people,' he murmured, kissing the lobe of my ear. 'Love and friendship conquers all, even Terry Meadows.' He chuckled.

Yes, we were on an emotional high.

When Terry did arrive I was surprised to see that he was accompanied by two men about his own age, all three immaculate in evening dress. But, from the look on Terry's face I immediately decided that he was the "parcel", they the "delivery boys". I detected a certain amusement on the latter's part, together with deference to Patrick, who thanked them warmly without calling them by name. Other than that, no one spoke until the two had departed.

'I don't think I'll stay either if you don't mind,' Terry said through his teeth.

'Daws will be joining us later,' Patrick told him.

'Whom you have briefed with every last little detail.'

'No. I've only asked him to dine with us.'

Terry sat down, obviously feeling a little conspicuous

standing up. 'What precisely is your game?' he enquired
furiously.

'I've no axe to grind. Call it friendship.'

'Friendship! You had me bloody well lifted.'

'For your own good.'

'Who the hell are those people?'

'You ought to have worked that out for yourself.'

'Men you once commanded in that special unit you were
in?'

Patrick nodded urbanely.

'They did me over. You ordered that, I suppose.'

'Did they hurt you?'

'No, not at all. But – '

'I asked them merely to make you feel vulnerable. Just so
you know what that's like in future.'

'I know what it's like. I was kidnapped, remember?'

'Your kidnappers didn't want any information from you.
What will you have to drink?'

Terry breathed out hard through his nostrils.

Patrick took an envelope from the inside pocket of his
jacket and laid it on the table. 'That's a very comprehensive
report I've written for Daws. There's a lot more detail there
than we gave the police. But it stops short of the conversation
we had in the kitchen afterwards. That's just between us.'

'Okay,' Terry said at last. 'I do appreciate that you
were dragged into this in the first place. But I'm still not
happy that Lyndberne's walking around with my name in
his memory.'

Patrick patted the envelope. 'I don't suppose Daws will
be exactly delighted either when he reads this.'

Terry settled for a gin and tonic.

Daws is too old and wily a campaigner to take the invitation
at face value. But he is also too much a gentleman to give
any hint that he thought there might be any subterfuge on
Patrick's part in requesting the pleasure of his company. He
arrived, exactly on time, and greeted us with genuine warmth.
Patrick immediately drew his attention to the envelope.

'D'you want me to read it now?' Daws enquired. 'What
the hell's that you're drinking, Meadows? I thought you were
a real ale man.'

'This place only serves posers' beers,' said Terry, looking embarrassed.

'Oh, well, if it's G and T I'll have one too.'

'In reply to the question,' Patrick said, 'I thought you ought to read it now from the point of view that it might affect the *tone* of the evening.'

Daws gave him a sharp look. 'Why, have you busted my cover?' He reached for the report, his hand pausing when Patrick did not reply instantly.

'Yes,' Patrick said, having had to clear his throat before speaking.

Daws slit open the envelope. 'Well, it had to happen sooner or later. As every soldier knows, you can't stay in the hills forever.'

He was given his drink by Terry and there was silence for perhaps fifteen minutes while he read. From anyone's viewpoint it was interesting reading – it would make an excellent novel – and I had typed it twice, the second time round giving it the same care and attention I would one of my own works. Parts of it had been very difficult to write and Patrick had had equal difficulty in dictating some of it to me. For I had left nothing at all out. But Daws did not pause in his reading, nor glance up at us, nor even exclaim under his breath. I reasoned that such an old soldier had probably read far grimmer accounts of assignments. When he had finished he folded the sheets of paper carefully, put them back into the envelope, tucked it into the pocket of his dinner jacket and stared into space thoughtfully, sipping his drink.

'I wanted to shoot him, sir,' Terry blurted out.

The steely blue gaze came to rest on the speaker. 'Why didn't you?'

'The Major stopped me.'

Daws transferred his gaze to Patrick. 'Ethics?'

Patrick said, 'D12 wasn't set up for its operatives to shoot people in police custody.'

The Colonel signalled to the barman. 'No.' He ordered a bottle of champagne, this development causing the rest of us to exchange glances.

'So what'll happen to Lyndberne?' Terry persevered.

'Just for this evening, he's at home with his wife and twin daughters.'

'Eureka!' Patrick chortled, slapping the table with an open palm and causing several alarmed glances from others in the room. 'He works for the Anti-Terrorist bunch and his name's Brian and he's a model citizen of Wanstead Flats. If I'd known that I'd have shot the bastard myself.'

Daws actually looked annoyed. 'He's a senior officer with the police branch you've just mentioned. This operation had been planned for several years and *your* arrival on the scene caused some agitated telephone conversations on the highest level, most on a plane higher than mine. I only got the full story this morning after complaining to the Prime Minister personally.'

'He could have given the Major the nod,' Terry protested. 'Not *used* him like that.'

'He didn't know the Major's game,' Daws said. 'Nor even who he was working for now. There was enough publicity after his departure from MI5 to fuel a thousand rumours. But you can rest assured you didn't give my name to an enemy.'

'And when he'd pasted hell out of both of us and got the truth, he let me help him achieve what I assume was his goal and finish the lot off?' Patrick said wonderingly. 'Yes,' he went on, frowning. 'It was brilliant. He never faltered for a moment.'

I said, 'He suggested they switch on the television. D'you think he'd noticed your little modification?' Yes, he would go far in his chosen career, I was thinking bitterly. A man who could torture the wife of a man he knew to be a British army officer, the woman herself well-known as a writer, was exactly the right sort of person to succeed. Then I remembered what Patrick had just said. *If I'd known that I'd have shot the bastard myself.*

'Sure to have done,' Patrick said. 'Do tell us the full story, sir,' he begged Daws.

'The idea wasn't to, as you put it, "finish the lot off",' Daws said distastefully. 'But to arrest as many as possible. It was the Commander's idea – and I think he had better remain nameless – he masterminded the whole operation.

211

The idea of schools for terrorists isn't a new one, as you know. He reckoned that if he created a character black enough and then set up shop he'd get some worthy customers. And he did. He also worked quite alone − no other police were involved.'

Terry said, 'And neither MI6 nor MI5, nor even the local police, were informed in case the plot was leaked?'

'And caused the fish to slip through the net,' Daws added. 'Yes, precisely.'

'But it created mayhem,' I said. 'Two children were killed as a result of those abominable people coming into this country.'

'It was very regrettable about Anton Friedrich,' Daws said. 'I don't think anyone realised that he'd be one of the takers. The Commander says he was forced to shoot him.'

'So one must assume that the immigration authorities had been ordered to let such people in,' Patrick said. 'I did wonder about that. It was the only part of it that didn't quite fit − ' He broke off, his expression hardening. 'You've recently spoken to this man?'

'Yes, this morning. I attended his de-briefing.'

'I'd be very interested to know whether his account of events tallies with mine,' Patrick said.

'By and large,' Daws answered. 'Major, I know you're angry but − '

'I don't think there's ever been an occasion when a free-lance agent has blundered into one of my set-ups,' Patrick said, speaking very crisply. 'But if it did happen I think the last thing I'd do is string them up from the ceiling and plug them in to the mains.'

'You're right,' Terry murmured. 'I'd say the guy lived under his cover just a little too diligently. Almost as though he enjoyed being like that.'

The Colonel shook his head. 'No. That wasn't the impression I received at all. I'd say he is a dedicated officer, but no more.'

And glib, I thought, a man of many faces. I shivered.

'He'll be tried and sent to prison,' Daws said. 'To preserve his cover. It took years to create the character so I can't blame his superiors for not wanting to lose it. Presumably arrangements will be made for him to escape in the not-too-distant future.'

'So he can start up again?' Terry asked.

'Somewhere else,' Daws replied. 'A neutral country. I don't know — it's no concern of mine really.'

I said, 'And everyone — you included — are quite happy with his method of operation. If he nets the world's most wanted men he has *carte blanche*?'

'I wouldn't go as far as to say that I'm *happy* about it,' Daws said kindly. 'But as I said, it's no real concern of mine. And the second time will have to be the last. He'll have no credibility amongst the criminal element by then — word will have got around. Afterwards he'll have to be given a completely new identity.'

'He had little credibility first time round,' I remarked. 'If we'd been writing our report from the angle that Lyndberne was a "friendly", it would have been quite different in places. He was inept, the students thought very little of him. It was Patrick who made it succeed — if he hadn't been there, most of them would have packed up and gone home.'

'But they would have been arrested at airports,' Patrick said. 'He did succeed in what was probably the most important thing — lured them into the country and provided the means for safe entry. That must have taken some organising.' He saw the way I was looking at him and added, 'You have to give credit where it's due.' To Daws he said, 'You've already said that he didn't just step into the identity of an existing Lyndberne but that the character was created. How? Did the police forces of Europe allow him to shoot a few of their people who were due for retirement? Were a few elderly planes with no one important on board downed?'

Daws should be used occasionally to being on the receiving end of Patrick at his most acerbic but again he looked annoyed. 'It was all fabricated,' he said. 'And he was blamed for a few real crimes. He himself suggested the Brecon Beacons National Park as a suitable venue for what he wanted to do. Good access by both road and sea, plenty of wild countryside, not many people to interfere with the project.'

'God forgive me for what I'd like to do to him,' Patrick

whispered and I was shocked to see that he had gone quite white. 'Only a few kids on school trips and hill walkers to get in his way. If he was here right now I think I could break his neck.' He left us abruptly.

'Oh dear,' said Daws. 'This has all had a very bad effect on him.'

'We picked up the pieces,' Terry said slowly. 'Literally. We tried the kiss of life on the girl who was fatally injured, talked to the parents, slogged our bloody guts out to find out who was behind it all. And now we're told it's some smart-arse on the *right* side of the law. No, correction, he *is* the law. If I was the Major I'd sell the story to the Sunday papers.'

'Meadows, you're prejudicing your own position by making such wild statements,' Daws told him sternly.

Terry leaned forward and spoke very quietly. 'And it could be, sir, that you're right out of touch with real life. I never thought the day would come when I'd hear you talking like a politician.' He rose and said to me, 'Please give my apologies to the Major.'

I discovered that tears were pricking my eyes as I watched Terry walk away.

'The Major trained him,' Daws said under his breath.

'*You* recruited both of them,' I pointed out.

'They're both good men,' Daws insisted as if to exonerate himself.

I looked him squarely in the eye. 'You'll have to choose whether you want good men who occasionally lose their tempers or people like the one calling himself Lyndberne. He's a thoroughly bad man. He might get the sort of results that are wanted but he's bad all through.'

When Patrick returned with menus a couple of minutes later Terry was with him.

'I refused to accept the apologies,' Patrick said, smiling at Terry who, in spite of everything, did not seem angry. 'A lot is at stake here and I have a few more questions.' He seated himself and dealt out the menus briskly. 'The first is – why weren't the so-called students arrested on the first day instead of dragging the whole bogus thing out for so long?'

'I asked him that,' Daws replied. 'He hoped to gain

214

sufficient intelligence by prolonged contact with them — information about hostages, future plans and so forth — to make the added work worth while.'

'Okay,' said Patrick. 'I'll allow him that. The second question is, where was his back-up? Where were these people going to be arrested?'

'There was no close back-up,' Daws said. 'That would have been too dangerous. As you know, even the local police hadn't been informed what was going on. And the arrests were going to be made at sea. When they were all on board the specially chartered vessel that would take them from Tenby to Southern Ireland. This was to avoid publicity and decrease danger.'

'To himself,' Patrick said. 'My third question concerns the whereabouts of video recordings made of interrogations. The interrogations when I gave him your name and also Terry's when I was under truth drug and the two occasions when I gave him useless information after he'd hung me up for a while with electrodes inserted in my rectum. If the recordings come to light, and assuming they didn't get blown to pieces in his office, you'll find them interesting. You might even like to show them to a psychologist I know who works at Scotland Yard. My point is that the information wasn't anything to do with the Anti-Terrorist people and that our friend was merely doing it to amuse himself. And you can be sure of one thing. No arrests would have been made — he intended to finish the whole lot off himself.'

Daws said, 'According to him your interference forced him to change his plan.'

'That's rubbish,' I said. 'And so is the business of arresting them at sea. We were *underground*. Any number of police could have raided the place at any time. It was quite secure. And the students weren't armed — only The Greek.'

Terry said, 'It was a perfect venue, sir, to have made arrests. It could have been done at virtually any time and would have resulted, probably, in no injuries, never mind deaths.'

'So what is your opinion?' Daws said to Patrick.

'He's a maverick — the power he's been given has gone to his head. He's very dangerous.'

215

'Isn't that a little harsh? I'll tell you what he said to me. He made no sign that he'd heard my name before when I introduced myself to him, by the way. As far as you were concerned, he said he felt it his duty to satisfy himself that you were still on the side of law and order, as he put it. He had gathered a little intelligence concerning your presence in the area but had no real idea why you were there. He insisted that he felt that anyone drawn to his enterprise was immediately suspect. In that I agree with him absolutely. He didn't know whom you *represented*. I admit that if I'd been in possession of your full account of what happened then, I might have tackled him more strongly about his treatment of you. But I don't think you can question his *motives*. Methods possibly. But the man has been positively vetted. He's on the line − there's no need for concern in that direction.'

Patrick is not often lost for words.

Postscript

We returned home the following day to find that we had visitors, Larry and Lorna.

'I understand congratulations are in order,' Larry said. 'You nabbed the so and so.' He then gave Patrick a bearhug, surprising him greatly. Patrick responded to this bonhomie, when released, by giving Lorna a kiss with raffish overtones.

'When you've finished eating each other ...' I started to say but was interrupted by Larry.

'Dawn's gone into Tavistock to stock up the fridge but we'd already told her we weren't staying. Justin's having his afternoon nap. We only popped in to see if you were back and she asked us to babysit for an hour.'

Patrick looked at his watch. 'Too late for lunch, too early for tea. That means its time for a beer.'

'Good', said Larry. 'Brought you a couple of bottles of Ruddles.'

'What a saint,' Patrick breathed. 'Let's go to a comfortable room.'

We gave them the gist of the story, leaving out all the unpleasant things, and also, of course, the real identity of the culprit.

'So it's safe now,' Larry said with relief.

'Yes, it's safe,' Patrick told him.

After a little silence Larry said, 'Shirley's left me. She said she was fed up with being the wife of a dozy schoolteacher. Gone home to her Mother.'

'What about the children?' I asked.

217

'They refused to go with her. They're at Hinton Littlemoor with Mum and Dad.'

Lorna tucked an arm through Larry's. 'So he's mine now,' she said, laughing.

'The kids get on well with her,' Larry said, slightly defensively. 'I think we can make a go of it.'

'Your health,' Patrick said, raising his glass. 'At last, Larry, you have a woman I enjoy kissing.'

They stayed to dinner — cooked by Dawn — and it was only afterwards that I noticed three official-looking envelopes propped up on the mantelpiece. They were all addressed to Patrick. Dawn had placed my post on my desk.

'Give it to me on the chin,' said he.

'In postmark date order,' I said, opening them quickly. 'Number one is from the library threatening you with a fate worse than death if you don't return your books. Number two ... yes, I thought so, it's from the army. They say they haven't forgotten you and your career is being reviewed and until you hear further you are to remain on leave.'

Patrick groaned.

'Number three, dated the day before yesterday ...' I fell silent, reading it again.

'Well?' Patrick demanded.

I said, 'It's from a different army department. In London. They're pleased to say that your name's been put forward for promotion.'

'That's why his career's being reviewed,' Larry said excitedly. 'If he's made up to lieutenant-colonel he can be the commanding officer of a regiment.'

'Or head of D12,' Patrick said softly.

The problem of bringing Lyndberne to "trial" was overcome by the neat arrangement of having him extradited to West Germany, there, ostensibly, to answer for crimes he had committed in that country. The entire episode faded from public memory. It was some months later, when Patrick and I were in New York, that we heard that a senior British policeman had been drowned in a Scottish

218

loch. He had been on holiday and had gone fishing in a boat alone. The local worthy who had found the body reported that a dead rook had been lying on the shore beside him.